LITTLE
THINGS
BIG

DAVID M. SALKIN

Crystal Lake Publishing
Where Stories Come Alive!

www.crystallakepub.com

WELCOME
TO ANOTHER

CRYSTAL LAKE PUBLISHING
CREATION

BY DAVID M. SALKIN

HORROR

Forever Hunger
Deep Black Sea
Dark Tide Rising

MILITARY & ESPIONAGE

The Team
Team II – Into the Jungle
Team III – African Dragon
Team VI – Shadow of Death
Team V – The MOP
Team VI – Dangerous Ground
Crescent Fire
Necessary Extremes
Battle Scars

CRIME

Blood From A Stone
Hard Carbon
Deep Down

ADVANCE PRAISE

"Geneticists inadvertently create super-sized skin mites—and humans are on the menu! This story burrowed into my flesh and ate me alive from the inside out—and I loved every minute of it! If you like Michael Crichton and James Rollins, you'll love David Salkin." – Toby Tate, Screenwriter, Producer, Author of *Lilith* and *The Lilitu Trilogy*

"If this book doesn't give you nightmares, nothing will. You'll be captivated, entertained, and terrorized all at the same time." – Lisa Black, *New York Times* Best-selling Author of the *Gardiner and Renner* and *Locard Institute* series

"*Little Things Big* is a terrifying, yet believable thriller that will have you reading well into the night. It begins like the slow climb of a roller coaster, but when the action kicks in, David Salkin doesn't relent. Don't bother washing your hands—it's already too late! But really, wash your hands... this is a story." – Master Sergeant Chris Grall, U.S. Special Forces (Ret.), Award-winning Author of *Trigger Guard: A Writer's Guide to Firearms*

AUTHOR'S NOTE

Back in 1976, when I was too young to be going to horror movies, I saw a movie called *Food of the Gods*, which gave me nightmares for weeks. I'm pretty sure some of the imagery from that movie is forever burned into my brain, and appears reimagined on these pages. That movie and my book have nothing to do with each other, but the idea of making everyday, harmless creatures big enough to eat people is the stuff nightmares are made of. Take a peek under an electron microscope some day and see what lives on your skin and eyelashes. We're constantly surrounded by micro-terrors. "Something evil coming out of a lab" is still a sensitive topic in our post-Covid world, and I'm pretty sure will remain so forever. This book maybe isn't such a far leap. I hope you enjoy the story. Now go wash your hands.

ACKNOWLEDGMENTS

My books are always dedicated to my family and friends, and to those who have served our nation in uniform. Of course, this book is no different. Some of my friends appear in the book by name. Their characters don't always resemble them at all, it's just a "shout out" for being a buddy. If I kill you horribly, don't take it personally.

I'd also like to add the Azario Readers Club to this dedication page. My neighbors and friends in the club reminded me that people still love to read, and chat about books and authors. That inspired me to get off my butt and start writing again. This is novel number sixteen, with two others right behind it!

And remember the rules... if you love my book, please write a review. If you hate it... forget you ever saw it! I write military espionage, crime, science fiction and horror... all thrillers meant to provide you with high quality entertainment. I hope you'll check them all out.

Lastly, my heartfelt thanks to the team at Crystal Lake Publishing. A special "thanks for the opportunity" to Joe Mynhardt. Editors Alex J. Coyne and Andy Baldwin did a great job reminding me that grammar, spelling and punctuation do still exist in the English language. Charlene, appreciate your constant communication and keeping the ball rolling. Crystal Lake... thank you for getting this story off my hard drive and onto the bookshelves!

1

Central Pennsylvania: Global Tech World Solutions Laboratory

ANDREW RETURNED FROM THE feed lab in building two to the micro lab located in building one. He carried a large box full of various crop samples, including alfalfa, corn, wheat, and soybeans, which he dropped off at the specimen desk. The lab techs would spend a few days under the electron microscopes and spectroscopes examining the latest genetically modified plants.

Glancing around to make sure no one was watching, he shuffled past a desk that was covered in stacked Petri dishes. The dishes were sealed and in the process of being labeled with a black Sharpie marker which had run out of ink, causing the tech to leave the desk in search of a replacement. Andrew swiped one of the unmarked clear containers, a little smaller than a hockey puck, and slid it into his lab coat, never breaking his pace as he walked past the desk.

From there, he headed to the men's room where he locked himself inside a stall. He took the seeds and crop samples he had hidden in his pocket and transferred them to a small plastic bag which he then slid into his underwear. Security was tight, and smuggling samples out of this place had been a bigger pain in the ass than he had anticipated.

Getting raw meat samples would be an even bigger challenge, but for now, he was going to take things one problem at a time. He removed the Petri dish from his pocket and squinted at its contents. Whatever was in there was tiny. Some type of seeds? Whatever they were, they were smaller than grains of sand. Some type of flaky white pieces were mixed in with whatever kind of seeds were in there. Pieces of the seed husk? Maybe something to keep them dry? He didn't have time to figure it out.

He removed the tape seal and dumped the contents into another small baggie, tapping the plastic to knock the contents out into the bag. He wiped the last remainders out with his finger and then sealed the baggie. After shoving that into his underwear like the other sample, he crushed the plastic with his foot and wiped up the pieces with a handful of toilet paper, then left the stall where he shoved the garbage deep into the trash.

Andrew washed his hands, tightened his ponytail, and then walked back to the lab as though nothing ever happened.

———

As the Learjet banked and came in on its approach to a tiny, private airstrip, Paul Dodds looked at the green countryside below and flashed back to his last trip to Ireland, where he had taken care of other corporate business making sure the company's tax liabilities would be lessened to the greatest extent of the law. This trip would be different, and he was excited beyond all measure.

"Pretty country, isn't it?" asked his right-hand man, who happened to be a woman.

"Sure is. I was just thinking the same thing."

He gave Connie a quick smile.

Constance Whitcolm. MBA from Wharton after an undergraduate degree in biology from UPenn. With her smarts, looks, and family money, she could have set her career goals for the White House. Instead, she had opted to chase the almighty dollar. It was working; at twenty-nine and single, she was what they called a "power broker" at Global Tech World Solutions.

Every man at Global Tech, married or single, undressed her with his eyes, and she knew it. She used her looks as just one weapon in her arsenal, and if it took the "slight hint of future possibilities" with the male members of the senior staff to move up the corporate ladder, she had no problem flirting with men she found completely unattractive. She had only slept with one man and one woman in the company so far, but hadn't ruled out Paul yet, as his star was on the rise and he made no attempt to hide his attraction for her.

Connie crossed her legs and adjusted her skirt, taking her time so that Paul could admire her legs for a brief moment before he quickly looked away to avoid being obvious.

"Reminds me of Ireland," he said, gazing out the window.

"How did that go? I meant to ask," she replied.

"Excellent. One of these days, the federal government will realize that a different tax system will make them billions a year, but until then, I get to go visit our money in Dublin once a quarter. Great city. I love it."

"Maybe you'll take me one of these days," she said, smoothing the hem of her skirt.

Paul looked at her and held her eyes an extra second. Damn, she was gorgeous.

"Well?" she asked.

"It's not your department, but I guess you can ask Smith if you could go."

"Oh, you mean go *officially*," she said.

Paul's face turned red. Being bald gave him a lot of face to change color. "What did *you* mean?" he asked, his mouth suddenly dry.

She shrugged, faking her innocence.

The pilot's voice broke the moment. "Final descent, folks. Please make sure your seatbelts are fastened and I'll have you on the ground in a few minutes. Seventy-two degrees and perfect sunshine in central PA. Looks like another beautiful September day."

Connie opened her purse and checked herself in her compact mirror, spruced her long blonde hair, and then quickly put it away as the jet touched down on the tarmac with only a slight squeak of rubber kissing asphalt.

Paul was rattled by her comment, but now had to change gears and get ready for the biggest meeting of his life. The latest discoveries at GTWS just might make the company so many billions that they'd *buy* Ireland. And if the rumors were true, and the company was bought out by Prosanto, with the stock options he'd get, he could retire in a couple of years with millions. A beach house and Connie might become two very real options.

The jet stopped moving and the grounds crew chocked the tires with heavy wooden blocks. The co-pilot emerged from the cabin and opened the door, extending the small staircase to the runway. Paul watched Connie walk down first, her hair gently blowing in the late summer breeze, and followed her down. A black Escalade was parked nearby with another equally beautiful young woman standing in front of the SUV. The driver stood behind her, looking more like a Secret Service agent than a limo driver. He was easily two heads taller than she was.

"Welcome to the farm!" said the very peppy woman. "Kim Hendricks, C.O.O."

They were being met at the tarmac by the Chief Operating Officer? Paul was impressed. The driver introduced himself as Mike, no last name, end of information. He roared off the tarmac like a race-car driver.

Kim half turned in her front passenger seat to address her guests.

"We're very excited to have you here. Everyone just calls it the farm. This division of GTWS is highly secure. As soon as we get the usual non-disclosure forms, documents, and badges out of the way, I'll give you the full tour and update you on everything that's happening. I apologize in advance for all the formalities—you know lawyers." She faked a laugh. "Right...you're lawyers..."

Paul smiled. "Just me. She's the smart one. But no worries, I know the drill."

With the speedometer never reading less than ninety, Mike sped along a narrow road that smelled like it had been newly paved.

"We don't get much traffic," Kim explained. "In fact, the only time we ever drive on it is when visitors arrive by private plane, which only happens a few times a month."

"The farm" was located in cattle country in central Pennsylvania, at least an hour from anywhere. The staff lived at the facility, which was enormous. What had started as an animal research facility had slowly grown into the company's largest project in the world. With a staff of seventy and an annual budget of sixty million dollars, the progress had been incredible. The breakthroughs of the last two years, in particular, would change the world.

2

The Farm

THE ESCALADE STOPPED AND Mike waited for the automatic plate reader to unlock the heavy metal front gate.

Paul noticed the concertina wire and cameras along the top of the fence. "You guys don't mess around with security," he said quietly.

"No, sir. We have laser sensors and plenty of cameras. Internal controls on the facility itself are even more stringent," replied Mike matter-of-factly.

Once the gate rolled open, they headed up the long driveway to the front entrance of the massive facility. The SUV stopped at the front entrance and Mike hopped out to open the rear doors for their guests. Kim swiped her access card and opened the front doors, leading them through a lobby. Mike remained with the SUV, his facial expression never having changed once since the moment they met him.

The décor of the facility was clean and modern, sparse though it was. The three entered a room enclosed in glass, where a file sat on a long table next to a plastic tub that contained ID Security badges. Kim invited them to sit as she pulled out papers for them to sign and issued them their badges.

With their badges now around their necks, Connie and Paul followed Kim down a very long hallway, their heels echoing through the white tiled hall. It had the feeling of a hospital corridor—cold and sterile, but brightly lit.

Kim opened a door with her access card and showed her guests inside. "You're entering the visitor center. Here's where you'll get a brief orientation before I take you inside. You'll be given full access to all of the labs and animal enclosures. I think when you see our progress, you're going to be as excited as we are."

Kim pressed a button that began a motion-picture quality film. With an opening music score and soaring shots of farmland, deserts, table full of food, starving children, fishnets being pulled onto boats full of fish, and mass graves of African villagers, the film immediately painted a gripping picture. The narrator's voice began talking over the subsiding music:

"With eight billion hungry mouths to feed, pressure to produce food has never been greater. Climate change means some areas of farmland experience drought and crop failure, while other farms are being washed away by massive floods. New diseases affect crops

and livestock, some which are now resistant to pesticides or herbicides. With over five billion of the world's people living in poverty, how will humanity move forward? How will we feed the future children of the world while billions are already dying of starvation and malnutrition..."

"Maybe stop pumping out so many kids," Paul muttered under his breath.

Connie elbowed him. "You mean *customers*," she whispered back with a smirk.

The film continued with footage of starvation and failing farms, painting a horrid scene of a miserable future. The music then changed to a much livelier score, and the scene cut to families gathered around tables full of food.

"Here at Global Tech World Solutions Laboratory, we've solved the world's food shortage! While no new discovery is without controversy, we believe that fears based on a lack of knowledge can be overcome with education. The scientists and researchers at GTS Labs have changed the future of farming and animal husbandry, and have ensured a future of hope and promise..."

The film ran for another few minutes, and when it ended, both Paul and Connie felt obligated to give Kim golf-claps.

"Impressive," said Paul.

"An exciting presentation. The carrot on the stick. When do we get to see the big surprises?" asked Connie.

Kim smiled and stood up. "Now."

Kim led them to the hallway where a golf cart was already waiting. "Hop in," said Kim. "As I warned you, this place is enormous. We have these golf carts stashed all over the facility."

She drove them down hallways that seemed to go on forever. Colored stripes on the white walls served as guides to which section they were in, and occasional maps showed "you are here" icons. She pulled up next to several other golf carts and parked.

"This is the micro lab. This is where it all started. I'm going to introduce you to Dr. Lamont White. He's the genius behind most of what you see here, although nowadays he has a lot of help. In the beginning, it was just him and a few researchers. He now runs a team of thirty research scientists—some of the brightest minds in the world. If he starts talking hard-science and loses you, remind him you aren't scientists. Brilliant guy, but not always on the same planet as most of us."

Kim swiped her badge, and Paul and Connie each had to swipe theirs as well. They found themselves inside a tiny man-trap, between double glass doors.

"Okay, this is just a quick decontamination process. Take a breath, hold it, and close your eyes just for a couple of seconds." She pressed a button on the wall marked "ENTER," and they felt a blast of warm air rushing over their bodies. The second door opened to the lab clicked open. "Thanks, that was it. You'll have to come with me to the locker room area. It's time for 'suits and boots.' I know it seems a little dramatic, but this is a very clean facility," she said apologetically.

They put white jumpsuits over their clothes. Paper booties went over their shoes. The next stop was a cavernous room full of scientific equipment on a massive scale. They both said "wow" under their breath at the same time. Out in the room, researchers worked under microscopes of every kind, including a giant electron microscope in the back of the room. Kim made a beeline for a jacketed man that was typing away on a computer.

"Dr. White, our guests have arrived."

Dr. White stopped typing and stood up. He was, in fact, tall, dark, and handsome.

"Welcome! Welcome!" He shook hands and began speaking quickly, obviously excited to speak about the facility. "So glad the office sent you down. If you can work the lobbying end in D.C. and help us with all the approvals, we can start production of the livestock programs immediately."

Paul wondered how many cups of coffee the man had consumed, but he said nothing.

"Connie, what year were you born?" asked Dr. White.

She was a bit taken aback, but said, "Nineteen eighty-seven. Why?"

He did a quick calculation in his head. "Okay, so almost thirty years ago..."

"Twenty-nine..."

"Right, so in 1987, the world's production of beef, pork and chicken was a hundred and thirty-two million tons. One thirty-two. What do you think it was this year?"

She shrugged. "No idea."

"Two-sixty. Almost exactly doubled in thirty years."

"Twenty-nine."

Dr. White ignored her and continued. "We've managed to double production of meat for a hungry world in thirty years, mostly through innovation, better feed, and line breeding of top stock, but that's not going to be enough. Most of that tonnage was chicken—from twenty-four million tons to almost ninety tons, which is great, but for beef, we only increased from forty-eight to fifty-nine million tons."

Kim tactfully touched Lamont's arm. "Dr. White, why don't we take them around the facility as we chat?"

He looked around as though he just realized he was standing in the middle of his own research area. "Oh, right, right. Great. This way."

They followed him through the lab.

"I'll tell you about this part in a second. Getting back to the beef problem..."

"People eating less red meat?" Paul asked sarcastically.

"No, no. That's not it. We can triple chicken production because they breed quickly and reach maturity for slaughter at six to twelve weeks."

"Wow, I had no idea," said Paul. "Always figured they were a couple of years old."

"No, no. Organic free-range chickens, twelve weeks. Mass-produced birds with special feed, six weeks! Amazing, right?"

Connie made a face and wondered about going vegetarian.

"And that's the problem we have. For prime beef, steers and heifers are almost thirty months old at slaughter. Thirty months. That's over twenty chickens in the same time period. Pigs run about the same unless it's fattening pigs for bacon, then maybe six months. But it's time—it takes time. In the meantime, people are starving, right? What if we could triple or quadruple the output in the *same* amount of time?"

Paul and Connie nodded. This was the whole reason for their visit. Output equals profit, and time is money.

Lamont pointed to the electron microscope. "Here's where it all started. Genetics and gene mapping." He walked to a computer and started typing. Some type of monster appeared on the large screen with armored scales and horn-like hairs. It was terrifying. "A common dog flea." He switched slides and began rattling off names of various creatures blown up to millions of times their actual size. "Dust mites, larvae, copepods... We're surrounded by an infinite number of creatures so small we can't even see them. Well, we *couldn't* see them. Until we made them bigger."

Lamont began walking at almost a jog across the lab, with Paul, Connie, and Kim trying to keep up. The man certainly was excited about his work. He brought them to a large cabinet and opened a drawer, removing a glass box. Inside was something so horrific-looking that Connie jumped back a step and put her hands to her face.

"It can't hurt you," said Lamont calmly. "It's dead."

"What the hell *is* it?" asked Paul, his face showing revulsion.

"A tiny creature that lives on the hairs of your eyelashes. They're there right now."

Connie wiped her face without even thinking about it. "Oh my God, that's disgusting!"

"Well, yes and no. I know that Walter—we named him Walter—is less than handsome, but he and his kind haven't changed much for a billion years, and we need them all around us. We're all covered in tiny dead skin cells. And also tiny creatures that *eat* tiny dead skin cells."

"I swear I'm going to throw up," said Paul. "I thought we were going to see pretty cows. This is absolutely disgusting."

"We will, we will. But I have to explain the history of what we've unlocked here! It's beyond amazing!"

Kim tried to help her guests. "Lamont, our guests aren't scientists. How about if we skip some of this and show them section three?"

Lamont shrugged. "Okay, okay. I was just making a point. Discoveries like this don't just happen by accident. It was years of research, and then gene mapping, and then starting with tiny organisms and finally working our way up to mammals. It all began with figuring how genetics could change growth rates and sizes."

Kim started walking, looking at her guests, who slowly followed her as Lamont kept talking, and put the creature away before following them.

Kim smiled at her guests and whispered. "He's very excited about his work. And he has a right to be. Wait 'til you see section three."

"Is this section one?" asked Connie.

"Technically, yes. But we just call this building the mic lab. Microscope laboratory. But yes, it's Building One on the maps."

"What's in Building Two?"

"Building Two is the farm within the farm. It's flora only," Kim explained "We grow feed for our animals, which, as you'll see in a little while, need either a lot of food, or very special food. We also do our genetic modification experiments for all plant life there as well."

Lamont caught up to them, still rattling off numbers. "The average steer goes about fourteen hundred pounds today. That's up three hundred pounds from twenty years ago."

"Genetically modified?" asked Paul.

"Not the way you're thinking, no. Genetically *managed*, so to speak. Line breeding is for keeping the traits you want and eliminating those you don't. Today's beef industry is very efficient. But what if in that same thirty-month time period, you could grow cows to ten or fifteen *thousand* pounds? Or better yet, hit that goal weight in *ten or twelve months*? It's the same story for chickens bigger than turkeys and hogs the size of cows. An order of magnitude larger in less time than it takes to grow into current sizes! This, my friends, is how we can feed the world!"

Paul and Connie looked at each other and smiled.

They'd done it.

Super-sizing the cattle, pigs and chickens wasn't the answer in and of itself. Larger cattle, for example, cost more per acre than smaller ones. There had been many arguments in the cattle industry about "ideal size," but it was a very complicated equation, which also had to take into account the grazing area, transportation costs, calf production, and meat quality. Just "making them bigger" wouldn't do it. But, making them super-sized in a fraction of the time it would take to grow to today's "normal" size could change everything.

Lamont's excitement was contagious. "Look, the cattle industry folks that I've spoken to were resistant to the idea of going over fifteen-hundred pounds. We had lots of long talks about their industry problems. I'm very proud to say that we've worked very closely with industry leaders to address their real concerns and built a program around exactly what they wanted. The fact that we can now grow these animals to enormous sizes in less time than they can currently raise their herds changes *everything*!"

"But won't they need much more food and water to reach these sizes? I mean, isn't there a trade-off on what they consume versus the output of beef?" asked Paul, always considering the bottom line.

"Of course! Excellent question. And that's where our genetic alterations come in. As we studied smaller creatures, we began experimenting with growth rates and manipulating the genetic coding. The results have been astounding. It took us years to get here, Paul, but we've made these animals so efficient they can not only grow ten times larger but ten times *faster*, with almost the same amount of cost!"

"Don't they eat a lot more?" Paul asked.

"Grazing on grass, yes. But we've developed our own feed. Which we can sell, of course, that's packed with the exact amino acids they need. They eat it happily, and you can almost *watch* the damn things grow!"

Lamont paused thoughtfully, then began speaking again with such passion it was contagious. "If you've ever been around teenage boys, you know all they do is eat and sleep. When they hit their high school growth spurt, they become a bottomless pit for food. My nephew never ceased to amaze me. At a hundred and twenty pounds, he could eat more than any three-hundred-pound man I'd ever seen. Then go take a nap and start over again. When we started on the super-sized mammals, that was a real consideration. I mean, what good are super-sized cows if they cost a hundred times more to raise, right? There'd be no economies of scale, so to speak. But then we began experimenting with our own feed. The amino acid mixture is designed at the genetic level for their exact dietary needs. Anyone growing our livestock will need to buy their feed from us unless they have unlimited grazing areas."

Connie smiled. "So Global Tech will sell them the livestock *and* the feed. I love it."

"Precisely. At some point, when these animals start reproducing and the farmers no longer need to buy animals from us, we'll still have the feed industry to generate huge profits. They'll always need us for the feed."

Paul smiled. Dr. White had done more than the scientific research—he'd thought about the practical applications in a real world of profits and losses and addressed the company's bottom line.

"You've really outdone yourself, Dr. White," Paul said. "While we've been monitoring the progress here, we really didn't expect you to have reached this stage so quickly."

Dr. White nodded, looking very proud of his work. "The breakthrough on the rate of growth was the real game-changer. The disgusting-looking little mites you saw earlier provided the insights into unlocking the genome issues. You have to remember, you're looking at creatures that are many orders of magnitude larger than what occurs in nature. They normally can only be seen under an electron microscope, and now they're as big as hamsters. While they may be rather primitive-looking, they will have a tremendous impact on the future of the planet."

Paul nodded thoughtfully. Cattle, pigs, and chickens, growing to enormous sizes in less time than it would take a farmer to raise normal size animals. It really could feed the world. And make the stockholders at Global Tech very, very rich, indeed.

Lamont continued. "In explaining the growth rates and adult sizes, sometimes it helps to use this analogy. If our heifer was a human, she'd be born weighing about ten pounds, at twenty-two inches. Just slightly larger than average. By the end of the first week, she would weigh twenty-five pounds and reach twenty-six inches. By the end of the first month, she would be larger than its mother."

The group exchanged glances. It was a mixture of amazing and uncomfortable. Picturing a newborn trying to nurse at six feet tall, two hundred pounds was more than unnatural, it was unsettling.

Kim caught the fake, nervous smiles and jumped in with her chipper self. "Okay! Let's continue our tour, shall we?"

3

Building Three: The Zoo

THE GROUP SWIPED THEMSELVES through another set of double doors, still wearing their white jumpsuits. Kim forced a smile as the doors slid open. "We call this building the zoo. Don't be alarmed. I know it's a little weird at first, but they're just cows, albeit really big ones."

A few other employees, also in white jumpsuits, said quick hellos as they went about their business. The four of them walked down a small hallway to yet more doors and, after swiping through, stepped into a giant enclosure that could have served as a football stadium. Inside, under an open roof, a herd of cattle the size of African bush elephants roamed about eating grass that was growing in the dirt, as well as animal feed and hay that was stacked everywhere.

"Holy shit," exclaimed Paul before he could stop himself.

Connie's mouth hung open.

"They're really something, aren't they?" asked Lamont proudly. "They're not quite two years old yet. They're still putting on weight. The bigger ones go about fifteen thousand pounds each." He smiled.

Paul stared in disbelief. "I know this was the goal, but wow. I don't even know what to say. They're enormous. It's incredible."

Lamont looked proudly at the cattle. "The only downside is the amount of dung, but we use that for fertilizer over in building two. Big cow patties help make big stalks of corn, hay, wheat, alfalfa, you name it. We're changing everything in the world from this humble little lab in the countryside."

"I'm not sure I'd call this place a humble little lab. I think it's bigger than the Pentagon," said Connie.

"Not quite. The Pentagon is a million and a half square feet. We're less than half that size."

Connie looked at Paul. Sarcasm was wasted on the good doctor. Brilliant, yes—but a total geek. She stared at the cattle, then asked Lamont, "The meat, uh... Has anyone ever tasted it? Is it like regular steak?"

Lamont smiled. "Next stop, the butcher shop! Building five."

"Seriously?" asked Connie.

"Of course. What's the sense in raising cattle if you can't eat them? That *was* the whole point, right?"

"Well, yes, of course. I just, uh… I don't know. They're just so gigantic. What would a steak even look like?"

"Yes, yes, that *was* originally an issue. You're one hundred percent correct, of course. You can't just slap a hundred-pound steak down on the kitchen table. We brought in a butcher and actually had him relearn his trade. The basics are the same. The cuts of beef and so forth. But making the finished meat product look appetizing enough for folks to want to eat it required some thought. Basically, the butchering and aging process starts the same as usual, but then the butcher figured out a way to keep cutting the steak into smaller pieces until they resembled regular steaks. The only downside is that everything has to be boneless, because a bone-in ribeye steak would have a bone attached to it the size of a baseball bat. But, as long as you don't cry about not seeing any T-bones or porterhouse steaks, you'll find the finished product as good as anything in the world. We've been able to produce beef that has enough well-marbled fat content to be USDA Prime. That's a big deal for the cattlemen."

Connie looked at Paul. "Incredible."

Paul shrugged. "I dunno, I've always been a *bone-in* kind of guy."

"I'll show you the bones, and then you'll understand what I mean. Follow me," said Lamont.

The group left the zoo and hopped into another cart and drove off to building five. Inside building five, they were taken to the meat preparation room, referred to by the staff as the butcher shop. It was the same as most butcher shops, except the scale was increased in size to be able to deal with fifteen-thousand-pound cattle instead of fourteen hundred pounders. Giant hooks hung from automated overhead belts, and carcasses the size of elephants hung below. They had been gutted and skinned already and looked like regular sides of beef except for the size.

They followed Lamont and watched in amazement as a team of butchers used giant band saws and heavy machinery to take apart one of the animals. It was systematically butchered into smaller and smaller parts and sent down a conveyor belt until at the end a man with a regular butcher knife was cutting pieces into smaller, recognizable sized steaks.

"See the problem with the bones?" asked Lamont, pointing to some scraps on the floor. The heifer's rib had been stripped and was bigger than a two-by-four.

Lamont approached the butcher at the end of the conveyor belt, who, like them, was dressed all in white. His uniform also included a hat and apron. The apron was fairly well-covered in blood.

"Morning, Vinnie. We have some guests this morning from corporate."

Vinnie waved, holding a sharp knife. "Sorry, a bit of a mess at the moment. Welcome to the farm."

Paul and Connie said hello. "So, you've actually eaten this yourself?" asked Paul.

Vinnie looked at Lamont with surprise. "Seriously?" he asked.

Lamont looked a bit nervous and shrugged. "Look, the FDA would have our heads, of course. But honestly, why would we waste the steaks? Best I ever had. We feed the staff with what we produce here."

Vinnie pointed to a large steel door. "Doc, show them the aging room."

Lamont nodded and walked them to another door. Inside, it was cold and sized like an airplane hangar. "The meat locker," he said, pointing to shelf after shelf of aging beef. "When it's dry aged, it's the best USDA Prime beef you've ever had. The chef and catering company that runs the kitchen here says it's the best they've ever worked with. I'd love for you to have lunch here. Best steak, *ever!*"

Connie made a face at Paul and looked back at Lamont. "You've been eating it, like, *regularly*?" she asked.

"Every day. Thank God for Lipitor. I think my cardiologist would be pissed if I told him I ate steak four or five nights a week, but it's so damn good."

Paul looked hesitant. "Doesn't the FDA have to approve everything for human consumption first?"

"For sale to the public, yes. And maybe, to be technical, even for us. But those idiots wouldn't have the first clue about what we've actually done. These animals are extremely healthy."

Paul made a face at him, with his eyebrow raised.

Lamont became animated. "I mean, after the original problems. Of course the early experiments were primitive by today's standards. But after what we call 'Trial AL-27,' we were perfect. The 'AL' was for the hybrid—the Angus-Limousin cross breed. It was the twenty-seventh attempt. Anyway, the AL-27 was successful, and we've been reproducing them ever since. They're healthy, and quite frankly, delicious. Remember, they eat food that's been specially designed to work with their genetics. We can predict the muscle-to-fat ratio and actually control it for the proper marbling in the beef. Fat *is* flavor."

Lamont began walking with Connie and Paul close behind. Kim walked behind them and whispered, "He's not kidding. Best steak you'll ever eat. I think the aging process does it. Try it. Our cafeteria is first class. We even stock great red wine."

They continued the tour, discussed outputs and profits, and ended up, as planned, in the cafeteria. They grabbed a table in the cafeteria, which looked every bit like a restaurant you'd find in any decent sized city. With seventy employees, give or take, and nowhere else to dine, mealtime was busy.

"We're the original farm to table," said Lamont with a grin. "I'm having the ribeye, which I suggest to you as well. It *is* different than what you're used to seeing, because we obviously only use a tiny portion of the cut. VJ—that's Vinnie, the butcher—Vinnie Jackson. Anyway, VJ figured out a way to cut it so that the shape mimics a ribeye. The grain pattern is different since you're only eating a small portion of the cut, but the aging process guarantees a tender and juicy steak."

Connie and Paul agreed to try what was recommended, as did Kim, and the four of them sat at the table and chatted about the day's tour and briefing. When the server arrived, Lamont ordered a bottle of red wine for the table and four ribeye steak specials.

Lamont looked back and forth at Paul and Connie. "You seemed a little nervous about eating the steak. Look, I get it. Fear of the unknown. But GMOs are nothing new. The media hypes it up and terrifies people, but in the meantime, we have eight billion people to feed. Ninety-four percent of soybeans grown today in the US are genetically modified. Eighty-eight percent of all corn, ninety percent of all canola oil, the list goes on. Hell, if not for GMOs, you probably would have watched papaya disappear from Hawaii. If the GM version hadn't been introduced to withstand the ringspot virus, they'd *all* be gone. Giant-sized animals are unnerving when you first see them—I get it. But once folks are educated, they get comfortable with it."

Connie forced a smile and wondered if she could actually eat the steak.

4

Time Off

"Take it easy, Mike," said Andrew, waving as he exited the front of the building. Mike, the giant-sized security guard, returned the wave, barely looking up from his iPad where he caught up on sports.

Andrew had a few days off in a row to go home, which all employees got once a month. Most of the time, employees only had a day or two off between their three or four day shift, so they just stayed at the facility and enjoyed the pool, the free gourmet food, and various forms of entertainment from billiards to a small Irish pub where most of them went at night to wind down. "Going home" meant far travel for most of them, and it typically wasn't worth the effort. The dorms at the farm were spacious and beautiful, and the employees were happy to stay over in rooms nicer than most of their homes. In Andrew's case, it was different. He had an important meeting ahead of him.

Andrew walked to his motorcycle and put on his helmet, then started up the old Yamaha and roared out of the parking lot. He swiped his card at the main gate and when it opened, he took off down the rural road. As much as he was always stressed while at the facility, the drive in and out never failed to help him clear his head. Reaching speeds of one hundred twenty miles per hour on the straightaways, the ride to Harrisburg could be cut down to two and a half hours. He stopped only once, to take the plastic baggie out of his underwear and shove it into his jacket pocket.

As he roared down the rural roads, his mind wandered. What a strange life-journey he had taken. From Penn State College undergrad to a master's in microbiology at UPenn to the largest, most advanced research lab in the country, Andrew Booth had always been one of the brightest minds in the room. It wasn't until he met his current girlfriend, a California self-proclaimed hippie, that his views on science in America radically changed.

Hope Whitley had come into Andrew's life when he went to San Francisco on vacation after graduate school. He needed a little break before starting his exciting new job at Global Tech World Solutions Laboratory, so he hopped on a flight to San Francisco where he planned to spend four weeks riding down the coast from San Francisco to San Diego on a rented motorcycle. Instead, he met Hope on his third day in San Francisco and was instantly hooked on the free-spirited beauty who had been born and raised in the Haight-Ashbury section of the city by two very free-spirited parents who refused to stop being hippies.

After years of intense study, to meet someone so completely laid-back was mind-blowing. They had met in a small bar while listening to local musicians. He watched this beautiful woman with hair down to her perfect little butt dance around the bar without a care in the world and knew he had to meet her. Their conversation led to Hope introducing him to dozens of people in the bar, which led to him calling Hope "The Mayor." Everyone knew and loved Hope and seeing how everyone reacted to her made him want to know more about her. He asked her to dinner the following night and, as fate would have it, she and her boyfriend had broken up a few weeks prior, and she said yes.

Andrew and Hope had dinner in Chinatown, where he learned Hope was a vegetarian, followed by a long walk through the city. The evening ended with her staying over at his motel. He hadn't been with a woman in over a year, having devoted all of his time to finishing his master's degree, and Hope was nothing short of amazing in bed. Having just won the lottery of life, Andrew, now officially "Andy," asked her to go with him to San Diego. At first, she said no, so he just remained in San Francisco, seeing her every day and night. Eventually, she hopped on the back of his bike and they headed south for a beautiful five days of sight-seeing and getting to know each other on a deeper level. When Andy told her the following week he had to go back to Pennsylvania to start his new job, they were both heartbroken. After two solid days of begging her, she decided to throw caution to the wind and head east to see what Pennsylvania was like.

After coming from a city like San Francisco, Pennsylvania farm country was a culture shock. Hope missed her hippy parents, her beautiful city, and the ocean. But she had fallen for Andy and found herself drawn to the animals and farmland and decided to stay with Andy to see where life would lead them. It wasn't until he started telling her about what his new job was like that he discovered Hope's radical views on GMOs and "big government." It shouldn't have come as a surprise, coming from a hippy household of California ultra-liberals, but to see Hope so completely angry and upset about what he was doing at work was unnerving. He went from being excited about what they were doing in the lab to feeling guilty, like he was some sort of Dr. Frankenstein. When Hope told him that he had to talk to one of her friends in San Francisco about what he was working on, he found himself in a tough spot. He'd signed numerous non-disclosure forms and swore secrecy to his projects, but Hope was persuasive, and he eventually caved.

It was the phone call to Hope's friend Dean that would change everything, forever.

Chet and Li made an unlikely-looking pair of friends. While they were both brilliant scientists, Chet Smilek was a giant of a man who used his time off to train in the weight room. He'd put on ten pounds of muscle since starting his career at the lab. His beard was red like his balding head, but now showed some white streaks in the chin. Without his black nerd glasses, he looked more like a middle-aged Viking than a scientist. Li Chen, on the other hand, weighed less than the weights on Chet's curling bar. His off-time was spent playing Sudoku or reading computer magazines. Still, the two of them loved each other's company when they weren't working and shared a similar warped sense of humor.

"We're going to get fired," said Li quietly. His voice was timid, like his persona. At five-foot-six and barely one-twenty, Li was mousy for a man. He was also one of the most brilliant geneticists in the lab.

"Chill out, man," said Chet. The two of them had a buzz on after a few rounds in the Irish Pub where the workers had gone to unwind after a long day. Their discussions about the mites they had been working on had led to guesses on insect behavior, which led to cash bets, which led them back to the lab.

"Destruction of property, trespassing, violation of our contracts—oh yeah. We're fired and going to jail," replied Li.

"You're such a pussy. Besides, fifty bucks is going to be mine."

The two of them walked into the lab after swiping themselves in and putting lab jumpsuits and booties back on. The place was always sterile and immaculate.

"The fifty I'm going to take from you won't cover my bills after I get fired."

Chet ignored his whining and walked over to the cabinet where the live specimens were kept. He pulled out a Plexiglas tank that was sealed shut and placed it on a large table. He then pulled a different tank, much smaller, from another cabinet.

"After I win, we leave here immediately," said Li.

Chet placed the small container on the table and opened the top. Inside, a small lab rat was sitting nervously in the corner.

The two of them knelt beside the larger tank and looked inside. Half a dozen beetle-sized mites were feeding on a small piece of beef. They tunneled in and out of the bloody meat as they ate their way through it.

"Nasty little fuckers," said Chet. "I hope Lil' Clarence is hungry."

"You named the rat?" asked Li.

"Hell yeah. That's my champion."

"Wait—you've done this before?"

Chet smiled.

"That's cheating! You trained him to eat the mites?"

"You didn't ask if I'd done it before."

Li was pissed. "We had a gentleman's bet! This is bullshit, Chet."

"Hey, I told you that the mites wouldn't be able to go after bigger food until they were at least three centimeters. These are less than two. You took the bet."

"I took the bet based on their evolving feeding techniques and some new type of colony behavior we've been observing. You didn't say you'd already done this."

"You didn't ask me. Still think they can take Lil' Clarence?"

Li got down closer to the tank and jumped back when two of the creatures inside bounced off the glass after jumping at his face. Li stared at the mites. Once so small they could only be seen under a powerful electron microscope, they were now larger than Japanese beetles and looked much more menacing. With the same slightly iridescent armor as the beetles, the mites were also covered in small hair-like horns and razor-sharp teeth and claws.

When microscopic, the tiny creatures lived an unseen life on human skin. Normal dust mites were so small they could spend their days inside a pore or hair follicle. They would emerge at night and use their claws to climb hairs or pluck at dead skin cells. The "skin janitors" provided an essential service to their hosts in a symbiotic relationship that functioned much like that between a clownfish and a sea anemone.

Now super-sized, the once slow-moving creatures were as fast as cockroaches and as aggressive as wasps. The only reason they were still being used in the lab was because of their use in genetic coding experiments that were then carried over to the more complicated mammals. It was the cattle, sheep, and pigs that were the true aim of all the size experiments, but tiny creatures like these grew at amazing rates and reproduced rapidly. They were useful, if not horrific-looking.

Li stood back up trying to look calm after jumping when the tiny bugs tried to attack him through the glass. "The bet's the bet. Fifty bucks. Clarence has to eat all six."

"Fine," said Chet, smiling. He hadn't fed Lil' Clarence in three days.

The two of them shined a light under the lid to make sure none of the mites had climbed under it and then tapped it hard to knock off any that might be too small to see. Chet picked up the rat by his tail and nodded at Li, who quickly opened the top of the tank. Chet dropped the rat inside, and Li slammed the lid closed, and the two of them stooped over, hands on their knees, to watch the micro-gladiators go at it.

The rat's nose twitched, and he scurried towards one of the mites that was skittering around inside. Chet smiled and whispered, "Good boy."

What happened next was so fast that the two of them would be processing it in their brains for the rest of the night. From out of the beef, five more mites emerged and attacked Lil Clarence in an orderly fashion. They looked like a colony of army ants. As they converged on top of the rat, dozens more raced out of the meat. These were much smaller—babies of the original six, barely the size of sesame seeds, but they were lightning-fast and streamed across the floor of the tank disappearing into the rat's fur.

Clarence spun in circles a few times as he tried to bite at his attackers, but the much smaller creatures tore through his fur and burrowed into his skin, instantly disappearing into the rat's body.

"What the fuck?" said Chet, his face showing his abject terror.

Li, having now forgotten about their bet, grimaced as he watched the rat spin around and flip in circles, making loud screeching noises that neither of them had ever heard before. The rodent was obviously experiencing a whole new level of pain.

"Oh my God," whispered Li.

The rat dropped on its side and died as blood oozed out of its orifices. Within seconds, the rat's body began to disappear in some kind of bizarre vanishing act as it deflated. The mites emerged through the shredded skin and continued their feeding frenzy. Chet and Li just watched silently, disgusted beyond words. Chet had been sure the rat would just eat the small critters. Li thought they might attack him like they did when they were fed beef, but even he didn't expect such an immediate and violent destruction of the lab rat.

After five minutes, there was nothing left except a few of the rat's teeth. No fur, no blood, no nothing. Just a few tiny, white teeth. The mites went back to the piece of beef, still not satiated, which seemed impossible for their size.

"Look," said Li, pointing to one of the mites in the corner.

The mite's exoskeleton split in the back, and out of this emerged an exact duplicate, now almost forty percent larger than the first. The mite ate its own exoskeleton, then proceeded to squirt a small stream of eggs on the floor of the glass.

"Jesus," whispered Chet.

Li stood up and took a step back. "Okay, that's it. We're out of here. I'm going back to the bar and doing shots of tequila until I can't see that anymore. That was disgusting."

Chet, normally Mr. Macho, made a face and nodded. He quickly picked up the mite's tank, double-checked the lid, and slid it back into the cabinet again. He looked over at Lil' Clarence's tank and made a face, then dropped it into a bin for contaminated glassware.

"Fifty bucks," said Li, walking quickly out of the lab.

"Fifty bucks," said Chet quietly, then added: "Sorry, Clarence."

5

Micro Lab

"Jesus. Is that a new record?" asked Joyce, who was one of the many scientists working in the micro lab. She normally worked in the farm—building two—and was just dropping off samples. It was still early in the morning, and she looked much more chipper than Chet, who hadn't slept well thanks to the nightmares.

"Might be. Four pounds," replied Chet. He placed the abhorrent dead creature on the black slate countertop. Normally smaller than a grain of salt, now larger than a softball, the dead skin mite was a multi-legged creature with sharp weapon-like mouthparts and razor-sharp grasping claws. The hair-like horns extending from its back only added to the creature's ferocious appearance. It was black in color, with a grayish underside, but the face of the thing was slightly iridescent purple, an aubergine metallic warrior's mask.

"Lifespan?" asked Joyce.

"This one's four months. Thousands of molts. They're amazing. If they lived longer, no telling how big they could get." He adjusted his black nerd glasses on his nose.

"When are you going to start doing shrimp and lobster? *Then* you'd have something!" she joked.

He stared at her. "Seriously?"

She shrugged.

"No, really? You didn't know?"

"About what?" asked Joyce.

"We *did* do lobster and shrimp. The meat was nasty. Lobsters over ninety pounds and shrimp over thirty. All the meat was tough, and the texture was gross, no matter how we tried to prepare it. The chefs even tried cutting it into tiny pieces. It was just, I don't know, different. We stopped working with them three years ago. Thank God for that. Running the aquariums was such a pain in the ass."

Joyce nodded. She had only been working at the lab for a year and a half. "I didn't know. So why are you still working on these nasty skin mites?"

"They're the best organisms for the size experiments. Their size is undetermined. They'll just keep growing until they die. Rapid growth rates make for easy observations. It's been fascinating, albeit totally disgusting," said Chet, matter-of-factly. He held up a

Petri dish that contained flea-sized creatures that were feeding on minuscule pieces of cow flesh recovered from the butcher scraps.

"Yeah, you're not kidding. Most hideous looking things I've ever seen," said Joyce, making a face.

"Oh no, I didn't mean their appearance. It's watching them *eat*." He looked at her face, which showed revulsion. "Yeah. When they're the size of the head of a pin, and they eat your dead skin cells, you don't mind. Even when they get bigger and start eating meat, you don't mind so much. But when they're *this* big and attack lab rats, you could pretty much barf. They don't leave a scrap. Nothing. *Nada*. Give them long enough, you won't even find any blood in the tank. Course, the plus side is we don't have to clean out the tanks when they're done."

"You feed them lab rats?"

"Normally, we feed them raw beef. After a brief conversation about their behavior changing as their size increased, we did a live rat experiment. These things normally only eat dead tissue, like scavengers. When they became a few hundred thousand times larger, their eating habits changed. Little monsters attacked a live rat like piranhas. It was fascinating, if not disgusting. Quite efficient eaters."

Li's face fell. He was nearby and shocked to hear Chet talking about their screwed up late-night experiment. Joyce was cute though, and Chet was probably trying to impress her. Li shook his head angrily and walked away from them. Chet hadn't been nearly as cavalier about it last night when both of them almost puked.

Joyce held up her hands. "Okay, that's enough. I'd like to be able to eat and sleep again at some point in my future."

Chet shrugged. "Actually, I'm wrong about them eating everything. We did find the rat's *teeth*. That was it. Just the teeth. Guess they don't like to eat enamel. What are *you* working on?"

"Corn. Beautiful, non-meat-eating, sweet corn." She struck a dramatic, angelic pose with a huge smile.

"Gonna make popcorn the size of this guy?"

Joyce raised an eyebrow. "No. But instead of one marketable ear per plant, we'll have six that are all equally good quality. Unlike your disgusting little friend there, what I'm working on will actually feed the world."

"Yeah, he's more likely to eat the world," said Chet, not knowing how close to being right he just might be.

6

GTWS

THE GROUP SIPPED DELICIOUS Cabernet and chatted about their progress in the lab until the server arrived with their four steaks. He placed a plate in front of Paul, who quietly mouthed his amazement.

"This looks amazing," said Connie as she looked down at the thick, juicy steak on her plate. They each were also served a baked potato and asparagus. "Looks as good as any steakhouse in New York."

"Oh, it *is*," said Lamont with a smile. He then shifted to the role of analytical scientist again. "Notice the shape of your steak, though. Normally, you'd have the more muscular middle part of the steak around a fat eye in the center. Then on the outside, there would be a slightly fattier layer, the fat-marbled muscle called the *spinalis dorsi*, known as the lip or cap. What you're eating is just a very small portion of that outer cap, which is well-marbled and super tender."

Lamont refilled Paul's wine glass.

"No wonder you have the budget you do," said Paul, only half joking. "That bottle of Silver Oak your normal table wine?"

"Oh no, this was special for your visit," said Kim. "I saw a comment on Connie's Facebook page about her favorite wine, so we made sure we had some for you."

Connie laughed. "Big Brother is always watching! In this case, I'm glad. Thank you." She cut her steak, which was extremely tender, and tried her first small bite. Her face lit up. "Wow, this is amazing. Really, really great."

Paul was chewing his own mouthful. "Definitely," he said, his mouth still full of steak. "Best steak I ever had."

Lamont beamed with pride. "I told you, we'll change the world."

They finished their meal and sat back to finish Silver Oak bottle number three.

"For the record, we don't normally drink during the day," said Kim, her cheeks now rosy. She was a size two petite, and after two glasses of wine, was already a little buzzed. Connie was a glass ahead of her, and equally "happy."

"So, what happens next?" asked Lamont. "We're ready on our end. And now you can see for yourselves, the quality is there. The ball's in your court."

Paul wiped his mouth with the napkin and nodded his head. "I know I speak for both of us when I tell you how impressed we are." He looked at Connie, who smiled and nodded. "I'll be speaking with the C-Suite on Friday. We'll be planning with the lobbyists and PR folks and coming up with a timetable. It won't be easy, but the lobbyists we're using are top notch."

"Maybe we should just drive around America, giving people free steak samples. They'd demand the FDA approve everything immediately!" said Connie, a little louder than usual. She finished her glass, and Lamont poured her another. She started to say no, but then just laughed and waved him on.

"This will require more than just FDA approval. We'll need a serious PR campaign," said Paul.

"Like the movie we showed you when you arrived," said Kim.

"Exactly," replied Paul. "We'll probably end up using that same production company with our lobbyists. But what I'd really like, is to bring out some of the senators and congressmen and have them sit right here for a steak."

"And some Silver Oak!" said Connie, raising her glass before taking another big gulp.

"Amen!" said Kim, taking a sip herself. Lamont raised a glass, and so Paul did as well.

"I can see today is not going to be a very productive day after lunch," said Lamont with a beaming smile.

"I'm serious," said Paul, trying to stay on task. "We bring out some of the bigwigs from Washington D.C., wine and dine them here, and send them back to D.C. to start writing some legislation that will make production a hell of a lot easier than it is right now.

We pick up China as a client and it's a game-changer. Even poor people in China will be able to buy beef. We save the world, make a few billion dollars—it's a win-win!"

"Let's do it!" said Lamont. "Bring 'em over! We'll feed them steaks and start raising up a real herd!"

7

Harrisburg

ANDY PARKED HIS BIKE next to the tiny house and walked inside. Hope greeted him with a big hug.

"Hey, baby! I missed you," she said, leaning in for a very long kiss. They stayed kissing for a while. She eventually broke it off and asked, "Did you get them?"

He looked at her, feeling uneasy. "It's not cool, Hope. I could get fired. Hell, they could sue me for a zillion dollars. This is all really top-secret stuff. I signed like a million forms when I started working there, after a lot of background checks. That place is like working for the CIA or something."

She made a frown-face and gave him her sad blue eyes. "You said you would help."

"Yeah, I know. I just... I don't know."

"Look. Just talk to him, okay? I told him you'd be home today. He's coming by tonight."

"You invited Dean here? Are you crazy?"

Her face showed a flash of instant anger. "He's my friend, Andrew!" she snapped. She never called him Andrew. Ever. "I knew him way before I knew you."

He crossed his arms. "And what's that supposed to mean?"

"Oh don't give me any of that macho-possessive bullshit. It's not cool, Andy. It was a million years ago. God. Boys." She walked off into the kitchen in a huff.

Andy took off his jacket, pulling out the bag of samples as he took it off. He walked into the kitchen and held it up for Hope to see. She was at the kitchen table, filling up her bong with pot for a hit. She stopped and stood up. "You brought it?"

"I told you I would," he said quietly.

"I'm so proud of you," she said, coming around the table to kiss him. Within a few minutes, the fight was forgotten, and they were both stoned and having sex on the floor. A few minutes later, Hope began getting dressed again. "Dean's gonna be here soon. Get dressed."

Andy considered making a wise-ass comment about remaining naked and letting Dean know he had just had sex with Hope, who apparently had some sort of history with this dude he didn't even know, but held his tongue. Even he knew now wasn't the time, and he got dressed as he was supposed to.

"Doesn't Dean have a record?" asked Andy.

"What does that have to do with anything?" asked Hope, sounding annoyed again.

"Because if my employer ever found out I was meeting with a dude that was arrested and incarcerated, I'm screwed. I'm telling ya', this isn't cool."

"Just listen to him for a little while, okay? No one would ever know he was here. Jeez, Andy. You think your employer watches you twenty-four-seven? Even more the reason you should listen to Dean and Wally."

"Who's Wally?" asked Andy.

"Dean will tell you about him. I don't know him as well as Dean does. He was sort of a legend in San Francisco. Super cool, brave dude."

Andy crossed his arms in front of his chest and stood staring at Hope. There were times when she really pissed him off, but she was so beautiful, so sexy, so—something... "Okay. Fine. I'll listen to your friend, Dean. But I'm telling you right now, this was a one-time deal. I'm not smuggling stuff out of the lab again. Not for him or his buddies."

Hope walked over to him with the bong and exhaled a long stream of blue smoke. Her eyes looked like skating rinks. "Why don't you just hit the bong and chill, baby?"

He stepped away from her. "You know I can get random drug-tested at work! What's wrong with you? Jeez! Have just a little respect for my career!"

Even a contact high would be enough to show a trace amount, and to make it worse, he worked in a lab. She wandered out into the small den and turned on the TV, then proceeded to finish smoking until her head hit the back of the couch. She was, in her words, "feeling chilled out."

Andy fished a beer out of the fridge and sat in the kitchen feeling a mix of aggravated and stressed out. The moment had only been made slightly more tolerable by having just screwed like porn stars on the floor. He was on his second beer when the doorbell rang. By the time he was out of his chair in the kitchen, his still-stoned girlfriend was running to the door with just a little too much excitement.

"Heyyyy! Dino!" she exclaimed, and fell into his arms for a long hug.

When Dean looked up from the embrace and saw Andy watching him smelling her long hair, he stepped back. "Hey. You must be Andy." He smiled and extended his hand. They shook hands and Hope hooked Dean's arm and escorted him into the den, plopping down next to him on the couch.

"You look great, Dino. Man, it's been forever," said Hope, her big, blue eyes even shinier than usual. "Andy, could you grab a couple of beers for us?"

Dean smiled and looked her over. "Thanks, babe. You look awesome, too. Are you baked?"

She giggled. "A little. Want some?"

"No, let me talk to your man here for a bit first. Maybe after."

Andy emerged from the kitchen holding three beers. He handed one to Hope, then the second to Dean, staring right through him as he gave it to him. Dean was older, bigger, and tougher-looking than he was, with straight blonde hair and a couple of days of stubble on his face. With his jean vest on over his leather jacket, he looked like a biker from another era.

"Thanks, dude," said Dean as he took the beer. "And thanks for talking to me. Hope told me you weren't really too happy bringing the samples out of the lab, so I really appreciate what you did. You got them, right?"

Andy nodded, stone faced. He sipped his beer.

"Cool. Cool. Look, I don't wanna get into a whole thing about the company you work for, but I would like you to talk to a dude."

"Wally?"

"Yeah. Hope told you about him?"

"Not much. Just that he was supposed to be some kind of big shot."

Dean chuckled. "A big shot. Yeah, maybe." He looked at Hope, whose eyes were halfway closed. She was staring at the ceiling, a little too stoned to communicate. She was sitting closer to Dean than to Andy, and Andy wasn't happy about it.

Dean leaned forward with his elbows on his knees and looked at Andy with a serious face. "I want you to talk to him. Just listen to what he has to say. Be open-minded."

"I've already broken about ten laws just bringing you the seeds."

"Yeah, I know, and we appreciate your bravery. Really. But when evil men make laws, it's not evil to break them."

Andy just stared at him.

Dean broke the eye contact and fished out his iPhone. "You have Wi-Fi?"

Hope, half-listening, said, "Save the planet. Password 'healer'."

Sure enough, a Wi-Fi connection appeared that read "Save the planet." Dean chuckled. "That's so Hope. You're awesome."

Andy's jaw tightened, but he kept his mouth shut. Once Dean had a Wi-Fi connection, he checked his watch, opened FaceTime, and dialed Walter in New York City.

"Hey, brother," said a smoked-out and cracking voice on the other end.

"Hey, Wally. I'm with Hope and her man Andy in Harrisburg. Hang on, and I'll introduce you." Dean turned the phone around to Andy, and Andy could see a rough looking man with a shaved head and gray goatee. Dean leaned the iPhone against a book on the coffee table so it remained facing Andy. "This is Andy, Wally."

"Hello Andy. My name is Walter Bellville. Wally to my friends. Hopefully, we'll be friends."

"Hey," said Andy. He didn't use either name yet, as he was undecided.

"You ever hear of me?" asked Walter.

"Not really."

"Ever hear of the Nature Power Movement or NPM?"

Andy squinted and thought about that. "Sounds familiar."

"Yeah, well, in your line of work and all, it should. We represent the people against the companies that are destroying our planet."

Andy nodded as it clicked in his brain. "The Prosanto fire?"

"Exactly. Prosanto makes enough pesticide and herbicide to kill the Earth a hundred times, and no one says shit because they own every politician in DC. The bees are dying, man. And everyone knows it's the big Ag-consortiums. No bees means no food, bro. That weed killer they spray in the fields? Cancer-causing. And it kills the crops, too. So what do they do? They re-engineer the crops to be resistant to the weed killer. Now they can just dump a shit-ton of poison on our food and kill fucking everything, man. Everything except their profit. Then they harvest this poison wheat and soy and whatever the fuck they're growing and feed the planet. It's all one big experiment. And their CEO's are all eating organic because they can afford it."

"Right on," said Dean. "They don't give a shit about the regular people."

Andy shot Dean a quick look. Dean was sitting very close to half-asleep Hope, who finally had her head resting against his shoulder.

"It's a war, man. It's time to pick a side and get involved," said Wally.

"You guys fire-bombed an office and killed like ten people," said Andy quietly.

"People die in wars," snapped Wally. "How many millions of people are gonna die this year of cancer because of the shit they spray on our food, or the food itself? That's where your little company comes in, Andy. I've been following Global Tech for years, dude. These are some very evil fuckers, my man."

"And what is it that you think you know about GTW Solutions?" asked Andy, feeling defensive.

"I know they're fucking with DNA. I know that. I know they're engineering food and animals and will fuck up this whole planet dude. GMOs are gonna make humans extinct."

"Right on," said Dean. He relit the bong on the table and took a long hit.

"The work at GTW Solutions is classified. How is it that you think you know what they do?" asked Andy.

"Oh come on, man. You think every scientist on the planet wants to work for Dr. Evil? Get real, bro. There's plenty of people working on the inside who don't like what they see. So now we come to you. You going to be part of the solution, or part of the problem?"

Hope opened her glassy eyes and leaned forward to stare at Andy. "You had better be part of the fuckin' solution," she slurred. She stood up and slinked over to Andy, straddled his lap and started making out with him, grinding against him as she kissed him. Andy pulled away after a moment and whispered, "Chill out, Hope. You're stoned."

"So what? I feel good. And you're gonna be my hero, aren't you, baby?" She leaned back in and sucked on his neck.

"Quite a handful ain't she?" asked Dean with a knowing smile. Andy didn't like the question and pulled her next to him on the couch, on the other side, away from Dean. "So what's it gonna be, Andy? You going to join an army of people who are going to save this planet? Or are you going to side with the money and power and poison?"

Andy wasn't ready to commit to two men that made him uncomfortable. He changed the topic. "I brought the samples. If I get caught, I'm in deep shit."

"That's my man!" exclaimed Wally, a little too friendly. "Good job. Like I said, not every scientist in the country is some fascist power-broker. Plenty of smart people on our side, too, bro. You give the stuff to Dean, and he'll have our people go through it. We

need to see what your bosses are up to. I'm hearing some crazy shit, bro."

Andy cocked his head. "Yeah. Well. Me, too."

"Yeah? What are *you* hearing? What are you *seeing*? Your intel can be priceless. But *we* can put a price on it. We have money behind us. You get us good intel and we can get you some serious coin, dude."

Andy pondered that a moment. Dean interrupted his thought. "What did you see?"

"Genetic engineering. Lots of experiments. I don't get to see everything. But I hear stuff. They're working on animal mutations. Making beef and pork stock larger."

"Uh huh. That's what we hear. Big ones. Like *real* big. Can you get in there to see first-hand? Cop us some video?"

"No way. The zoo, that's building three, it's super restricted. Unless you're on the animal teams, you can't get in there. It was hard enough getting you this stuff."

"Okay. Well, it's a start anyway. Keep snooping around though. Dean's gonna' give you a little present for helping us out. Take it. Buy Hope a present or something. You get us some video, and we'll quadruple it. That's it for now. Dean, get the samples to Ross ASAP, bro. They're no good if they're not viable."

"Roger that, dog," said Dean. He reached into his vest and pulled out an envelope, which he plopped on the coffee table. He picked up his phone, said, "Later," and ended the video call. "Okay, Andy. That's it for now. I'll take the samples and get going."

"You're not staying over?" asked Hope.

Andy's face went red.

"No, baby. It's great to see you and I wish I could hang out, but I gotta get these to a dude right away. Maybe next time." He winked at her and she smiled, making Andy's jaw tighten again.

Andy stood up and walked to the kitchen, grabbing the baggies on the table. He walked out to the den, where Hope was still hugging her friend goodbye. Andy just stood there watching her hold some strange dude in his house.

"Here's the samples," he said coldly.

"Thanks, bro. This is awesome. I'll be in touch." He gave Hope a quick kiss and headed for the door. "I gotta fly. I'll call you soon. Hope, give him my number. Andy—you can text me any time."

He left and closed the door behind him, which Andy locked. He then turned to Hope, looking angry.

"Are you fucking kidding me?" he snapped at her.

"What?"

"What? *What?* You totally disrespect me in front of some old boyfriend and you have the nerve to ask me what?"

Hope walked to him, still feeling pretty high. "Oh, *Andy*," she said, with her pouty face. She slinked over to him, chin on her chest, looking up at him with big, blue eyes, and said, "I don't want to fight..."

She dropped to her knees and unzipped Andy's jeans, picking up where they had left off before Dean's visit.

8

26,000 Feet

Paul and Connie sat in the large seats of the Learjet, stretched out with their shoes off for the flight.

"What an amazing facility," said Connie.

"Yeah, that was something. Great steaks, huh?"

Connie laughed and tucked her legs as she got herself more comfortable in the big chair. "I was a little scared to eat it at first, to be honest."

"And then you had a bite," said Paul, knowingly.

"And then I had a bite. God—it was so good. And I can't believe they had Silver Oak! For lunch!"

"No kidding. I guess when you have a sixty-million-dollar-budget, sneaking in a few hundred for wine isn't so hard."

"I think I'm still buzzed," said Connie. She leaned out and ran her finger up and down Paul's arm. "It was a fun day."

Paul eyed her and cocked his head. "Yes it was." He watched her fingertip make little circles on his arm.

"I like working with you, Paul. If you had me moved to Riker's old job, we could work together all the time."

Paul laughed out loud. "Oh, *that's* what this is about!"

"What *what's* about?" she asked.

"The flirting, the innuendos. Don't try and bullshit a bullshitter, Connie. Riker's old job moves you over and up. Probably doubles your salary? Stock options? I guess that can even make a middle-aged bald guy attractive, huh?"

Connie faked shock and anger with an Oscar winning performance. "Paul! How can you even say that? Yes, the move would be an excellent opportunity, but that has nothing to do with us."

"Us?"

"Oh, stop. Don't even act like you don't feel something, too."

Paul crossed his arms over his chest and leaned away from her. "You're so full of shit your eyes are brown."

Connie unbuckled her seatbelt and lifted the arm rest between them. She leaned in until her face was very close. "My eyes are *very* blue, thank you very much." Her hand moved to his thigh. "Are you really going to tell me I'm the only one who feels something?"

"Connie..."

She slid off the seat to the floor, on her knees between his. "Tell me if the pilot opens that door!" she whispered, reaching for his zipper. Twenty-six thousand feet up and two hundred miles away, Connie began doing exactly the same thing as Hope was doing to Andy.

Paul's head dropped back against the seatback, and he whispered, "Riker's position needed to be filled anyway..."

9

Harrisburg

ANDY WOKE UP AT seven without an alarm, accustomed to his normal seven-to-four shift. He yawned and looked over at Hope, who was still out cold. Her long blonde hair covered half of her beautiful face and breasts. They'd had some serious make-up sex, followed by another small fight over Dean and Wally and their radical views, which led to more make-up sex. It had been a long night.

Andy stretched and scratched his hand and arm. It was still dim in the room, but his wrist looked red. He smiled. They'd been a little wild last night. She must have scratched him.

Andy got out of bed and pulled on shorts, then walked to the kitchen to make coffee. When he was home, he always made Hope coffee in bed. Just a little "I love you" in a mug. He set up the coffee machine and spotted the envelope on the coffee table. He'd forgotten about the cash in the midst of their sexual escapades the night before and hurried over to the envelope.

Twenty-five hundred in crisp new hundred-dollar bills. Andy smiled and just stared at it for a moment. Part of him felt guilty about what he'd done, but Wally did have a point. Prosanto and the other agriculture mega-corporations were cranking out lots of poison. Andy had read plenty of articles about honeybee colony collapse disorder, and the general findings pointed towards mites that were a bee parasite, viruses, and pesticides. While scientists couldn't agree on the exact cause, Andy couldn't dispute Wally's claims. The fact that Wally had firebombed a Prosanto office and killed innocent people didn't sit so well with Andy, however. The hypocrisy of the far left had a way of showing up with justifications of actions they'd otherwise themselves condemn.

Still, twenty-five hundred cash, and no one got hurt.

Andy scratched his wrist. It was an angry red.

The coffee maker hissed, signaling it was finished brewing, and Andy quickly grabbed two mugs and went back to the bedroom. He sat on the edge of the bed and put the mugs down on the nightstand next to Hope.

"Good morning, Sleeping Beauty."

Hope groaned and stretched and rolled on to her back, sweeping her hair out of her face. Even in the morning, she was stunning.

"Hey, you. I *like* when you're home. I missed my coffee in bed." She sat up and gave Andy a hug and kiss. She pointed to his neck. "Sorry about that," she said with an evil smile.

"What?"

"I think I bit you last night."

He smiled. "It was worth it. I might bite you back this morning."

"*After* my coffee!" Hope said with a laugh. Andy handed her the mug, and the two of them sat sipping the nectar of the gods. "Mmm. You make better coffee than me."

"Guess what's in the envelope."

Hope smiled behind her mug. "Oh my God, I forgot about that!"

"Me, too. We were busy."

"It was an excellent fight," she said, still smirking.

"Yeah, well. It would have been nice if I had known that Dean was an ex-boyfriend earlier. Or maybe if you hadn't been all over him."

"Seriously? We already had this fight."

"You're right. So guess."

Her smile returned. "Five hundred?"

He shook his head.

"A *thousand*?"

"How about twenty-five hundred!" He reached into his pocket and pulled out the bills, then ceremoniously dumped them on the blankets.

"Andy, that's awesome! And Wally said he'll give you a lot more if you got him video!"

"I know. I was thinking about that in the kitchen. It'll be really hard, but I thought of a way."

"Oh my God! How?"

"Well, you know I work in the farm in building two most of the time. I have access to everything except the zoo—that's building three. I remembered that the zoo is open-air. They leave it open for sunlight and rain, *et cetera*. It's like a regular pasture from what I'm told. In building two, we have trees around the perimeter. A few of them are pretty big. There's one that could get me up into the steel catwalks and super structure. Once I was up there, I could get over to building three, take some video from up top, and never have to actually even go into the building."

"That's awesome, Andy! If you give him video, he'll give you like ten grand!"

"I know, right? And it's not like I'd even be stealing anything. Just a quick video, in and out, no one would know anything. The farm building is huge. I could definitely get up there with no one seeing me."

Hope smiled and put her mug down. "Why don't you come over here closer, so I can give you a hickey on the other side of your neck."

Andy smiled and put down his coffee.

10

GTW Solutions
Corporate Office
Washington, D.C.

PAUL AND CONNIE TOOK a company limo from Reagan Airport back to their "world headquarters" over on Pennsylvania and Tenth, conveniently located near every senator and congressman in the country. After their brief "interlude" on the jet, Paul decided he would be recommending Connie for the transfer and promotion into his department. He was still smiling as they drove towards the office.

"Enjoy the flight?" asked Connie, rubbing his shin with her foot.

"Unlike any flight I ever had prior. And after a great steak and wine to boot. Might be the best day of the year so far," said Paul. She was using him. He didn't care.

"When will you talk to McNally?"

"Very soon. Relax. I'll be doing everything I can to help you."

"It would be great if we were a team, wouldn't it? Maybe I could take that trip to Dublin with you after all."

"I do believe you'd like Dublin. Although the flight is longer and probably wouldn't be nearly as much fun."

She leaned close. "Well you just never know, do you?"

The limo pulled up in front of their building, and the driver hopped out to open their door. Paul walked quickly to the door with Connie close behind. On a date, he might be more gentlemanly, but this was all business, up to and including letting her know she worked for him, not with him.

The doorman opened the door and welcomed the International President of Development and Special Projects. Paul didn't need to show ID, which meant neither did Connie. They went straight up the elevator to the top floor and went to the conference room, where the CEO, CFO, and COO were waiting for them, having been alerted to their arrival.

They walked in and were greeted with excitement. "Welcome back. We're anxious to hear about your trip!" Exclaimed Roger McNally, the CEO.

"Yes, we've been talking about this all week," said Darla Daniels, the COO.

"Well, we've got a lot of show and tell for you, that's for sure," said Paul, as he took a seat at the long conference table. The table had been made from a cross-section of a giant redwood tree and probably cost as much as an apartment across the Potomac. Its grains took on different colors when it was stained and varnished, and it was a piece of art. Roger said the table served to remind them of their agrarian roots, and that they were a company which embraced nature. The fact that a five-hundred-year-old tree had been cut down to make the table was somehow lost on the C-suite.

"It's an exciting time for GTW," said Sean Smith, the CFO. "We've put a tremendous amount of our global resources into that facility. I think today's the day we find out whether or not it was the right move."

Paul enjoyed the moment, looking at each face in the room with dramatic pause. "Ladies and Gentlemen, I am pleased to tell you that we are ready. We've seen the numbers and reports for months, but after being there, at the site, I can tell you with one hundred percent certainty, Global Tech is about to change the world. When the poorest child in the most remote area of the globe is eating prime rib, we'll look back on this day and smile."

"We'll look back on this day from my carbon fiber mega-yacht, and smile," said Roger, with a wide toothy grin, sounding like as much of a wise-ass as he could muster, enunciating every syllable.

"Tell them about the steaks," whispered Connie.

The three executives looked from her to him.

"Yes, well I suppose I can jump around a bit. At the end of the day, nothing matters if the product doesn't have quality, right? We had the best steaks I've ever eaten. Steak from a fifteen-thousand-pound steer. That's ten times bigger than normal, and it wasn't finished growing. They've had the same results with pork and lamb. They're so good at it now, you can practically tell them how big you want the animals. They've got corn, soy, and wheat all in the works ahead of schedule. And, they've gone vertical, creating the necessary feed to sell to the farmers who raise the livestock. The work product has been outstanding. Allowing the scientists to have a hand in designing the facility was brilliant..."

"And expensive," said Sean, always about the bottom line.

"Yes, it definitely added to the costs. No doubt," said Paul. "But they've created an environment that's astounding. On the way back from the farm, Connie came up with a great idea. Connie—tell them about the launch."

Connie took a deep breath. They had discussed this in the limo, and now was her big break. She would make the presentation, and after she left, Paul would request her transfer and promotion to be his second in command to replace a retired "company original." It was a big move.

Connie stood with perfect posture and began. "Locating this office down the street from the capital was no coincidence. We need the co-operation of the government to make this happen. It's why we paid out over seventeen million dollars last year just to lobbyists. For a fraction of that cost, we can have much more dramatic results." She paused and looked around the room.

"A party. A first class, major event. We fly in every senator and congressman that will agree to come, and give them a real tour of the facility. Then we wine them and dine them on the best food they've ever eaten. We were just there, and let me tell you—they do it right. We wrap up with a video presentation that will make them cry as they watch starving children all over the world, feeling guilty with their own full bellies, and then we tell them how they can end world hunger, right then and there. We have sample bills prepared ahead of time for them to read on their flight home. With some pressure after the dinner, we get the bills introduced in record time."

She sat down and looked at the members of the C-Suite. They were all nodding.

"I like it," said Darla.

"Me, too," said Roger and Sean simultaneously.

"Excellent," replied Paul with a smile. "Connie's already begun the process of crafting a bill with legal. We'll get the invites out right away. The sooner the better. Roger, how long, start to finish, did it take to get the law changed on food origin labeling?"

"It wasn't so much the time, as the money. Three months and eight million dollars."

"Chump change," said Sean. "We made the eight million back the first two weeks we moved the chicken processing to China."

"We also downsized over three hundred jobs, which saved us another fifteen million in salaries and benefits," added Darla.

"Sounds like a winner," said Paul with a grin. "Connie, why don't you get started on this right away?"

Connie saw the invitation to leave and stood up. "Thank you all very much. I look forward to working with you all closely on this going forward. I'll get the wheels moving at full speed."

She left the room.

"A mover and shaker," said Darla, happy to see another successful woman in a male-dominated company. Paul jumped on her comment.

"Yes, she is. Which is why I wanted to chat with you all without her in the room. I'd like to move her to Bob Riker's old position. She's a bit young, but she's sharp."

"Wow. Quite a jump, don't you think?" asked Roger skeptically.

"I think she'd be great," said Darla.

"She'd probably be happy with sixty percent of Bob's salary. You could fill the position and save us some money," said Sean.

Darla snapped at Sean. "Because she's a woman?"

"No, no, because she's a kid! Bob was here for twenty years before he was pulling down that kind of salary."

"She does his job, she gets his salary," said Darla.

"I'm hearing two things," said Paul. "I'm hearing we all agree that she's qualified, it's just a matter of money. Is that right, Roger?"

Roger shrugged. "Paul, it's your department. If that's your choice, I'll back you up on it. Salary is always a negotiation."

"She should be making what anyone else in the company is making in that position," said Darla coldly.

"Of course," said Paul. "And I think, just starting out, it's fair that she'd come in making less than what Bob was making when he left after twenty years." He looked at Sean, then back at Darla. "But she'd almost double her current salary, have stock option potential when this thing runs, and in a year or two, be looking at Riker's numbers if she can perform as I expect she can." Paul's mind wandered to how she had just performed on the plane, and he snapped himself back to the present. "So—do we have a consensus? I'd like to tell her now, and have that fire her up as she gets going on this party idea. We tell her she just doubled her salary, and I wouldn't be surprised to see the president at the damn party!"

They all chuckled, exchanged nods and smiles, and told Paul he could deliver the happy news. Paul decided he would take her to dinner to tell her, and her first "bonus" would come immediately following.

11

Harrisburg

ANDY STEPPED OUT OF the shower and looked in the mirror. His skin was irritated in a few spots, and only one of them looked like a hickey. He leaned in closer to the mirror and wiped off the steamy haze. He had several red blotches that itched and burned, and looked like they were getting worse, not better. He walked out to the bedroom where Hope was still in the process of getting dressed.

Andy spotted the rash on her lower back and butt cheeks and felt his face get hot with anger.

"Hope." He snapped, his voice sounding cold as ice.

"What is it, Andy?" she asked, looking confused. She could sense his anger and had no idea why.

"Let me ask you something, and just tell me the truth. No bullshit."

"What?"

"Promise me—no bullshit!"

"Andy, what is it?" she asked, now feeling alarmed.

"This!" he snapped, showing her his arm, then lifting his chin to show his neck. "This rash. It's all over me. And I see it on your ass. Were you fucking Dean?"

"What?" she screamed.

"Did that fucking dirtbag give you some kind of shit that you gave me?"

"Andy! What are you talking about? I hadn't seen Dean in years! And he's not a dirtbag! He's an old friend and a great guy!"

"Swear to me!"

"I am swearing to you! Why are you being such an asshole?"

"Because I've got this shit all over me and it burns! And I see it on you, too. I haven't been with anyone else, Hope. Have you?"

"Oh, fuck you, Andy!" There was real spite in her voice this time.

"Don't bullshit me, Hope! I know how you are. You like to be 'Miss Free Spirit' and fuck on the first date. You been banging anyone else while I'm working my ass off?"

"Oh that's it! Because we had sex on the first date, now I'm a whore? You can get the fuck out of here!" She threw her hairbrush at him. "Get out! Get the fuck out!"

Andy stormed out of the room and slammed the door behind him. He stood in the den, pissed, and thought about what to do next. What if it was some kind of creepin' crud from some dude she was screwing? What if it wasn't and he was just being a jealous asshole? He heard her crying and breaking things in the bedroom and then suddenly felt like an idiot. He wasn't thinking clearly. He had been jealous of Dean.

Andy walked back to the bedroom and opened the door. Hope was on the bed crying. When she saw him, she told him to leave, still crying, but he ignored her and knelt down between her legs.

"I'm sorry, Hope. I'm really sorry." He hugged her, but she tried to lean away. "I was just really jealous of Dean. You were flirting with him, and I got pissed. Then I see this shit popping out all over me, and then I see it on you..."

"You're an asshole," she said quietly, then hugged him back.

"I know. I'm really sorry."

"Show me how sorry," she said.

Andy pushed her back on the bed and dropped his towel.

When he was finished "apologizing," Andy held Hope close and felt her heart pounding. "We've been fighting too much," he said.

"The making up has been really good, though," she said, grinning.

Andy smiled, too. "I have to go back tomorrow. If Wally will give us ten grand, I'll take that video. No one gets hurt, nothing gets stolen, and we get ten grand in cash."

She rolled over to face him and threw a long silky leg over his hip. "That's my man," she said. She looked at his rash. "That is really red. Poison ivy maybe?"

"How would I get poison ivy? How would we both get poison ivy? I work inside a lab that's totally controlled. Nothing grows in there that isn't planted on purpose."

"You didn't get it until you got home. Maybe it was from around the house?"

"I wasn't outside much. And you have it, too. Does it burn or itch?"

"No. I didn't even know I had it until you told me."

"I wonder if I got it from you or you got it from me?"

"You're not going to start that again, are you?"

"No, no. I didn't mean like that. It just burns. It's getting worse."

She made a face. "On your way back to work, stop and get some cortisone cream. Maybe take a Benadryl."

"Good idea. I'll stop and get some. You should too. I'm sure it'll be gone in a day or two..."

12

Philadelphia

WALLY AND DEAN MET in a dump of a bar in south Philly and took a small table in the back of the pub. They drank pints of Guinness while they spoke quietly about the latest lab results. It was fairly busy for the middle of the afternoon, but Irish pubs didn't follow the same schedule as the rest of the world. The sawdust on the floor and the smell of old sour beer soaked into the ancient planks verified the authenticity of the joint.

"The seeds were the same GMO crap we see all the time, but that's not why I drove all the way out here to meet you face to face. There's some seriously fucked up shit going on in that lab, bro," said Wally as he leaned closer to Dean.

"What's up?" asked Dean, white creamy foam in his mustache hair from his Guinness.

"Hope's boy…" mumbled Wally, as he placed a Camel cigarette between his lips. He wiped a few tiny pieces of tobacco off his tongue and thoughtfully stared at the small, dried fragments.

"Andy?"

"Yeah, Andy—he stumbled on some crazy shit, my man."

"The seeds?" asked Dean, a little confused.

"No, man. At a quick glance, one of the samples looked like seeds, but the shit was alive, bro. My boys in the lab freaked out. They said, and I will try and repeat this as close as possible… The samples in the bag were genetically modified microscopic skin mites that are already thousands of times larger than normal, and apparently still growing."

"Thousands of times larger? I don't get it. There was only tiny seeds and shit in those bags."

"No man, that's what I'm saying. One of the bags had seeds and corn kernels and leaves in it. The other bag had what looked like seeds, but they weren't. They were skin mites." He lit the cigarette with a Zippo, clicking it open and closed, and inhaled the unfiltered cigarette. Smoking wasn't allowed in the bar, but they were in the back, and no one was going to approach these two and tell them to put it out.

"What the fuck is a skin mite? Sounds nasty, man," said Dean, taking another long drink of his beer.

"It is nasty. Look, human bodies are covered with millions of tiny microscopic bugs that eat dead skin cells and bacteria and shit. Everything on the planet is covered with the stuff. But those

Frankenstein dudes at Global Tech modified them to make them way bigger. You normally need an electron microscope to see these things. The ones that the kid brought home are big enough to see with your naked eye. They just keep eating and growing and reproducing. It's some crazy shit, bro. Regular horror movie stuff."

Dean's face showed his disgust. "So what happens when they get big?"

"No one knows. That's the fucked up part, bro. No one knows. These mad scientists can end the whole planet with what they're doing, and the government just hides it and acts like nothing is wrong."

"The government is behind it?" asked Dean. He waved at the waitress and held up two fingers, then finished his beer.

"Of course! You don't think these billion-dollar companies aren't tied into the government, do you? Did you see how they changed the food import rules?"

Dean shook his head. He wasn't the activist that Wally was, he was just happy to get paid to occasionally break the law, kick some ass, and bang plenty of young and idealistic women who thought he was a soldier of the cause. Wally was a superhero. By being around Wally, he was almost a superhero, too—the closest he ever came to amounting to anything. Not having anything beyond what amounted to a tenth-grade education, Dean sometimes had a hard time keeping up with Wally's long tirades. As rough and scary as Wally was, he had learned a lot by reading while in jail and was actually the smartest guy Dean had ever met—which may not have been saying much with Dean's circle of friends.

Wally shook his head. "Man, you gotta' start reading more, Dean. You're like one of my top guys, and you don't even know half the shit that's going down."

"Yeah, I know. I don't read much, ya' know? But you know I got your back."

Wally nodded and gave him a fist bump. "I know. But listen—shit's about to get real. We have to take a stand on this one. I'm talking to some people. Getting some real big shit together. You gonna be my general in the field?"

Dean smiled. Kickin' ass was one of the few things he was good at. "You know it."

"We're taking it down."

"Taking what down?"

"Global Tech. I'm going to get so many of our people together it will be like an army. We're going to storm the castle, bro. Gonna destroy that place and everything in it."

"Whoa," said Dean, surprised. "Seriously? Like, that giant facility where Andy works?"

"That's the one. Andy is gonna get us some video, and we're gonna smoke that fucking place and everything in it."

The waitress came by and brought them two more beers. She eyed the cigarette but said nothing.

"Thanks," said Wally to the waitress. "Can I get a cheeseburger? You want something, Dean?"

"Uh, yeah. Cheeseburger is fine, thanks."

When the waitress left, Dean leaned closer to Wally. "Yo, man. Most of our people are like, you know, animal rights and shit. They'd freak if they knew we ate meat..."

Wally gave him a cold look—one that had been mastered in prison. "Fuck that, man. I ain't no vegan. We say what we have to say to build our army, you know? But listen—if a cow could eat you, it probably would. I don't like how they treat the animals—don't get me wrong, and I'm glad we keep the pressure on the big Ag companies. But at the end of the day, meat's meat and a man's gotta eat."

"This job out at the plant. Paying gig?"

"I'll take care of you. You know I always do."

"Yeah. I know you do, but you know, money's tight."

Wally reached into his jacket and pulled out an envelope. "There's two grand in there. Keep half and give the other half of it to Hope. Tell her it's a down payment on that video. We need it fast, man." Wally glanced around the bar slowly, taking in everyone around them then leaned in closer. "Dean, this gig is gonna be huge. And when it's all over, you and me are outta here with more money than you can count. I got a spot all picked out in Mexico, and we're gonna live large, my man. Never gonna work another day in our lives."

Dean smiled. "Now you're talking. How's this gonna get us money?"

"You let me worry about that part. Got it all covered. You just do your part and I'll take care of the rest. Big money, man. Big."

Dean smiled at the thought of going back to see Hope. She still looked amazing, and it was pretty obvious she still had a thing for him. Andy would be back at the plant when he paid her a visit. Maybe he'd stay a little while.

13

Making Plans

CONNIE WALKED OUT OF the congressman's office and headed down the elevator. When she got to the bottom, she called Paul, whose condo she had just left that very morning after staying over for the second time in three nights since her promotion.

"Hey, good-looking," he said when he saw her number light up on his phone.

"Three for three," she said, sounding happy.

"Oh yeah? Nice start."

"It'll keep getting easier. Once one hears who's going, the next one wants to make sure he's there, too, you know?"

"Of course."

"There's a rumor that Casey will be going, so of course the junior congressmen jumped at the invitation."

Paul laughed. William Casey was the majority leader of the house. "A rumor, huh?"

She laughed. "Just a rumor. By the time I speak to Casey, I'll have fifty people coming."

"Get the Whips committed. If the Whips go, the parties will fall into line."

"Good idea. I'll go see Hastings next."

"You have a date worked out yet?"

"Two weeks. It's fast, which means schedule conflicts for some of them, but it's a weekend visit, which helps. Besides, I can be very persuasive."

Paul nodded. "That you can, my dear."

―――――

Andy called Hope when he got back to the plant and parked his bike. "Hey, babe, I made it. No traffic."

"Awesome, Andy. Dean just called. He's going to stop by with a down payment for that video."

"Shh! Not on the phone."

"Do you really think they listen to your..."

"Hope! I heard you. I'll get it. When's Dean stopping by?"

"I don't know. He just called a little while ago."

There was an awkward silence. Andy felt himself getting angry again, but what was he supposed to do?

"Fuck!" he snapped.

"Andy! Stop it!"

"No, not that! It's my arm. Hang on." He pulled off his gloves and jacket and pulled up his sleeve. The rash was raw and blistering. "Shit. I think the cortisone made it worse."

"Is there a doctor at the plant you can see?"

"Yeah. Like the whole place is full of doctors."

"No, I mean a real doctor. Is there a first-aid station there or something?"

"Yeah. I think so. I'll ask my supervisor. How's your rash?"

"I can only see it in the mirror, but it hurts. Tell me what your doc says. If he gives you medicine, get extra for me."

"Okay, will do." He paused. He wanted to say something about Dean's visit, but took a deep breath and just said, "I love you."

"Love you, too, babe. Call me soon. Bye."

Hope hung up and walked to the mirror. She was wearing only a thong and lace bra, having decided to get changed to look decent for Dean's visit. She looked over her shoulder at her lower back and butt. It was so red, it was almost purple. She touched it, and it hurt. She wondered if Dean would see it.

14
GTWS

ANDY SAID HELLO TO Mike the security guard and started to head back to his dormitory area.

"Looks like someone had an interesting few days off," said Mike with a knowing smile.

Andy looked at him, puzzled, until Mike pointed to his neck where Hope had left a big hickey. Andy laughed and shrugged. "She missed me," he said, trying to sound cocky.

"Apparently."

Andy walked back to his dorm and unpacked, then changed. He noticed blood on his shirt when he pulled it off. He'd have to go find out about a company doctor tomorrow. For now, he had other more pressing plans to take care of first.

Once he was changed into his company scrubs, he headed down to the farm in building two. He put on his jumpsuit and booties and went through the double doors into the massive building. He said a few hellos to his co-workers and headed to his workstation, where he had his computer and notes.

"Hey, Andy," said Puneet, one of the younger researchers with whom he occasionally had meals. "You just getting here? Working an overnight shift?"

"Not all night. I was home for a few days. Just catching up."

"Okay, well, you'll be the last one out. I'll see you at the pub later?"

"Sure," said Andy, thankful that everyone was finishing up for the day.

Andy made himself look busy with data comparisons and growth charts on the GM corn they'd been working with for the past year. When Puneet and the others were gone, Andy took a stroll along the outside perimeter of the field, which grew inside what looked like a football stadium. He walked through the cornfield on purpose, in the event anyone had watched him by closed-circuit camera. He wasn't sure if anyone actually watched the labs in real-time, but he wasn't taking any chances.

Once he was satisfied that he had "disappeared" from view for any outsiders, he moved quickly to the tree line that bordered the farm. The designers of the farm had decided that trees would help stabilize the soil and atmosphere inside the lab, as well as offer benchmarks for the growing seasons with their own leaves. A green mountain sugar maple had grown to fifty feet near the outside wall, and Andy quickly got around the back side of it and scaled up.

He climbed as fast as he could, and the branches that scratched his arms and back irritated the rash something awful. Once he got high enough, he climbed from the tree into the steel substructure of the building and then climbed and walked his way to the top of the building. It was darker up in the steel, and it offered some concealment from outside view.

When Andy was at the top of the farm's wall, he hopped over the dividing masonry firewall and came down on the other side, in building three—the zoo. It took ten minutes of careful climbing to quietly move into position to see the open field below. When he finally could see the cattle, his mouth opened and eyes went wide. It was like looking down on a herd of elephants.

"Holy shit," he mumbled.

For a few moments, he just watched in amazement at what looked like a herd of dinosaurs. Finally, he took out his phone and began shooting some video of the animals below. Looking at the recorded video, he realized that he was too far away. He climbed down slowly and carefully, feeling slightly panicked. While he could easily bullshit a reason for being up in the catwalk of the farm, he wasn't authorized to be inside the zoo—and especially not scaling down the wall. He moved slowly and carefully, barely breathing, as he climbed down.

Once Andy had climbed down to where the steel structure ended and the actual innermost wall began, he stopped and looked around. It was later in the day, and almost everyone in the building was ending their shift. A few departments and special projects had crews that worked twenty-four-seven, but in the zoo, the animals went to sleep at night—and so most of the researchers did too.

The open roof of building three was similar to building two, although the roof of the farm in building two was covered in glass to control the climate. Here in the open-air zoo, the sun had set and it was getting chilly. The elephant-sized cattle were starting to settle down for the night, and some immense hogs and sheep wandered freely in the open pasture as well. Andy looked at his pictures and video and realized it was useless without something in the picture for scale. There was no way to know how big anything was unless it was compared to something else. He decided he needed to get down to the field and take some real close-ups.

Andy climbed down to the top of the wall and looked around for a long time, making sure he was alone with the animals. When he was satisfied, he dropped down to the soft earth and sprinted to a large bale of hay for cover. The pasture smelled like a barnyard—hay, manure, animals, and grass. It was cozy in its own way, with the lowing of cattle, even with animals that looked like dinosaurs.

At first, Andy was going to get close and take a selfie next to an animal, then realized that using himself for scale guaranteed he'd get busted putting himself in the evidence. He decided to use his hand on a cow for scale and then try and find something else that might help prove the massive size of the animals.

Andy crouched and moved quickly across the open grass to one of the cattle that was curled up for a night's sleep. The animal was terrifying in its size, but all of the animals were calm and gentle in appearance, and they seemed to be more interested in sleep than anything else. Andy spoke softly to the giant steer as he approached, using a gentle, almost babylike voice as he got closer. When he was next to the steer, he pulled up his sleeve and placed his hand on the animal's chest, which was shoulder-high to him even though the animal was lying down.

As he pulled up his sleeve to take the picture, his skin cracked and bled near his wrist. He flinched, cursed at the pain, and took a quick picture. He quickly checked the results, then took a short video of the animal, trying to get his hands and feet in the shot to show how massive the creature was in comparison. He narrated what he was seeing as he took the pictures. After a few seconds, he had to stop and get out of there—his wrist was on fire.

Andy looked at his wrist and cringed in horror. It looked like his wound had gotten infected. What the fuck was that? Maggots? He felt his knees buckle, and he tried not to scream—but something was definitely moving on his skin. He grabbed his ID card from his lanyard and used the edge to scrape off whatever was on his skin. Something must have gotten on him when he was climbing through the steel sub-structure and had likely been attracted to the blood. That had to be it.

Whatever it was, it appeared to come off easy enough, falling into the grass next to the heifer. He scraped at it a little more, just to be sure, because it was disgusting, but stopped when his skin started bleeding. He wiped his skin off against the soft hide of the cow, then pulled his sleeve down and moved over to a large sheep. Normally knee or waist-high, this sheep was as tall as he was. He shot more video and then took some pictures of the hogs nearby. Something about them was more intimidating than the cattle or sheep, and he didn't venture too close to them. The giant hog locked eyes with him and held his stare, and Andy backed off towards the hay bales again.

The steer that he had originally videoed made him jump and almost scream when it leapt to its feet and charged across the grass, mooing as it ran. Andy crouched and waited, afraid that someone might see him, and then made a beeline for the wall where he had come in. Climbing back up was extremely difficult, but once he made it to the wall, he raced up the steel structure back to the top and escaped the same way he had come in.

15

D.C.

"OH, *SENATOR!*" CONNIE EXCLAIMED with a toss of her hair, as she held his forearm. "You're hysterical! If you ever give up the senate, you could go to Hollywood."

Senator Carr laughed, a little too loudly, and then threw back another Scotch. "The Ha'Penny Lion" was packed with Washington power brokers, elites, politicos, and lobbyists. It was the hottest spot to see and be seen in D.C., and although almost every congressman and senator ate and drank there regularly, the popular theory was that none had ever reached into their own pocket to pay for anything—ever.

"So you'll join us then?" asked Connie, leaning in very close, perhaps because it was so crowded. The senator, a third-termer from South Carolina who was often looked at as a possible presidential candidate, had a great view straight down the deep "V" of Connie's little black dress.

He laughed. "I told you, it's very short notice. I'll try my best. I have to check with my chief of staff."

Connie moved her hand to his waist and looked up at him with big, dramatically sad eyes. "But who will I dance with if you don't go?"

The senator's face turned a little pink which made her smile. He laughed nervously. "Well, you never said anything about dancing."

"I didn't?" she replied, still looking way up at him with her bottom lip pouting. "I love to dance." She pressed closer to him. The bar was very crowded, almost too much.

"You do make it difficult to say no," he said, smiling.

"I never take no for an answer," she said, a slow and evil smile spreading across her face.

The senator took out his phone and sent a quick text to his chief of staff. When he hit send, he held up the phone to Connie. "Done. I just told Scott that I have plans for the twenty-second!"

She leaned in without warning and gave him a quick peck on the cheek. "That's such great news! And you, Senator, are going to be on the right side of history! This is a big deal. Just wait. You won't believe what you're in for this weekend." She wiggled her eyebrows at him.

"Can't wait," he said.

Another patron began yelling the senator's name, and their conversation was interrupted, which was fine with Connie. She just nailed down her twenty-sixth VIP guest, and with the newest big names, it would make the junior politicians all want to join in on the fun. Connie slipped away from the bar and called Paul as she walked briskly towards her next stop. She caught him up on the latest additions to their guest list, and the two of them celebrated over the phone.

"You know, I'm thinking we get luxury buses! We pack the D's on one and the R's on the other, and just let them party their way to the lab," said Connie.

Paul laughed. "That's because you're still young enough to think a bus trip with an open bar is fun. No, dear, these folks will expect luxury private jets and stretch limos. This little shindig of yours will cost a few million. But no worries. We'll make it back faster than you can say 'legislation.' You're doing great work, Connie. Putting you in Riker's spot was a great move."

"You're only saying that because you like our special one-on-one meetings."

Paul smiled on his end of the phone. "Well, there's no denying that. And we do have to be careful. If the board finds out we're spending so much private time together, we'll have a problem."

"You want to stop?" she teased.

"I never said that! In fact, you should come by tonight to celebrate your outstanding work. See you around nine. I have a few late-afternoon meetings."

"As fun as ours?"

"Hardly. Keep up the good work. See you at nine."

Connie ended the call with Paul and smiled. Everything seemed to be going just as she planned.

She called the next number on her list.

"Senator Warner's office, Lydia speaking..."

"Oh hi, Lydia. Connie Whitcolm from Global Tech. The senator is expecting me..."

16

Harrisburg

"IT'S OPEN!" YELLED HOPE from inside the house.

Dean entered the house and closed the door behind him. He could smell the strong odor of pot in the dim house. It was almost ten at night, and he'd had a long drive through heavy Philly traffic.

"Hey," he yelled as he walked in.

"Back here," she answered.

Dean walked into the house and found Hope in the kitchen. She was sitting at the table smoking her bong and drinking a vodka on the rocks.

"The party started without me?" asked Dean smiling.

Hope smiled. "No, I was just, I dunno. Nervous, I guess. Just wanted to chill out."

"Nervous? About what?" asked Dean. He walked over and gave Hope a little kiss hello, then took off his coat and put it over a chair.

She looked at him and made a face. "You know."

Dean smiled and suddenly felt optimistic. "Bar still open?"

"Yeah, there's vodka or beer. Mixers in the fridge. And..." She pointed at the bong.

"Cool." Dean poured a vodka and added some tonic water from the fridge. "You talk to Andy yet tonight?"

"Not yet."

"Let's give him a call. I brought a down payment for you guys." Dean pulled out a thousand dollars and put it on the table in front of Hope, who touched his hand and looked up at him, then pocketed the money.

"Right now?"

"Yeah. Wally's in a hurry. Lots going on. We really need the video."

Hope took out her phone and called Andy, who picked up right away. "Hey!" he said, sounding breathless. "I was just going to call you. I just got back to my room."

"Did you get it?"

"Yeah. I was just going to upload everything to you when you called. When you get it, you can send it to Dean."

Hope placed her phone on the table and hit the button to put the call on speaker phone.

"Dean's here."

There was silence. For some reason, it made Hope smile. She liked teasing him. Their making up had always been so much fun.

"Dean's there now? When did he get there?"

"Just now. He literally just walked in."

"It's so late."

"Hi, Andy," said Dean, letting Andy know he was on speaker.

Hope looked at Dean and smiled at him. She didn't answer Andy's comment, but said, "Dean brought us a down payment."

"Oh. Cool."

"Can you send the pictures and videos right now?"

"Yeah. You won't believe what I saw. Seriously. It was amazing."

"What was it?" asked Dean.

Andy lowered his voice, even though he was locked in his room. "Giant animals. *Giant.* Like—cows the size of elephants. Bigger, maybe. Fuckin' insane, dude."

"Nice. You have proof?"

"Yeah. It was hard to get. When I took the first video, they just looked normal. It wasn't until I got *next* to one of the cows that you can tell how big they are. It was lying down and it was *still* taller than me. I saw a sheep bigger than a horse. Giant pigs. It's crazy, man."

Hope interrupted. "You got next to it? How?"

"It wasn't easy. I had to climb a wall and jump down to this giant inside field. I bet you could fit at least ten football fields in there. It's open-air, but all enclosed on the sides. Security was tight. It was hard getting in and out of there."

"Wow. Sounds so cool," said Hope, staring at Dean, who tried to look unimpressed.

"Send it. Let's take a look."

"It was really dangerous, Dean."

"Ten grand."

"Okay. I'll send it. Call me back when you get it. Hope, take me off speaker."

She did and picked up the phone, staring at Dean. "What's up?"

"How's your rash?"

"Burns. Did you get medicine?"

"I stopped for cortisone, but it got worse anyway. When I was climbing over the walls, something got in it..."

He hesitated.

"What was it? What do you mean?" she asked.

"It was so gross. Like, I dunno. Looked like little grubs or something got into the wound. I swear, I almost puked. Burns like hell now."

"Go see the company doctor," she said.

"Yeah, I'm going to shower first and head there next. Leave your phone on and I'll call you first thing after I've seen the doc. Sending the video now."

"Okay. Talk soon." She made a kiss noise and hung up, still looking at Dean. "He's sending it now."

"Everything okay?"

"We got this rash. Poison ivy maybe. I think Andy's got infected."

"Where?"

Hope leaned forward and whispered, "On my butt."

"Maybe Dr. Dean should take a look for you."

"*Maybe*," she teased.

Her phone dinged as the video landed. Then pictures. Picture after picture of enormous animals, unlike anything the world had seen since the last woolly mammoth disappeared some ten thousand years ago. Dean put his arm around her and leaned closer to see the screen better. Hope played the video, and she and Dean sat snuggling together, watching the enormous steer behind Andy's tiny hand. The video panned around the enclosure and showed the other animals. It was amazing.

"Wally's gonna' shit when I send this. Forward this to me. I need to send this right now. Holy shit."

Hope took a few minutes to send it, and then Dean sent it on to Wally, who called immediately after he got it. They had a long, animated conversation and finally ended the call as Hope smoked another bowl. She dropped her head back and enjoyed her high.

Dean got up and walked around behind her, placing his hands on her shoulders. She held his hands with hers.

"Ten thousand dollars is a lot of money," she said, opening her eyes and looking up at him.

"Especially if you don't have to share it? That what you're thinking?" he asked.

She smiled and shrugged.

"We need Andy to get us inside." Dean cursed himself. He had just divulged way too much to her.

"You're going inside?" Her eyes widened. "What are you gonna' do?"

Dean grimaced. "Listen. This is really secret, you understand?"

"I can keep a secret," said Hope, her evil smile returning.

Dean leaned down and kissed her on the mouth, and she kissed him back for a long minute.

"Want me to take a look at that rash?"

"Could you, doctor? I can't see it, but it burns."

Dean slid her chair back with her in it, and she stood and turned around. They embraced in the kitchen, kissing and touching as they got reacquainted. It had been three years since they'd been together, but the time seemed irrelevant, as did her relationship with Andy. She took Dean by the hand and led him into her room.

17

Global Tech World
Solutions Laboratory

ANDY FINISHED UPLOADING ALL the videos and called Hope again. It went to voicemail after ringing a long time, and he guessed they were still downloading. He decided to shower first. When he went to his bathroom and took off his shirt, he was horrified at his rash. It had spread, and the maggots—or whatever they were, were back. He screamed and tried jumping away from his own arm, which he couldn't escape. He felt sick to his stomach and started panicking.

After a few seconds, he remembered they did have an emergency button on their phones in the room, and he pressed the number nine.

"Good evening, Andy." It was Mike, the huge security guard. "This is the emergency number. Everything okay?"

"Um, no. Not really. Do we have, like a doctor here I can see?"

"What's wrong, Andy?"

"I... I... I dunno. There's an infection on my arm. It's getting worse. I need to see someone now."

"Okay, sit tight. I'll be right there and bring you to the first-aid station."

Mike hung up the phone at the security desk and hopped into his cart, which he rode full speed back to the dorm area. With perhaps the most boring job on the planet, running someone over to first aid for a Band-Aid was the highlight of the week. He was on his headset talking as he drove down the empty hallways.

"Hey, it's Mike at the desk. I've got a first-aid call from Andrew Booth. Picking him up now. I'll meet you in the med room in a couple of minutes."

"Okay, I'll be expecting you," said Dr. Laurel Hayes, the doctor on duty.

When Mike arrived at Andy's room, he announced himself and keyed in. He found Andy, near to hysteria in his bathroom. He was in jeans and no shirt, and had his arm under the sink running hot, soapy water on it.

"Hey bud. I'm going to run you down to see the doc, okay. Just relax."

Andy looked up, his eyes wide with panic. "I don't know what it is!" he blurted.

Mike smiled and spoke in a soothing voice. "It's okay there, bud, I got ya. Come on with me."

Andy rinsed off his arm and turned off the water. When he turned around and held up his arm, Mike's eyes went wide.

"Holy shit," Mike stammered. He stared at what looked like shiny, black bugs tunneling in and out of Andy's flesh. His red and infected skin was oozing white matter, and the small insect-looking things were crawling all over his arm.

Mike's stomach did a backflip, but he tried to remain calm. He grabbed a towel off the rack by the shower and wrapped Andy's arm in it, then escorted him to his cart. The second Andy was seated Mike took off down the hall at full speed, rubber tires squeaking on the clean floor at every turn.

"Just hang on, Andy. We'll have you at the doc in a minute. What happened, Andy?"

"I don't know. I just got a rash a couple of days ago and it got infected."

Mike shook his head. He still felt queasy, and he had served two combat tours in Afghanistan. "We're here. Come on, let's get you to the doc."

Mike walked Andy into the infirmary where Laurel was sitting at a desk reading a report.

"Hi, doc. Andy here has a wicked infection. You need to take a look."

She stood and smiled and extended her arm towards the examination table. "Come have a seat, Andy." She saw the towel wrapped around his wrist and looked at the red welts around his neck.

"Doc," said Mike, making a face. He was trying to figure out how to prepare her. "His arm. It's uh…"

"Okay. It's okay. Let's take a look." She gently unwrapped his arm which was resting on his knee. The second she unwrapped it, small bug-like creatures tried to tunnel back under the skin to avoid the light.

"It hurts!" said Andy. "It really *hurts*!"

Laurel swallowed hard and looked at Mike, then back at Andy. "Andy, where do you work?"

"The farm."

"Anywhere else?"

"Just the farm. I'm pretty new. I do mostly gopher stuff. Just bringing samples back and forth and stuff."

"Okay. So... No time doing actual work in micro?"

"No, I'm not a tech yet. Still training and doing grunt work."

"Okay. Okay." She smiled as she talked to herself, trying to decide what to do next. "So, have you traveled out of the country recently?"

"No, I just got back from a couple days off. Oh shit. I gotta call home. I wonder if Hope's is getting worse, too."

"Hope is your significant other?"

"Yeah. She has a little rash, too. Just not as bad. Well, it wasn't. Mine got real bad all of a sudden, you know? Like, I had it for a couple of days, and then suddenly, bam! It just got so much worse, and now—what is that doc?"

"I'm going to take a closer look. Why don't you call home and see if Hope is feeling okay?"

———

Dean liked it rough. Unlike Andy, he wasn't loving or gentle. Dean was all about Dean, and he liked to make it hurt. Hope loved that about Dean. He was a bad man and knew it, and his forceful animalistic manner was a huge turn on.

Hope had led him into her room, and Dean instantly spun her around, tore the front of her jeans open, and bent her over.

Out on the kitchen table, her phone buzzed and vibrated and moved across the table, unanswered.

"Doctor's gonna take a look at that ass," he growled.

Hope arched her back and let him pull her jeans down.

"Holy shit, Hope," he said, the moment lost.

She looked over her shoulder at him. "What is it, baby? What do you want me to do?"

"You weren't kidding. That rash is really bad."

"It hurts. You said you'd make it better." She stepped all the way out of her jeans and pulled down her thong, then climbed up on the edge of the bed on all fours, with her face to the bed and her ass held up high.

Dean stared at her perfect ass. He wondered if he could catch anything from her.

"That ass ain't gonna spank itself," she said.

"Shit," mumbled Dean, admiring her perfect little body. He pulled off his shirt and unzipped his jeans.

———

"No answer," said Andy.

"Okay. Let me just take a closer look," said Laurel. She had a light on her head and a magnifier in her gloved hand. She held his hand and lifted his arm, looking as closely as possible at the infected wound. Her stomach turned.

"Mike, would you mind calling Dr. White for me?"

"*Lamont*? You want me to wake up Dr. *White*?" he asked, surprised and intimidated about waking up the head of the entire facility.

"Now!" she snapped.

Whatever it was, they both knew it was bad. Mike called Dr. White from his mobile as he walked into a neighboring room. Lamont picked up after a few rings, sounding groggy and tired.

"Good evening, Dr. White. It's Mike Dempsey, head of security. I'm with Dr. Hayes in the infirmary. She's asked me to have you come here right away."

"Now? She needs me now?" He was out of it.

"Um, yeah. Medical emergency, sir."

"Okay, I'm on my way…"

18

The Zoo

THE FIFTEEN-THOUSAND-POUND HEIFER JOGGED around the pasture, agitated and angry. The sheep, pigs, and other cattle that had been sleeping now moved out of her way as she trotted past them, snorting and throwing her head around.

Normally a docile member of the herd, the heifer—a female that wasn't called a cow because she hadn't given birth yet—was now throwing a fit. She was so agitated that even the larger steer kept out of her way.

When the pain and itching became too much, she rolled on the ground and tried to scratch herself against the grass. She was making loud noises when the overnight worker showed up for the usual check-in.

Emmet Waters looked out into the field and saw one of the giant females crying out in pain and rolling around on the grass. *That* was a first. He hopped into a cart and drove out to take a closer look. The animals were used to people being around and didn't fear their presence. When he pulled up alongside, he stopped but didn't get out. He shone a flashlight on the animal and stared at an oozing, bloody mass on her flank. The open wound appeared to fester, and it obviously was bothering the stricken animal.

Following lab protocol, he called his supervisor, Jeannie Davis, and reported the problem. "Hi, Jeanne, it's Emmet over in the zoo. We have a problem with a sick heifer. Looks like some kind of infection. Nasty wound."

"Got a tag number?"

"Yes. One-fourteen. Penelope."

"I know that heifer. We were just talking about considering her for the new breeding program. She's never been sick for a day in her life."

"I know. But I'm looking at a *nasty* wound. Infected as hell and she's in pain."

"Damn. Okay. Try and isolate her and I'll be over in a few minutes. As soon as you get her in a pen, check the others."

"I'm on it... But..."

"But what, Emmet?"

"She's freaking out, Jeannie. Moving her to where she doesn't want to go is going to be interesting. Let me see what I can do."

He hung up and watched fifteen thousand pounds of pissed off beef flip back on to her hooves and begin pawing the ground.

19

Infirmary

LAMONT PULLED ON SOME green scrubs that were handy and ran down the hallway to an available cart, then drove straight to the infirmary. It took him ten minutes to get there, by which time Andrew Booth was sitting up in a hospital bed with his arm resting on a pillow. Dr. Hayes had given him a mild sedative to calm him down and had considered taking one herself. For the first time in her medical career, she was so disgusted that she was actually afraid. Mike stood outside the examination room looking fairly pale and nodded to Dr. White as he walked past. Dr. White mumbled a quiet greeting in return and strode inside.

"Evening, Laurel. What's up?" asked Lamont as he strode into the room.

"Sorry to wake you, Dr. White. But I, uh… You need to take a look at this."

Lamont walked closer to the patient, and Laurel handed him a magnifier. "Take a look at the wound up close."

Andrew dozed.

Dr. White leaned closer and jumped back instinctively.

He caught his breath and looked again, studying the creatures that were gnawing through the flesh on Andy's arm. He took a peek at his neck and saw similar activity there, although it was not quite as heavily infected yet.

"Any idea what it is?" asked Laurel.

"Yes. I know *exactly* what it is. I just don't understand *how*." He gently nudged Andrew's shoulder. "Hey there, Andrew. Wake up. I need to talk to you."

Andy opened his eyes and looked at Dr. White.

"Andy, you work in the farm. Were you doing anything in micro?"

Andy stared at him with heavy eyelids.

"In the micro lab. Did you touch anything? Open anything?"

Andy felt his stomach tighten. "I didn't mean to."

"Didn't mean to *what*, Andy? What did you touch?"

"Some Petri dishes were on a table. I was just looking at it."

"Did you open it?"

Andy felt scared. He could lose his job. He could get arrested. He looked at his arm, now resembling an infected piece of raw meat. "I'm sorry. I just opened one of them and looked inside," he lied.

"Okay. Okay." Lamont closed the towel over his arm.

"Treatment?" asked Laurel.

"Let's step outside for a moment."

The two of them walked outside. Lamont pondered his words and then spoke carefully, choosing his words. "That young man is infected with genetically modified skin mites. We take every precaution in the lab, and that idiot just wanted to open up and handle a live sample because he was curious? Jesus Christ, Laurel."

"Skin mites? Some type of parasite?"

"Technically speaking, yes, some type of parasite. They feed off a human host. Normally you wouldn't even know they were on your skin. We're both covered in them right now. You and I. They're so small they're practically invisible, and it's a symbiotic relationship. These dust mites were altered during experiments while we were unlocking the genetic codes for growth. It's how we super-sized the livestock and plants. And now this man has them feeding off of his flesh."

She tried to hide her horror. "So what do we do?"

He took a breath and thought a moment. "In the lab, these things grow to a few pounds each and they're known to eat everything in sight. But it's *controlled*! We need to kill these things without *killing* him. In the lab we use high doses of Nitazoxanide and spray it on them. We'll give him a dose of five-hundred milligrams intravenously and spray some on the open wound. I've got fifty congressmen and senators coming here in a few days! This is no time for this type of drama!"

His phone buzzed again. "Dr. White, it's Jeannie Davis. I'm sorry to bother you so late, but we have a problem in the zoo..."

20

The Zoo

DR. WHITE DROVE THE cart to the zoo as fast as it would move. When he arrived at building three, Jeannie Davis was already standing outside the security door with a worried expression on her face. He squeaked to a stop in front of her and stepped out of the cart.

"I'm sorry to wake you, Dr. White..."

"It's okay, I was up. What's the problem?" His stomach was already in a knot.

"Sick animal. Heifer number one-fourteen. Penelope." She made a sad face.

"Penelope? She was chosen for breeding because she's a perfect specimen. What happened?"

"I don't know. But I think she'll have to be destroyed," she said, her voice cracking.

Lamont walked past Jeannie and swiped his card, then walked through the double doors of the zoo. Jeannie followed him inside and caught up, giving him the update as they sped down a hallway.

"Emmet called me. Penelope was fine this morning. At evening rounds, he found her racing around, highly agitated. When he examined her more closely, he found a gaping wound. It's bloody and infected, doctor. And spreading quickly. We isolated her immediately."

"Any other livestock showing problems?" asked Lamont, his face showing his deep concern.

"No, sir. Not that we can see. I've called out the entire crew for a physical examination of the entire population."

"Excellent. Where's Penelope?"

"Pen seven."

The two of them hustled down to the pen where Emmet sat outside the door on a small stool. His face looked pallid. When he saw his supervisor arriving with the director of the facility, he hopped up to his feet.

"Evening, Emmet. I understand we have a sick animal," said Lamont dryly.

"Yes, sir. It's bad. Really bad. She went from normal and healthy to this in just a few hours." Emmet opened the pen door and the three of them stepped inside the room. The pen was forty by forty feet with a forty-foot-high ceiling. Bars separated the three of them from the animal inside. Hay was strewn on the floor to provide more comfortable bedding. They stood outside the bars and stared in horror at a heifer that looked partly eaten, but was still alive. Her hide was missing in a few places, exposing raw beef that was shredded and oozing.

"My God," said Lamont quietly.

Jeannie's hands went to her face. "She's so much worse!"

Emmet stared at the animal sadly. "I'm telling you, whatever she has is going through her so fast. I have no idea what it is. Never saw any disease like this before."

"I'm willing to bet it's no disease. You two know Andy from the farm?"

"New kid? Booth?" asked Jeannie.

"Yes. He's in the infirmary. It's why I was awake when you called me. The idiot opened a live sample of skin mites from micro and got himself infected. Now it looks like he somehow contaminated the whole damn zoo." Lamont kicked a box of supplies on the floor across the viewing area and snapped. "*God damn it!* If this gets into the other animals we'll have to destroy the entire stock!"

Kim had walked in behind them and headed to Lamont. "Everyone just take a breath. No one's destroying anything until we know what's going on, okay?"

They all turned to face her, surprised to see her. "Mike called me. He told me you were down here," she said, answering Lamont's unasked question about what she was doing there.

Lamont was clearly upset. "Kim, you have no idea what's going on here. We have a possible lab-wide contamination."

"Is that confirmed?" she asked calmly.

"No! I just walked in!" he snapped.

"Well then, no reason to get hysterical. Let's go slowly and thoroughly and see how bad this is. We've got quite a large, important, group coming through here in a couple of days. We need to be ready for it. What's that animal's status?"

Lamont stared at her in disbelief. "Kim. Seriously? You're worried about some politicians coming here? Did you hear anything I just said? I'm talking about a possible level five contamination! You don't have to be a scientist to look at that animal and see the gravity of this situation!"

Kim crossed her arms over her chest. "Lamont. You *just* said you just got here a few minutes ago. Level *five*? Seriously? You need to calm down and see what's happening here before you start talking about level five *anything*!"

"I'm in charge of this facility," he reminded her.

"Actually doctor, you are in charge of lab operations. *I* am in charge of this facility. Let's be real clear about that. Now—what's the issue?"

Lamont crossed his own arms and mirrored her pose. "Do you see that animal?" He sneered.

"Of course. And it looks quite ill. Now I'll ask you again. What's the issue?"

"The *issue*, Mrs. Hayes," he replied, reminding her that she was a Missus and not a doctor, "is that one of our new techs decided to contaminate himself and this animal with skin mites from the lab."

"So fire him and destroy the animal. Then make sure the rest are healthy and we move on."

"Just like that?" asked Lamont, incredulously.

"Just like that."

"Kim," said Jeannie softly, "Penelope was a perfect animal. We were getting ready to attempt breeding with her. We need to see if she can be saved and observe how she responds to treatment. This isn't an instant fix."

"Actually it is. Destroy her. Have this pen sanitized. Get that idiot out of the infirmary with his packed bags and tell me everything's fine in twenty-four hours. Contain this." She stared hard at Lamont, then at Jeannie and Emmet. "Any questions?"

Lamont pointed his finger in her face. He was much taller and a little intimidating to anyone other than Kim. "I'm in charge of the lab. Nothing gets destroyed without my say-so."

"Fine. We'll call Paul Dodds at corporate in the morning."

"Fine," snapped Lamont.

"Fine," replied Kim between clenched teeth. She walked out without saying goodbye.

The three of them turned back to Penelope, who was laying down and breathing hard in the hay. Even on her side, her flanks were taller than Lamont, the tallest of the group. Dark, sticky blood ran down her black-and-white hide. She let out a long "moo," as if to ask for help.

"Let's get her started on Nitazoxanide. Apply topically to all open wounds and give her fifteen hundred units. That's a lot, but she weighs fifteen thousand pounds. Who the hell knows what a lethal dose is for her."

"The rest of the crew should be here soon," said Jeannie.

"Good. Let's get a visual exam on every animal out there. We go one at a time. Very thoroughly. If it's just one animal, then Kim's right. We destroy one-fourteen, and as soon as Booth is well enough to travel, we throw his ass out of here and forget this ever happened." He paused. "Full hazmat protocols. You treat this like its Ebola."

21

Harrisburg

DEAN WOKE UP EARLY in the morning and looked over at Hope. She was still asleep and tangled in bedsheets and covers. They had enjoyed quite a wild night. Just like old times. Now it was time to get home and call Wally before she woke up and asked him any questions about their non-existent relationship. She was a great piece of ass, no doubt, but Dean didn't have time to deal with his crazy ex.

He dressed quickly in the dim morning light and left. A couple hours later, he was back in Philly and calling Wally to check in. Wally was preparing to start World War Three over at Global Tech. Arson and destruction of property wasn't anything new to Wally or Dean, but they'd never tackled anything on this scale before. It was one thing to spray-paint some fur coats inside a retail store or burn down a small office—but going after a facility the size of Global Tech was intimidating, even to Dean who loved destroying things.

Their phone conversation was kept short, since Wally didn't trust phones. Wally merely said he "wanted to go to the game within a week. Everyone was going. Pick up supplies. Probably Saturday night." Dean understood, and that meant getting his hands on some weapons and explosives, which was nothing new to him, either.

He undressed and ran the shower, catching sight of himself in the mirror. He had a red rash on his torso, from his privates to his chest. "You fucking bitch! If you gave me some kind of crotch rot, I swear I'll drive back there and kick your ass," he snapped at his reflection.

He stepped into the shower to scrub himself real good and potentially get rid of whatever crap Hope had shared with him.

After his shower, Dean dressed and made some calls. They'd need at least eight vehicles for his private army of thirty-five loyal followers. The average age of his people was nineteen. Mostly animal rights activists, a few anti-big oil, anti-big pharma activists, and a few plain old nut-jobs that just wanted to belong somewhere. Anywhere.

Most of them had more tattoos and piercings than Dean could count, and in their quest to rebel and be unique, they all looked exactly alike to Dean. He could care less. Whatever their individual motivations were, they loved being outrageous and "cutting edge" as they liked to call it. They were a rebel army, and Wally was their badass leader.

They would be saving the planet. How could they say no to that?

The blood soaked through the sheets of Hope's bed. She only moaned once.

22

D.C.

THE RINGING PHONE so early in the morning woke Paul up in an immediate state of confusion. He blinked and looked around. Connie was starting to stir from the noise as well. He grabbed the phone and mumbled a quick hello without looking at the screen.

"Sorry to call so early, Paul, but we have a serious situation at the lab, and a difference of opinion on how to proceed," said Kim.

Connie rolled over and looked at Paul. Even first thing in the morning, she *still* somehow looked sexy and beautiful to him. She mouthed, *"Who is it?"*

Paul put his finger up to his lips and pressed the speaker button. "What happened, Kim?"

"Seems a new employee contaminated himself and one of our animals. They're both pretty sick. I want the heifer put down and destroyed immediately. Hell, I want the idiot that's responsible put down and destroyed, but that's probably not possible. Anyway—Dr. White and Jeannie want to try and save the animal and monitor progress. Quite frankly, I'm much too worried about any other contamination. I have zero sentimental attachment to this hunk of beef and want it dead before it ruins the entire facility. Lamont is already crying about level five."

Paul and Connie exchanged horrified faces. Level five was the worst case scenario—one that required the total destruction of all animal subjects and sanitization of the entire facility. Basically, burning all the work of the past several years and hundreds of millions of dollars.

"You said contaminated. What happened?" asked Paul.

"One of their genetically modified micro-organisms from the lab ended up on Andrew Booth who must have had contact with the heifer. These little organisms are normally harmless, unless you make them a few million times larger than normal. Then they start eating people and animals."

She said it as such a simple fact that Connie and Paul just stared at each other with horror, shaking their heads.

"So what happened to this Booth person and the heifer?"

"He's in the infirmary, under sedation and getting treated for the parasites. The animal was much further along. I'm guessing they were infected around the same time, but the mites are fed meat from the cattle most of the time in the lab. I'm guessing they recognized it as a food source immediately, and so they were more aggressive."

"So there's a cure, then? At least for our employee?"

"Well, in theory, the same anti-parasitic drug they used in the lab should work. But the heifer looks to be beyond saving. As in, partially eaten. I disagree with Lamont about more scientific experimental bullshit. I want that animal put down immediately and incinerated. I need your help in making that happen. He won't listen to me."

Connie made a pleading face at Paul, and he put the call on mute.

"I've just killed myself to get the party arranged for fifty congressmen and senators! We can't cancel now! Get that animal into an incinerator and straighten this mess out! *Now*, Paul!"

He unmuted the call and spoke to Kim. "If you need me to speak to Lamont directly, I will, but you have the authority over that facility."

"Lamont says he has control over the lab, and therefore the animals."

"Call me back when you're both in the same room. We'll conference this and get everything straightened out. We can*not* screw up our VIP party, you understand?"

"Of course. That's what I told Dr. White."

"Call me back."

Paul looked at Connie and ripped the sheet away from her body so he could admire her. "We have a few minutes before they call back," he said.

23

Infirmary

"How are you feeling?" asked Laurel. She stood over Andy's hospital-style bed where they'd set up an IV of antibiotics, painkillers, and fluids. Still, Andy looked white and clammy.

"It hurts. Everything hurts."

That answer bothered Laurel. "Andy. I'm Doctor Hayes. You remember me?"

Andy stared at her. He was on morphine and half out of it. "Yeah."

"Where does it hurt?"

"Everywhere. My arms. My stomach. Everything burns."

"We're treating your rash, Andy."

"No. Inside. It hurts *inside*."

He screwed up his face, and suddenly vomited blood over himself. Laurel hit the alarm button on the wall which rang right to Mike at security.

"Yes, Doctor Hayes?"

"I need help in here! Call Doctors Alonzo and White and get them here now! Emergency!"

Andy continued spasm after spasm, convulsing as he threw up more blood and moaned in pain. He flopped back against his pillow, choking. Laurel grabbed rubber gloves and snapped them on, then quickly pushed her fingers into Andy's mouth and cleared out the bloody vomit so he could breathe. She didn't notice the small critter that ran across the floor from the pool of vomit.

"Just relax, Andy. I've got you. You might have had a reaction to the medicine or the morphine. Just relax while I get you some water."

She used a sheet to wipe his face and clear away the mess as best she could, then grabbed a cup of water from the sink. As she held up his head and helped him rinse his mouth, Dr. Peter Alonzo—the other company doctor—arrived on the run from the gym. He was wearing only gym shorts and a tank top with sneakers.

"Mike called. Catch me up," he said, grabbing a small metal bowl so Andy could spit the water out once he rinsed his mouth.

"Gloves," said Laurel quietly, taking the bowl from him. "Parasitic infection from the lab. He opened a live sample. Infected one of the animals, too. We're running Nitazoxanide through him now. May be highly contagious, so please follow precautions." She stared at him hard.

Pete understood that while she didn't want to alarm the patient, she was driving a point home. He scrubbed, put on gloves, and grabbed a gown. Walking back towards the bed, he let out a surprised curse and slapped at his ankle.

"What's the matter?" asked Laurel, focusing on her patient as she helped Andy change out of his soiled gown.

"Nothing," replied Peter, returning quickly.

He ignored the nasty bug bite.

Dr. White entered the infirmary for the second time in just a couple of hours. "What's the latest? You called me down?"

"Patient vomited blood. I'm concerned he's having a reaction to the Nitazoxanide or the morphine. I think we need to transfer him out of here while there's time."

He sighed. He'd have to call Kim for authorization. They hadn't had a pleasant conversation the last time.

"Give me a sec," he said, stepping outside. He dialed Kim's cell and she picked up right away.

"Good timing, I was just calling you. We have a conference call with Paul as you requested."

"Okay, fine, but I need your authorization to have Mr. Booth moved by ambulance to a Harrisburg hospital."

"Why?"

"He may be having a reaction to the Nitazoxanide. Or maybe the morphine, we're not sure. But he looks worse. He's vomiting blood and needs a hospital."

"Meet me in the main conference room. Let's get Paul on the phone before we do anything else."

Lamont shook his head. It was typical corporate bullshit, where no one wanted to take responsibility for making a decision. He hopped back into a golf cart and raced to the conference room.

———

In the conference room, Lamont and Kim sat down at the long mahogany table and stared at the phone in front of them. Kim pressed the speaker button when it rang.

"Good morning, Lamont and Kim. Paul Dodds here with Connie Whitcolm in D.C. I understand we have a few issues to sort out first thing this morning."

Kim raised an eyebrow at Lamont and spoke. "Yes, thank you, Paul. It's just Lamont and I here. We have a problem. One of our new employees got himself infected with a microbial parasite and spread it to one of the animals. I want the animal put down immediately and the area sanitized to avoid the risk of spreading. Dr. White seems to have some sentimental attachment to the cow..."

"She's a heifer. Paul—you see the problem here? With all due respect, Kim isn't a scientist or doctor. She doesn't even know the difference between a cow and a heifer. How can I have conversations with her about proper lab protocols? This isn't some industrial engineering question, we have an infection here."

"Right, I understand. Which is why the problem needs to be eliminated as quickly as possible," said Paul.

"Sir, we need to *understand* the problem. We can't just destroy a prized specimen and not even understand what happened here."

"I appreciate your desire to learn from your mistake..."

"It wasn't my mistake..."

"Do you run the lab?" asked Paul coldly.

"Yes, of course, but..."

"Then it was your mistake. And I want it fixed. We have fifty very, very important people coming over there soon."

"Sir, I suggest you cancel immediately."

"What?" exclaimed Connie, sounding genuinely angry at the suggestion.

"I think it's a mistake to bring in a bunch of outsiders while we're having a contamination problem."

"We're not going to have a contamination problem," said Paul. "Because you're going to destroy that animal and incinerate it immediately."

"Sir! We need to take a closer look at this heifer, even if we do have to put her down."

"Negative. You're to destroy it and sanitize."

"Jesus, Paul! That's not how the lab works! And I have a man in the infirmary that needs a hospital!" he blurted.

"No!" screamed Connie. "No one is going *anywhere*. We will not have some reporter doing a story on a lab accident before the big event!"

"She's right," said Paul. "Deal with it there."

"Paul! We have a very sick man here."

"And whose fault is that, Lamont?"

"It's not my fault! The kid opened a live *goddamn* specimen!"

"Right. So it's the kid's fault. And he can tough it out over there," said Paul. He winked at Connie, who was still wearing the same blue teddy she had slept in.

"And if he dies, are you going to be responsible?" asked Lamont, sounding more agitated.

"No one is going to die. You have two medical doctors on staff. Between them and yourself, I'm sure you can come up with something. Destroy that animal and take care of the sick employee on site. Have I made myself clear?"

Kim replied, sounding peppy as ever. "Quite clear, Paul, thank you. We'll have this all taken care of immediately. We should prep for fifty on Saturday?"

"Yes, Connie was quite persuasive. We'll have a great turnout," said Paul, running his hand up and down her smooth and bare thigh.

"I'll be sending you the guest list today," said Connie. "We'll really need to roll out the red carpet and put on a great show. Our production people have outdone themselves."

Lamont got up and walked out of the room without saying goodbye, slamming the door behind him.

"Dr. White just left," said Kim. "Thanks for backing me up. He's brilliant, but stubborn. I'm sure everything here will be fine. He just doesn't understand the political end of what we do sometimes."

"And the kid?" asked Paul.

"He's pretty sick. But like you said—he did this to himself. He can gut it out until at least after the party. Let's give the VIPs a night they won't forget and get some legislation passed."

Paul and Connie smiled at each other. "Perfect. See you Saturday."

They hung up with Kim. "That wasn't so bad," said Connie.

"Nope. And I think we can be a little late for the office..."

24

Philadelphia

DEAN AND WALLY SAT in the front of a small warehouse as their people began arriving and filing in. Wally had bought a few cases of beer and some pizzas, making sure not to order anything with meat on it. The "soldiers" arrived in small groups and said hello to their leaders before sitting down to eat, drink, or get high. When all thirty-eight of them had arrived, Dean closed the door and locked it. Walter Belville strode out to the center of the warehouse, where his followers went silent.

Dean made eye-contact with a kid smoking a joint and whispered, "Put that shit out." The kid hurriedly complied. Dean barked like a drill sergeant. "Listen up!"

He knew that it was more important to look bad-ass and remind everyone that he was in control more than anything else. They'd already gone silent waiting for their legend to speak to them. Dean sat and looked to Wally.

Wally smiled and eyeballed the crowd. "Welcome. Welcome my warriors, to the biggest mission the Nature Power Movement has ever conceived. You're all about to be a part of history." He walked slowly and dramatically through the crowd, locking eyes with each member, making them feel important.

"Why is it, do you think, that the cops and Feds are looking for me? If you think it's because I firebombed an office and damaged some property, you're wrong. It wasn't because of a few thousand dollars of damage—they couldn't give a shit! It's because Prosanto *owns* the government! It's because I threatened their profits, which means less money to the powerful politicians. And any threat to their power has to be dealt with. They tried to silence me once. Eighteen months in a shithole jail to make me fall into line. Bullshit. I just waited and counted the days and thought about how to make a real statement. And now I have the way. But you all need to understand first."

Wally had referenced only the first firebombing he did jail time for—the one in which no one had been injured. He didn't make mention of the last one—the one that killed a few people and had the authorities on his tail for questioning.

Wally walked over to a laptop and turned on a video that showed up on a projector screen. Dean lowered some of the lights, and the group watched in amazement as a voice narrated over images of giant animals. Wally announced over the video's narrator, "This is my warrior, this is Andy! Working on the inside! Look at what your government is hiding!"

"...and inside this building is where they keep the animals. I work in the farm in building two, and sometimes in the micro lab in building one. Here in building three, what we call the zoo, is where they keep cattle that weigh between fifteen and twenty thousand pounds. Pigs and sheep bigger than cows. It's insane. This cow is laying down, and it still towers over me..."

The video went on for a while longer, then the computer started showing photos. When it was finished, Dean put the lights back on. Wally walked back into the center of the room.

"You're a fucking *experiment*, people! An experiment! These scientists are making Franken-cows and they're gonna' feed it to people who have no idea what they're eating! Who knows what these things will do to anyone who eats them? Twenty-thousand-pound cows? You wanna eat that? You want your children to eat that? Your grandchildren?"

Screams and cheers from the crowd fired up Wally even more.

"Prosanto keeps telling us that the chemicals they spray are safe. Yet their rich owners shop in the organic section where we can't afford to shop! Then they get the government to change the laws so they don't even have to label shit anymore! You don't know what country your food comes from, what chemicals are in it—you don't know nothing! And now Global Tech is breeding some kind of freak-zoo? I don't know about you, but I say no fucking way. It's time we do something about it!"

The crowd started cheering louder.

"This will be the biggest thing we've ever done. I'm not gonna kid ya—some people are gonna get hurt. Maybe even killed. But we're going to burn down this whole fucking lab and everything in it! Who's coming with me?"

The crowd was on its feet, screaming obscenities and ready to go to war.

Wally enjoyed the moment, then called Dean over. When Dean reached Wally in the center of the crowd, Wally grabbed him by the wrist and lifted it up into the air. "We're going to war! Dean is going to teach you how to use some of the weapons we have. This is the real deal."

The two of them stood with raised arms and looked out into the faces of their rebel army. Wally smiled and wondered how much he'd make on the GTWS stock options he'd shorted. This was his last gig. The Feds would be after him for sure after this one—but with the few million he stood to make on the stocks, he would spend the rest of his life chilling out on the beach in Mexico with Dean, living like rock stars. Every dollar he'd ever stolen was riding on this. And when Global Tech was belly-up on Wall Street, he'd be belly-up on the sand, looking at palm trees with a cold beer in his hand. He'd be rich.

Wally roared and shook his fist again to more cheers.

Wally knew that they'd do whatever he told them to.

25

The Zoo

EMMET, JEANNIE, AND LAMONT stood outside the pen and looked in at their dying heifer. Bloody ooze was running out of the massively gaping wounds in her hide. The pained animal occasionally cried out with long, low, mooing sounds.

"I don't think we could have saved her with our best efforts anyway," said Jeannie, stoically.

"Maybe not, but with an actual scientific approach to the problem instead of just a quick incineration, maybe we'd *learn* something," said Lamont.

No one spoke for a moment as they watched the animal suffer. Jeannie broke the silence first. "The team's been taking inventory. So far, all the other animals appear to be fine, thank God."

Lamont nodded. "Maybe we dodged the bullet. Okay. Emmet, euthanize her and get her on to a truck. Incinerate her and sterilize the pen, the truck, and everything along the transfer route. Use a bio suit for yourself and anyone helping you. Better be safe than sorry."

Emmet nodded, happy to hear that he was being ordered to wear a suit he wanted on anyway.

"What do you want to do after the inventory is finished? If all of them are clean, just back to normal schedule?" Asked Jeannie.

Lamont nodded. "Yes, but I want them observed carefully. Random spot checks every few hours. Those mites grow extremely quickly when they have a food source, and they evolved on beef. I'm theorizing that the cattle will show infestation quickly if there's a problem, just like Penelope did. We need to be ahead of this."

Lamont looked at Emmet, who took off to gather his crew and equipment. Lamont walked out feeling dejected. The breeding plans would be set back weeks or months, no doubt, and he'd have to start over with genetic testing on a new heifer.

Jeannie walked over to the edge of the open pasture and looked out at the animals. They'd been poked and prodded and now looked agitated. She made a spontaneous decision and cut the lights by fifty percent to calm them down and help them rest. It worked, and she watched as—one-by-one—the animals pawed the soft earth and settled down.

Jeannie walked out before the tiny, hideous creatures in the grass, now freed from the blinding lights, emerged and began finding their way to new hosts.

132

26

Infirmary

Andy was getting worse. Much worse.

Laurel called Peter and asked him to return for another consultation. Andy was heavily sedated, and his rash was covered by bandages that had been soaked in the anti-parasitic medicine, but he was still a ghostly white and covered in sweat.

Dr. Alonzo walked in and looked at Andy, then asked Dr. Hayes if she'd arranged for transport to a hospital.

"Kim Hendricks and Paul Dodds had a conference call. No one leaves."

"Quarantine?"

"Not exactly. More like, no leaking this mess to the media before the VIP visit."

"Laurel, that's ridiculous, and you know it."

She shrugged. "Not my call. You want to talk to Kim, be my guest."

"What about Lamont?"

"He was on the call, too. Overruled I think. But we should talk to him anyway. Andrew looks worse, and I think we have to increase the Nitazoxanide. We're already giving him a very high dose, which is why he looks so sick, but something's not right. Lamont knows about the anti-parasitic medications and whatever he's got crawling around inside him."

"I'm calling him right now."

Peter called Lamont on his cell, and Lamont answered right away. After a brief conversation, Lamont agreed to come right over. Ten minutes later, he was in the room with the three of them. Andy was dozing under sedation.

"You're right. He looks worse," said Lamont.

"He's doused in the medication. Why isn't it working?" asked Laurel.

Lamont stared at him. "I told corporate that I wanted to study the heifer, but no. Now all I have is a theory with no proof."

"Well?" asked Pete.

"You have him wrapped in a poison that will kill the mites. What if it drives the mites deeper into his flesh to get away from the poison?"

"You think these little bugs are smart enough to recognize a chemical and move away from it?"

Lamont shrugged. "I don't know because the damn suits won't let me do my job! But let's pretend that it's possible. It'll drive the mites into his system where they can end up anywhere. They move to his brain or major organs and he's dead. Remove the bandages and wash off the applications, then double the IV dosage. Maybe we can reverse this."

"So they'll start moving back *out* of his skin?" asked Laurel, feeling queasy.

"I'm hoping they just *die*," replied Lamont. "As soon as that's done, I want him moved to a private room and quarantined."

"We were just discussing that," said Peter. "I agree a hundred percent. He should be isolated."

"And the last thing we should be doing is bringing in a bunch of visitors!" snapped Laurel.

"That's not my call. Call Kim. Call corporate in D.C.. Hell, call the CDC in Atlanta for all I care." He took a deep breath. "Look, the good news is, it appears we've got this incident isolated to one animal that's now destroyed and incinerated, and this man, who caused the problem with his own stupidity. We up the Nitazoxanide, he recovers in a few days, and then he's sent packing. I hope to have the lab and zoo back to normal in another forty-eight hours. We're observing the animals and so far, we're okay. Everyone just remain focused and vigilant, and we'll get through this unfortunate incident."

Lamont looked over at Andy and shook his head. He felt a combination of pity, worry, and anger at the individual responsible for the biggest mess in their history. He grumbled under his breath and left.

After he was gone, Laurel spoke to Peter carefully and quietly. "I haven't asked anyone about this yet, but don't you think we should notify his emergency contact? We have an obligation."

Pete made a face. "And then what? What if they want to come visit or demand he's transferred out? What if they have questions about why he's here?"

Laurel looked at Peter. "We both know he belongs in a hospital. If we notify his emergency contact and they insist on transfer, then we'd have to do it, right?

"Laurel…"

"Let them fire me. You know it's the right thing to do. We're doctors, not politicians."

Peter shrugged and threw his hands up, then walked out. Clearly he wanted no part of her decision. Laurel checked his records and found the number for his emergency contact, listed as "significant other: Hope Whitley." She looked around the room for reassurance and found none there, took a breath, and dialed for Hope.

In Harrisburg, Hope's phone buzzed and vibrated and danced along the table until it fell off onto the carpet next to the bed. The bed was soaked with fluids and blood, and twenty-eight teeth were scattered near the pillow. A hundred or so mites, ranging in size from peas to baseballs, chewed the sheets and blankets as they tried to find the last bits of nutrition before turning on the other for food.

27

D.C.

"I'm getting nervous," said Connie, adjusting her little black dress.

"No reason to be nervous. You look fantastic as always, and the VIPs are already being shuttled over to the airport."

"Shouldn't we be there to greet them?"

"You and I will fly out on the corporate jet and make our grand entrance. Kim and her staff have everything taken care of at their end already. She literally had a red carpet flown out there yesterday. They'll be greeted like kings and queens, given a welcome toast with Dom Perignon, and then taken to see the new video production."

Connie smiled. "I had the studio add 'We Are the World' as the closing music."

Paul laughed at the irony of her song choice. "Well, aren't you full of surprises."

"I'm hoping if this goes as well as it should, perhaps you'll remember me around bonus and stock time."

"You know I will. Come on. Let's get moving. Limo is downstairs."

"Limo to our private jet. I could get used to this, Paul."

"You and me both. You just flirt and tease them the way you tease me, and I'm sure we'll get whatever we want."

She put her hand to her chest and gave a dramatic throw of her long hair. "Why, Paul! I have no idea what you're talking about!" She slid her finger into her mouth and withdrew it painfully slowly.

"Right." Paul smiled broadly.

They were in for an unforgettable weekend.

"How is he?" asked Laurel, arriving for her shift.

Andy was being isolated in a private room that was off-limits to everyone except a few medical staff.

"Same. I keep waiting for some God-awful thing to come crawling out of him, but so far, it's been uneventful. He's just been sleeping. The Nitazoxanide's been running for seven hours. I'm not sure what his liver is gonna look like when this is all over."

"Lamont says it won't cause damage."

"Lamont can say whatever he wants. We're pouring a can of Raid into a human being and hoping it kills some bugs without killing the patient. That's *all* we're doing, Laurel." He stood and arched his back, groaning.

"You okay?"

"Yeah, just stiff as hell. Getting old ain't for sissies. Must have been sitting too long. My back's killing me."

"Advil's in drawer three."

"Thanks," he said, walking over to the drawer as if powered by batteries. "You ever call his emergency contact?"

"I tried twice. No answer."

"It's just as well. Now you can sleep well knowing you did the right thing and you still keep your job." He smiled and turned, then grabbed the counter as his knees buckled. "Damn!"

"Pete?"

"My back. It's worse than I expected. Jeez. I'm going to go back to my room and crash for a few hours. I'll stretch later. I'm sure it'll be fine. Maybe high school football wasn't such a great idea."

She smiled and nodded, then patted his shoulder. "Poor baby. Call me when you wake up."

Peter left and Laurel stepped closer to Andy. She whispered something to him, but he didn't respond.

She pursed her lips and looked at his rash, which was raw and still oozing pus. At least the white blood cells were doing their job. She snapped on gloves and began gathering what she needed to clean his many open sores. She hoped Lamont was right about leaving them open instead of covering them with the Nitazoxanide. At this point, she couldn't tell if anything was helping.

Pete could barely walk by the time he reached his room. The pain in his lower back radiated down his leg. He'd never had sciatica before, but he was pretty sure he had just been hit with it.

Pete closed the door behind him and got down on his floor to stretch. He laid back and pulled his right knee up to his chest.

"*Jesus,*" he muttered. It hurt.

He pulled his leg higher against his chest and tried to stretch his lower back. The movement put pressure on the mite that had burrowed up his leg and irritated his sural nerve. The armor-plated bug slashed and tore as it pushed and crawled its way further into the leg muscle, past the knee and across the sciatic nerve. As its eight clawed legs cut through the nerve, the pain intensified and Pete dropped his leg and fell back flat on the floor. He let out a long groan of agony and remained still. The mite, now free from the pressure, stopped moving, and lessened the pain in Pete's leg and back.

"Oh my God," he mumbled, thankful it had subsided.

Deep inside his thigh, the mite released her microscopic eggs into his bloodstream.

28

VIP Day

Global Tech World Solutions wasn't playing around when it came to its events.

All that was missing from this one was a marching band. Twenty employees lined each side of the long red carpet and applauded as the long line of senators and congressmen walked up to the building's main entrance. Most of them were already fairly buzzed after having drinks in their private jets and limos.

Kim wore a red business suit, flashing her smile as she shook hands and welcomed each and every one of their guests. She had been up all night trying to memorize the names of every congressman and senator. They couldn't well ask them to wear name tags at a red carpet event, now could they?

It was a daunting task, but she was doing extremely well for herself as she spoke to each of her VIPs. She made each of them feel important, keeping their gaze for just a few seconds. Enough to lock eyes, but not enough to intimidate. They were practically eating out of her hand.

Each were handed a glass of champagne and promised an unforgettable day, and they followed their guides to the main amphitheater where they'd be shown a movie that was created just for them.

The air was drunk with anticipation. "Hell," Connie thought, looking at the lines of important people lined up like big ants. "So were they."

As they took their seats, Paul and Connie entered the room and took front and center stage. Secret Service had insisted on sending along a protection detail because of the number of senators and congressmen that would all be together at the event.

They didn't normally protect senators and congressmen unless there was a direct threat, but the director of Homeland Security had still thought it was important to have such a large group accompanied by a small security team. The agents were excellent at fading into the background, and their presence was all but forgotten by the VIPs. For everyone else, they stood out like magnified mites on a red carpet.

"Welcome. Thank you all so much for taking time out of your busy schedules to come to Global Tech. We're changing science, and with your help, we can all change the world. It's now my honor and privilege to introduce our director of global operations, Mr. Paul Dodds."

Paul waved to the applause and repeated his thanks, then gave a quick summary of what they'd be doing and seeing in the coming evening before their huge dinner party.

He stepped aside with Connie as the lights dimmed and the production began.

It was similar to what Paul and Connie had seen on their first visit, but Connie had pushed the production team to take things up a notch—if they were going to get any donations out of these bastards, she'd have to.

With cinematic quality and inspiring, sappy music, she had the crowd near tears when the music finally faded out.

As the lights slowly came back up for dramatic effect, Paul gave Connie a wink as she walked back out to the stage. "It's difficult for us, here in America, to understand the devastation of hunger and famine that is so common all over the world. It's terrifying to think that all that separates us from total extinction is six inches of topsoil and some rain. Even here, in the world's greatest superpower, we have people that go hungry every day. And now, you—all of you—are in the position to change all of that. For the first time ever, we can truly end world hunger..."

She went on for another five minutes. Paul watched with admiration as this beautiful, intelligent woman delivered the presentation of her lifetime. When she was finished, everyone broke into applause, including Paul, and it was genuine.

"We'll now break into three smaller groups and give you a tour of this facility. When I first saw what you're about to see, it was reminiscent of the wonders of Willy Wonka's Chocolate Factory. Well, we don't make chocolate here, but when you see how we'll provide every human being on the planet with affordable beef, pork, and chicken, you will share my excitement. Please make sure you receive your gift bag on your way out of the theater."

As the senators and congressmen walked out of the room, staffers handed them leather bags containing chocolate, expensive fountain pens, and various other little treats.

Their packages also contained one more thing, a sample bill that would change the laws regarding genetically modified foods, imports and exports, and disclosure labeling. It just needed introduction and a vote.

29

On the Road

WALLY AND DEAN WERE sitting in the back of a van with their highly illegal M4 carbine rifles resting across their laps. They'd been purchased from a dirty arms dealer in Philly that Wally had met while he served time in the joint. The rest of the crew would have pistols, pipe bombs, Molotov cocktails, and a few shotguns.

They had a long drive and used the time to load magazines, clean their guns, and practice changing the magazines. The drive gave them time to discuss in detail who would be doing what.

Because it was a Saturday night, they figured most of the staff would be off work. Of course, there would always be a few guards and lab rats working every day, but it shouldn't be nearly as busy as a workday during the week. Simply, they would have less to deal with, and less to shoot at.

Wally gave Dean a hard stare. "You okay? You look nervous as shit."

Dean didn't like being called out in front of three of their lackeys. "I'm not nervous, you know me." He tried to sound brave.

"Yeah, I do know you, that's why I'm asking. You're sweating like a pig and you look pale as a sheet."

Dean tried to play it off with his usual machismo. "Yeah, I'm worried. Got myself a crazy piece of ass the other night. I think the bitch gave me the clap or something."

Wally leaned away from him. "Damn, dude. Move the fuck away from me. I don't need your infected shit anywhere near me. Go see a dick doc and get that shit taken care of."

Dean forced a smile. "Yeah, after all this shit goes down, I'll make an appointment."

"I'm serious, dude. Don't wait. I saw dudes in the joint that had all kinds of VD. Some of them even got crazy from that shit. I'm not kidding."

One of the kids behind them said, "Yeah, I read syph causes insanity."

Wally and Dean simultaneously shouted: *"Shut the fuck up."*

The kid went back to listening to his music.

Wally leaned closer and spoke in a whisper. "Ya know, when this goes down, some of these punks are gonna freak and lose their shit, right?"

"Yeah."

Wally stared hard at Dean. "Nobody flips on us."

He nodded. "Understood."

"Andy said the place was locked up tighter than Fort Knox. That means we'll need to grab some of these fuckers to have them key us into places. I hope you ain't afraid of getting your hands dirty."

"If I didn't wanna get my hands dirty, would I be doing this in the first place?" Dean leaned forward on his elbows and spoke through clenched teeth. "I told you. I'm just feeling sick. I *got* this, alright? I'll waste any fucker that gets in our way."

Wally smacked Dean's knee. "That's what I wanna hear. I ain't going back to the joint for this shit. We get jammed up, we kill everything we see, and then we get the fuck out of there." He leaned in even closer and added, "I've got a car stashed about ten miles outside the facility for you and me."

Dean nodded. "Nice."

He dropped his voice to make sure the others couldn't hear. "*Just* you and me. In two days, we'll be knee-deep in cash on a Mexican beach. Now just chill out and try and get some sleep or something. We'll get there after dark and turn that place upside down."

Behind them, in the second van, two of the college dropouts from California were talking in the back of the van while the others around them slept or listened to music.

"Wally said there's going to be animals there."

"Yeah, giant ones."

"Chloe, I can't kill an animal. Neither can you."

"I know. We don't have to do that. We're just lighting some fires."

"Oh my God, you're so stupid. What happens to the animals if we light the place on fire?"

"Won't they let them go first?"

April put her face in her hands. "I can't believe you got me into this."

"I didn't get you into this! You wanted to join!"

"You said they were vegans and were trying to stop animal cruelty."

"They are…"

"By lighting them on fire and killing everyone? We should split first chance we get."

The kid sitting in front of them turned halfway around and flashed a black combat knife. "You two aren't going anywhere. And you better pray I don't tell Dean or Wally what you've been talking about. You're in this until we're done here, just like the rest of us. Now shut up…"

They did.

30

GTWS: The Zoo

The tours had started, and the VIPs were more than impressed. They broke into three groups, and each started in a different section. Connie made sure that Senator Carr was in her group. She hooked his arm in hers and chatted as they strolled into the zoo.

"This is *really* what it's all about. Right here, I can't wait to show you." She turned to address her group of six senators and five congressmen. "Ladies and gentlemen, you're about to see something that will amaze you. It's classified and considered top secret for now—so please, no pictures. Scout's honor!" There were a few chuckles. All of them had signed a non-disclosure agreement before they'd even seen the front of the building. She swiped her card, and they entered the zoo.

"Just a reminder, these animals are very gentle but they're extremely large. Please don't get too close, but don't be afraid." She opened the second door and stepped through, holding it open. The eleven guests filed past her and walked out onto the grass. The first person to see one of the cattle stopped short and blurted, "Holy shit!" then said a quick "excuse me."

"Yes, Congressman Sullivan, that does best describe them, doesn't it?" said Connie with a big smile.

The crowd gave a few nervous chuckles, and a few of the guests were reluctant to walk in any further.

Connie saw their hesitation and the hum of hushed conversations and walked briskly past them. "Don't be shy! Follow me. They don't bite!"

A fifteen-foot sheep bleated from far in the pasture with her flock.

"One sheep produces enough wool to keep a factory busy for a long time." Connie said as she moved through the zoo.

The hogs had been removed from the pasture and penned, since they could be a little more aggressive and didn't put up a good show for the event. Several large heifers mooed so loud that it echoed far across the stadium-like pasture.

Senator Carr, trying to be brave, followed quickly behind her. "Would make a helluva steak," he joked.

"You have no idea how right you are," said Connie, locking eyes with him as she continued slowly. "In fact, you'll be eating it tonight, and I promise you, it'll be the best thing you will ever put in your mouth."

Senator Carr turned red as she teased him, then moved on to the next guest. "Step right in folks, don't be bashful and don't be scared. Let's go see one of the steers..."

She felt almost like a circus performer leading the crowd through the ring.

The dozen of them strode across the grass out into the pasture as Connie began reciting facts and figures. She was extremely well-prepared for her guests and sounded as though she had worked at the facility herself for years. A few of the employees were spaced out in the pasture, keeping an eye on the animals should any of them get spooked and terrify their guests.

It was all about the look, it was all about the image, and—Connie knew—it was all about the money.

It was twilight, and the darkness had soothed the animals into their typical sleeping patterns. One of the steers had laid down and was already dozing. Connie headed for the animal, chatting as she walked with her line of followers. Of course, the sedation helped.

"Our cattle are bred to produce the world's most excellent beef, and in the largest quantity per animal the world has ever seen. Because we cross Angus and Limousin, we produce polled cattle—that is, cattle without horns..."

"Yeah, that's probably a good idea for an animal bigger than an elephant," quipped Senator Carr. "I can't imagine a bull with twenty-foot horns running around out here."

Connie smiled and addressed the group as they walked timidly towards the steer. "This is a male, called a steer. If he wasn't castrated, we'd call him a bull. There are only steers out here in the pasture with our heifers..."

"And that's no bull," said Senator Carr, very pleased with his joke that got only a few polite smiles from the crowd.

"If a heifer has a calf, she is then called a cow. None of these have been bred, so they're all considered heifers."

A representative from Colorado raised her hand. "Excuse me, but if there's no bulls, and only heifers, then how are you breeding these animals?"

"Excellent question, Congresswoman Danfers..." Connie was amazed that only one person out of eleven guests had thought to ask the question. These people were allowed to be politicians?

"Please, just call me Lisa, we're off duty!" she said with a warm smile.

Connie returned the smile, "Oh thank you, Lisa! I'm honored. Well, so far, all of these giant animals started out in very small Petri dishes."

The congresswoman's eyebrows went up. "These are test-tube babies?"

"Exactly. And they were birthed by regular Angus-Limousin cows. Believe it or not, when they're born, they're almost the same size as regular cattle. The difference is, their genetic code has been modified to speed up their growth rates and then continue growing. That's no small feat, because unless it's done perfectly, they'd have all kinds of problems as they outgrew their natural sizes. Through genetic engineering and multiple generations of perfecting these animals, we're now ready to allow them to start breeding naturally."

Connie thought it was a good thing that nobody knew what *else* they had been growing in the lab.

There were a few nervous glances and chuckles from the crowd. They were hanging on her every word—as she expected they were going to.

Connie jumped right in with a wisecrack. "Yes, that's right. When you get reports of earthquakes from out here, you'll know it's just our animals mating."

Senator Carr whispered to Connie. "Maybe I'll get invited back out to see that."

She gently punched his arm. Such a kidder.

"So where's the bull?" asked Congresswoman Danfers.

Connie smiled. "Would you all like to meet Goliath?"

"If he's behind strong bars," said one of the other senators. "I saw King Kong!"

Connie flashed another PR smile. "Yes, well, he is isolated and secured in another part of the building. He weighs over twenty thousand pounds, and unlike these males, he is intact and a bit feisty. You'll be happy to know he is also polled."

She was met with several confused stares.

"Without horns." she reminded them.

There were happy nods.

"But still horny," she added, with a big white flash of her teeth.

Connie moved closer to the giant, sleepy steer nearest to where she was walking in the pasture. "It's okay, he's very calm." Calm and sedated, she imagined.

Emmett, who'd been observing both humans and animals, stepped forward and placed his hand on the animal's front leg, speaking softly to him. "Hi there, folks. Step right up. We call him Shorty, and that's because he's *only* thirteen feet tall. It's much easier to pet him when he's lying down."

Senator Carr was terrified, but looked at Connie and swaggered forward as though driven by all the Dom Perignon. He made kissy noises like he was talking to his dog and started rubbing the animal's leg.

Senator Carr felt something bite the side of his hand, and he pulled back in pain. He laughed, partially out of shock, and said, "Whoops! Sure is big, isn't she?"

The group around Senator Carr laughed, and Lisa joined in.

"Oh, you big baby!" said Lisa, stepping forward to rub the giant animal.

The mite that bit into her was so small it was almost invisible, and she didn't even notice as it burrowed into her skin.

31

GTWS: The Farm

Paul led another tour group of important and rich people with Kim Hendricks assisting. Unlike Connie, he didn't know a damn thing about any of the plants and animals, only the profit picture and potential for their stakeholders. He smiled, made small talk, and tried to look interested as Kim walked the group through the farm and its output.

"...and we can produce six times the amount of corn per acre as regular corn. Notice the number of ears on our white sweetcorn stalks. The taste is outstanding, and we can produce the same high-yield crops with consistent quality. And because we've engineered the corn to be resistant to most pests and diseases, we can use less pesticide and herbicide…"

They were attracted to the prospects, and Paul could tell that they were thinking about the money too.

Paul followed them around for twenty more minutes and kept an eye on the faces of his guests. They'd already seen the animals, so seeing the farm was extremely anti-climactic. He made a mental note to himself, on the next tour, that everyone started at the same place and ended the tour in the zoo—it would be much more riveting than looking at giant wheat stalks or soybean pods that produced six beans instead of two or three.

Paul waited until Kim took a breath, then cut into her speech. "How many of you would like to see the Irish Pub we have right here on campus? I mean, even mad scientists need to have a Guinness, am I right?"

The audience's faces changed and perked up.

"Do they have vodka?" asked Congressman Steel.

"Yes, they have vodka! They have it all! A pre-dinner cocktail, or more talk about crops? Your choice…"

It was unanimously decided, and the newly-energized group followed Paul with a lively pace as they headed out of the farm to the pub. Kim was happy to follow them as well, having done the same speech for three groups in a row she was feeling ready for a drink herself.

When they entered the bar, Kim was surprised to see Lamont already seated by himself. He looked instantly embarrassed to be seen having a drink, which was a rarity for him.

"Oh, my, look who we have here," she said with a huge, impressive fake smile. "Honored guests, it's my pleasure to introduce you to our lab director, Doctor Lamont White. It's been Dr. White's brilliant work that has taken this facility from obscurity to the leading animal research and development lab on the planet that it is today!"

The group clapped politely.

Lamont forced a smile, but was horrified to have been put on the spot. He had gone to the pub to hide from the VIPs—the pub was never supposed to have been part of the tour. He stood up and glanced quickly between Kim and Paul. His boss and his boss' boss and a group of VIPs. Super. Fantastic, in fact.

"Good evening, everyone," he said, standing up slowly from the bar stool. "I guess the secret is out—even scientists have a drink sometimes."

The truth was, Lamont had almost never gone to the bar after work. But they had euthanized and incinerated Penelope, they had an extremely sick man in the infirmary and were under orders not to take him to a hospital, and were still trying to understand the extent of the damage Mr. Booth may have done to the lab.

Even for Lamont, it had been a rough couple of days.

Paul walked over with the group and began making introductions. Lamont gave his best fake smile.

His quiet night of escaping the realities of the last few days had just turned to shit.

32

Dr. Alonzo

LYING ON HIS SIDE, curled up in a ball, Dr. Alonzo groaned and tried to will himself across his room to reach a phone. The nerves in his legs had been cut by the creature inside, whose offspring now feasted on the insides of his spinal cord.

His legs were useless for anything other than providing mind-numbing agony. He cried softly and called out for help, but the rooms were constructed well and sound didn't travel very far at all.

Being the "second generation" of wild mites, the creatures instantly recognized human flesh as food. Like all infant creatures, they wanted only to eat and grow and were beyond voracious in their feeding and growing habits. As they shed their exoskeletons and excreted waste, Dr. Alonzo's blood turned more toxic by the minute. He spiked a fever and grew weaker as the nausea increased.

"Please... Someone..."

When the adult female released her second round of eggs, which she produced every twenty-four hours, the microscopic mites flowed through his blood to his brain. While he couldn't feel it yet, they were making their way into his brain matter—and his reactions were slowing down.

Like many arthropods, a fertilized female could continually produce fertilized eggs from a single mating. As the tiny creatures burrowed into the rich proteins of his brain, Peter began hallucinating. He saw his mother, he saw his father, and he saw his little brother. They were all dead. The creatures burrowed until he felt a blinding migraine and—mercifully—lost consciousness.

Thankfully, he couldn't hear the munching and crunching of a hundred armor-plated mouths and claws as they turned a human being into pulverized meat that was easier for them to digest.

Five hours later, a little after seven o'clock in the evening, as the VIP guests began assembling for an amazing feast, his skin burst open in dozens of places. He was on his back, his midsection now hollow, when the mites began burrowing through his skin in search of more meat.

The largest of them was bigger than a golf ball, and ready to shed her exoskeleton yet again. Her offspring appeared in two sizes, a generation apart—dimes and quarters. Their backs split wide open as newer, larger versions of their former selves emerged, now hungrier than ever.

When they were their natural size, it might take all day to travel from one eyelash to another. Now, at millions of times larger than nature intended, they scurried across the floor faster than any cockroach they could find to devour.

33

The Zoo

AT THE REQUEST OF her guests, Connie brought them to see Goliath, their lone bull.

The guests were itchy after their walk through the grass and hay, a fairly common reaction for anyone who had never been outside the boardroom or corporate office for more than a couple minutes at a time.

Emmet accompanied the group and led them out of the cavernous pasture down a side-located hallway through to another enclosure.

"Follow this way, folks. We're going to enter Goliath's pen. He's separated, so there's no reason for anyone to be scared or intimidated. He's not aggressive as long as there aren't other cattle around."

The crowd gave another few appropriate, nervous chuckles.

"I hope we'll have time to shower before dinner," Lisa whispered to Connie as she scratched her arms. "I think I smell like cows. Heifers, I mean."

"See? You learned something today," she replied with her usual smile. "Actually, there won't be time for showering and changing, but we do have beautiful bathroom facilities to freshen up in before dinner. Don't worry, you look gorgeous."

Lisa kept scratching at her rash like it was a sin, hiding it as best she could. She was feeling itchy and gross. A tiny mite floated to the ground and raced out of the light into Goliath's pen.

A tremendous snort from Goliath made everyone jump. When he pawed at the soft earth, they could feel the vibration under their feet.

"He's something, isn't he?" asked Emmet proudly. "Over twenty thousand pounds of power and muscle and perfect genetic code. He can sire that entire herd and produce millions of pounds of future beef to feed the world. Just look at him—so powerful and gorgeous."

"Like all of our guests!" added Connie, ever the charmer.

Goliath tossed his head and began a circular trot around his enclosure. The pen, which could have comfortably held an entire herd of normal cows, was barely enough room for the bull to take a quick lap before ending up back at the bars.

"I always thought bulls had horns," said one of the freshman congressmen from New Jersey.

"City boys," said Senator Carr, somewhat snidely, to Connie.

Connie faked another perfect, PR-driven quick smile and looked over at the congressman. "I think most people think bulls have horns. Luckily for us, neither the Angus nor the Limousin have horns, and like we said before, no one would want that big an animal with two giant weapons on his head."

"Maybe you could make giant bull elephants with huge tusks. Might solve the ivory problem," joked Senator Carr.

Connie looked at him in amazement. Maybe he wasn't as dumb as he looked. She'd have to ask the lab about that later. Maybe Lamont could make them a side hustle and a few million out of this.

They stood and watched Goliath trot around his pen, making the ground shake for another few minutes. He was truly magnificent. Under the wrong circumstances, Connie also thought that he would be terrifying.

"Are we about done here? I don't want to go to dinner smelling like a farm," said Senator Beth Riccio.

Lisa leaned over to Connie. "See? It isn't just me. We're all going to stink at dinner!"

"Well then, we won't smell each other!" she replied with another million-dollar smile.

"Okay, folks. It's time to leave Goliath and head back to the employee lounges where you can wash up. After that, we go to our little Irish Pub, and then on to dinner. I promise you that you're going to have the best steaks you ever had in your life."

"Gonna be some big steaks!" said one of the congressmen with a laugh.

Senator Carr leaned over to the young New Jersey congressman and started his joke. "Ya see, this old bull and this young bull were up on the hill overlooking the whole herd of cows, and the young bull says, 'Let's run down there and fuck us a cow!' The old bull looks at him and says, 'Let's *walk* down, and fuck 'em *all...*'" He laughed harder at his joke than the congressman did.

As they walked, Connie explained to the group how they had to learn how to process such giant portions of beef and bring in butchers to make it all work, but promised they would be impressed. They shuffled out towards building one.

Back in his stall, Goliath snorted and jumped as something tiny burrowed through his hide into his flesh. It aggravated the colossal beast, and he ran in circles, faster and faster, until finally so aggravated he slammed himself against the bars, making the entire room shake.

Somewhere else, the crowd had already moved on to something else.

34

GTWS

THE EIGHT SUVs AND vans had driven out towards the facility on a lonely stretch of road that was used almost exclusively by Global Tech employees. There was nothing else out that way other than farms, forests, and the mega-facility that was Global Tech World Solutions. When they were approximately two miles out, Wally ordered all lights out.

The vehicles slowed to a snail's pace, driving in total darkness. It would take them almost fifteen minutes to drive the final two miles, but they didn't want even a hint of headlights to give away their arrival. Wally's driver had night vision goggles, and "blazed the trail" at five miles per hour, with the other seven vehicles trying to stay right on the bumper of the vehicle in front of them. In this slow tight pack, the eight vehicles arrived at the entrance road and entered the private property of GTWS.

There was no turning back from this now.

Inside the company's cafeteria, the employees had created an impressive venue for their guests. White tablecloths and flowers were placed on every table, and the lights had been turned down low with appropriate mood music piped in over unseen speakers. With plenty of extra budget to decorate with, the staff had turned a decent-looking cafeteria into a five-star resort-looking gourmet restaurant for the night.

The Global Tech employees had dressed up for the occasion and escorted their VIPs to their tables, careful to place the D's and R's together to avoid any issues. Paul and Connie had decided to split up to cover more ground, and Kim and Lamont each had their own table of VIPs as well.

Lamont didn't want to be there at all, but had to. After downing three coffees and washing his face with a quick change of clothes, he put on his best fake smile and sat with nine Washington D.C. big-shots. Jeannie Davis took table five, and each table had a company VIP with them for schmoozing purposes.

Lamont's phone buzzed right after he sat down. It was a text from Dr. Hayes in the infirmary, but he ignored it. Senator Riccio was rambling on about her work, and one simply didn't whip out a phone and read texts while being chatted up by a senator. When he didn't respond, the phone buzzed again—this time a phone call—but he simply ignored the vibration while never looking to see the text message that read, "URGENT."

Additional servers from the company's catering contractors had been brought in, and they understood well that it was a VIP night. They wore tuxedos and hustled out the salads for the first course.

As the food arrived, Kim stood up as planned and stood behind the small podium at the front of the room. She had a glass of champagne in her hand and watched as the servers brought each of their guests their own glass.

"Once again, I just wanted to thank you on behalf of Global Tech for joining us here today. Much of the food you'll be eating tonight was produced right here in our facility. We're the original farm to table..."

Senator Carr leaned over to Connie, who had made sure to sit next to him, and whispered, "Don't you mean *lab* to table?"

She returned a respectful though fake laugh.

"...and we raise our glasses to our senators and representatives, who give so much of their time and talent to serve our country. Like Global Tech, you all work to make our country, and the world, a better place..."

Everyone clapped and downed their Dom Perignon, and the servers were quick to return with bottles of red and white wine. Their instructions had been clear: Keep everyone drinking and eating and happy. The VIPs enjoyed farm fresh GMO salads, followed by pasta with homemade GMO tomato sauce, and then came the main course.

The room gave collective gasps as huge steaks were placed in front of the guests.

Paul and Connie had decided to go with double-sized portions to make a point, and each dish that was brought out could have been used as a serving platter for a family of four. The chefs had done a masterful job. Each hand-cut ribeye had perfect grill marks on it, and the GMO baked potatoes were bigger than anything that had ever been produced in the state of Idaho.

"Incredible!"

"Oh my gosh, this is insane! So delicious!"

"Wow!"

"Amazing steak!"

Connie, Paul, Jeannie, Kim and Lamont watched with great satisfaction as their guests ate like their own over-sized hogs, complimenting everything they tasted. Paul waited for his guests to slow down before getting up. Connie saw him and joined him at the podium.

"Jesus," thought Connie to herself. "These people are suckers."

Paul addressed the room with Connie standing at his side. "Well, I think you can finally see for yourselves. The products we make here are for real and can truly save the world. We know you are constantly harassed by lobbyists and pushed in a million different directions, so we really appreciate you coming out here today. And I think you'll agree, the quantity hasn't affected the quality. Isn't everyone enjoying their dinners?"

A thunderous round of applause made Connie and Paul smile.

"It is our sincere hope that by the time you finish dinner and coffee, we will have won you over to the world changing possibilities we have here at Global Tech. Thank you again for coming."

Lamont's phone buzzed again.

What the *fuck* was the problem?

"I'm so sorry. Please excuse me just for a moment," he said as he stood up.

He walked quickly out of the dining hall and opened his phone to see several missed calls and messages from Laurel. As he began to read the text, it rang in his hand, but this time the call was from Mike—the head of security.

"Doctor White, it's Mike. We were told that no one was to be disturbed, but you need to get to the infirmary right away. Dr. Hayes wants to call an ambulance for Mr. Booth, and Ms. Hendricks told me *specifically* that no one was in or out of here until after the guests have left at eleven."

"Okay, I'm on my way..."

35

GTWS

Dr. Laurel Hayes was freaking out.

Andrew Booth looked like he was something out of a horror movie, and Peter wouldn't answer his phone. When Mike finally walked back in, she screamed.

"Did you reach Dr. White?"

"Yes, he's on his way."

"I need you to find Dr. Alonzo. I've called his private phone and his room—nothing. I need him in here right now!"

"Okay, I'll run down to his room and ask around in his wing. I was working security at the door of the dinner when the VIPs went in. He's not over there."

"Go! And tell him to call me immediately! This man is going to die if we can't help him fast. Maybe if Pete and I both talk to Lamont and Kim, we can convince them we need a hospital."

Mike turned for the door. "I'm on my way to Dr. Alonzo's room, but then I need to get back to the security desk. It's the weekend, and I'm the only one on tonight."

"Jesus, Mike! No one's breaking down our doors to steal secrets! I have a man that's *dying* in there! *That's* a real emergency! Now do your fucking job!"

Mike ran off to find Dr. Alonzo, and he felt himself a little angry at being yelled at, but was also understanding that Dr. Hayes was under a lot of pressure right now. They all were. She'd never raised her voice to him before, so she got a pass. And she was right. In the four years that he'd been working there, Mike had yet to have to do anything that even resembled actual security work. In fact, a sick patient was the most exciting thing that had ever happened since he'd been working there.

Mike grabbed a cart and raced down to Pete's room, trying his cell and room phones repeatedly as he drove. When he got to his room, he keyed himself in and called back into the room.

"Doctor Alonzo? It's Mike, head of security. I'm coming in. Is anyone here?"

Mike closed the door behind him and walked back into Pete's bedroom. He stepped into the room and froze. The remains of what looked like a human being were on the floor. It was hard to tell. Mostly, it was torn-up hospital scrubs that were covered in blood. The remains of a human skull and a few bones were left on the floor, but that was it. He knelt down to take a closer look, hesitating for a moment, and reached for his phone.

The skittering of a hundred eight-legged creatures made him jump to his feet. Each of the horrid creatures looked like a giant armor-plated tick, with giant mandibles and horns. Each leg ended in razor-sharp lobster-like claws, and the speed of the things was unbelievable.

He screamed and tried to get his legs to run, but it was over in an instant. Even with his strength and size, Mike was no match for the speed or volume of the mites.

They flowed onto him like a bubbly black liquid, instantly burrowing through his clothes and into his flesh. They were all over his body. They were inside his body. He swatted at them and tried to pull them off, but they seemed to appear from every direction. They'd been hiding under the bed and furniture, out of the light of the room, but their hunger now drove them into the light straight towards the smell of human flesh.

Mike ran in circles like a wild creature, screaming and clawing at the multiple attackers who were all over his body and rapidly making their way into it. For a billion years, these tiny arthropods had evolved into the perfect eating machines. Now, genetically modified to the size of baseballs and still growing, they were like a pack of rabid wolves, except their claws were razor-sharp and their armor made them impossible to crush or kill with bare hands.

By the time Mike dropped to his knees, they had invaded deep into the cavities of his body and were eating their way through his vital organs.

He was dead before he hit the floor and—in less than thirty minutes—only his clothes, a few bones, and his teeth remained.

———

Dr. White entered the isolation room to find Dr. Hayes with a stethoscope in her ears listening to Andy's chest. He was unconscious, and he looked pale and sweaty.

"Laurel, what's going on? I'm supposed to be at this stupid dinner. His heart and lungs okay?"

"That is *not* what I'm listening to!" she screamed.

Tears spilled down her cheeks. She was frantic.

He made an inquisitive face and walked over. She handed him her stethoscope, and he put it on and listened. His face showed his horror. There was no question.

Yes, he could hear a heartbeat, but there was something underneath.

He could hear them too.

He could hear them chewing.

36

Nature Power Movement

THE VEHICLES STOPPED NEAR the fence and the invaders prepared for their assault. Walt looked around at his assembled "army." Mostly kids, their faces showed everything from extreme excitement to utter terror. They gathered around their leader. The sight was not unlike a battalion of young soldiers photographed about to ship off to Vietnam.

Wally spoke quietly as the group began gathering weapons. "We head around to the right side and cut the fence, then haul ass to the big building in the back. That's the building with the animals..."

Chloe nudged April. Maybe they could release all the animals.

"...I'll climb the wall and get inside the animal pasture and open the rear gate where they bring trucks in and out. You all get in fast and split into the teams we planned. Dean's team goes straight to building one, my team stays with me. Our guy inside said there are maps on the walls all over the place, so you'll know where you are going. Once we torch this place, we get out the same way we came in. Twenty minutes, tops! Then get the fuck out. Nearest cops are way more than twenty minutes away, but you never know. Maybe some state trooper rolls by or something and we have a problem. Now... Let's get moving and wreck this fucking place! Fast and quiet!"

Wally looked at Dean, who was pale and sweaty, his hands on his knees doubled over in pain. "You good to go, bro?"

Dean stood up and grunted a "yeah."

They started running along the fence line until they could see the giant building towards the back of the facility.

"Here!" shouted Wally, and one of his guys stepped forward with giant wire-cutters. They popped through each link of the fence until he created a door wide enough to slip through. Wally pulled a glow-stick from his pocket and bent it, then shook it to activate it. He shoved it into the links of the fence, marking their exit location in the dark. He slipped through the fence and started running, followed by his long line of quasi-warriors.

Once Wally and the group reached the back of the building, he told his people to get down low and shut up. He grabbed Dean by the shirt. "Any security shows up while I'm climbing, you waste the fucker, you understand?"

Dean forced a clenched grin. He wasn't ready to shoot and hoped he wouldn't have to. "I got your back."

Wally and one of the more athletic kids began climbing the steel structure that led up towards the open roof of the pasture that was the zoo. Once on top, after ten minutes of hard climbing, they made their way down inside. It was dimly lit inside, and quiet except for some sleepy animal noises. Occasionally, a steer would cry out and begin running around for a moment and then settle back down again.

The kid watched a few of the animals running. "Holy fuck, man! Do you see the size of that thing? We gotta get the fuck out of here!"

"Shut the fuck up! It's just a cow. Now get to that rear gate as fast as you can and open the doors. I'll cover you." Wally pulled up his M4 carbine and scanned the area through the scope, but there were no security guards anywhere that he could see.

The kid hopped down to the grass and started sprinting, followed by Wally, just a few steps behind with his M4 at the ready. The giant animals were an excellent incentive to run faster than the kid ever had run before in his life. He cursed under his breath the entire time he was running, completely terrified of the giant animals. As he neared the rear gate, a sheep stood up out of the grass, spooked by the two men running at her. The kid froze as the giant woolly animal rose up out of the grass.

Wally bumped into the kid and knocked him down, cursed at him, and kept on running. There was no time to stop.

The startled kid remained in the grass, frozen in terror as he stared up at the giant sheep. The animal bleated at him, and if Wally had looked back, he would have noticed that the kid literally pissed his pants.

It wasn't until he felt unseen insects biting in the grass that he found his legs and stood up, sprinting after Wally towards the rear gate. He had already made his decision—his part of the caper was over. He was heading out that fucking gate and never turning back.

Wally arrived at the rear doors, which were massive, and started reading the panels which gave instructions on how to unlock the door. He quickly pulled levers and turned cranks until the massive doors made a small hiss and creaked open. Wally started pushing and the kid caught up to him and slammed into it with all his might, pushing as hard as he could.

"Easy!" snapped Wally.

"I have to get the fuck outta here!" screamed the kid.

Wally wasn't about to allow some pussy to wreck his plans. He swung the heavy stock of his M4 around and smashed the kid's skull from behind. The kid flopped to the grass, out cold. Wally pushed the doors open further on his own, ordering his people to hurry up.

As the group ran into the pasture behind Dean, they started seeing the immense animals and whispering among themselves. They were excited and scared and in total awe all at the same time.

"I told you! They're doing fucked up things in this place! That's why we're here! Now follow the plan! Dean—take your group to the lab and burn that fucking place to the ground! My group, follow me! Hurry up!"

One of the young girls looked at the kid on the ground. "What about him?"

"Fuck him! Let's go!" screamed Wally. He was more intimidating than the steer and sheep, and his group jogged after him.

Dean ran as best he could towards the front of the large enclosure where he knew the front doors would be. His stomach pain had gotten so bad that he grunted with every stride. A dozen kids with weapons and incendiaries followed him.

Wally took his group and headed out the other way. They reached a hallway on the side and headed through the doors, then propped them open with a stool so they wouldn't need swipe cards to get back in. Wally ran full speed with the group following close behind, except for Chloe and April who had slowed down their pace. April pulled her by the arm, and they ducked behind a smaller side hallway waiting for their group to get further away.

April leaned close and whispered to Chloe. "We have to set them all free. You know Wally will kill them all."

"They're gigantic! They'll trample us to death!"

"Oh stop it! They're just big! They're cows and sheep, Chloe! Not tigers!"

The slamming of something heavy against metal bars made them jump. They glanced at each other and followed the noise down to the end of the small hallway where they opened a door marked "Goliath."

Inside, the largest bull to ever walk the face of the Earth was running and stomping the ground, slamming himself against the bars and snorting with anger.

"Oh my God!" said April.

"That poor thing! Look at him! He's bleeding all over! They put him in a cage way too small for him! He needs to be set free."

Sure enough, they saw the mammoth beast was bleeding from multiple gaping wounds. A mite crawled out of one of the open wounds and skittered across his hide only to burrow through his sleek, black hide to make another hole in his flesh.

"Eww! That poor thing! Look what they did to him!"

"There!" screamed April, pointing to a gate that led to the open pasture. "We have to set him free!"

The two of them ran around the pen and pulled the lever marked "release" by the "To Pasture" sign. An interior gate swung open. The bull spun around at the sound of the clanging metal and charged the opening, racing out into the pasture at speed that didn't match his enormity.

"Go!" squealed April, jumping up and down.

"That's so awesome! He's free!" yelled Chloe.

They watched him until he was out of sight, then looked at each other. "Now what do we do?" asked April.

"I don't know, but we need to get out of this stinky pen. The bugs in here are biting my legs like crazy."

37

Infirmary

Dr. Hayes and Dr. White stared at each other. He didn't want to say what he knew.

"They're eating him inside, Lamont! You know what that sound is!"

"That's impossible. He's been on meds..."

"*Then listen again!* You know damn well what that is! He needs a hospital, if it isn't too late already," she screamed.

Lamont's eyes showed tears for the first time since he had been a medical student.

He was the head of the lab, and even though it was the patient's own fault for touching the samples, somehow, Lamont still felt responsible. He was a doctor, he had sworn the oath.

"We can't have an ambulance come here right now. The place is full of VIPs. Mr. Dodds specifically said…"

"Paul Dodds is not a doctor, Lamont! This man is going to die!" She walked across, picked up the phone on the wall and dialed security. It rang into voicemail and she hung up.

She tried Pete's cell phone. Nothing.

His room phone. Nothing again.

In spite of herself, she panicked. "God damn it, Lamont! I can't reach Pete or Mike at security. We need help. If we do nothing, this man is going to die."

Lamont nodded, he knew it was true. "Listen. I'm going back to the cafeteria. I'll personally speak to Paul and Kim, okay? Just promise me you won't call for an ambulance until I get back."

"Then you better hurry, because this man can't wait!"

Lamont ran out of the infirmary and sprinted down the hallway back to the party. With his long strides, he could be there in less than three minutes. Back in the infirmary, Andy let out a long, low moan that seemed to go on forever, building in volume.

Dr. Hayes moved back to his gurney and looked down at him. "I'm so sorry, kid. I wish I knew how to help you." She placed the stethoscope back in her ears and placed it on his chest. When she placed her left hand on his stomach and palpated his abdomen, it opened in half a dozen places, sending mites the size of walnuts skittering across his body and up her arm. Andy's eyes went wide, and he gave a low hiss from his deflating lungs. She screamed and stumbled, falling backward to the floor.

As she landed on her bottom, a steady stream of mites flowed down the table from Andy's now dead body straight onto her. She screamed in terror and flailed her arms to get them off, but with their razor-sharp claws and vicious mandibles, they shredded through her clothes, burrowed into her skin, and began eating and slashing their way through her body cavity. Her shrieks were bloodcurdling, but there was no one to hear her. As she fell back to the floor, the endless line of mites from Andy continued to take her apart, bite by bite, until her screaming subsided.

Lamont ran to the dinner party as fast as his legs would take him. When he got to the outside doors, he stopped and caught his breath, straightened his sport jacket and shirt, and then walked in as casually as he could muster. He made a beeline for Kim, who was busy fake-laughing and fake-smiling while being fake-charming to her guests.

"A word, please? Just for a moment." said Lamont. He was fake-smiling himself, but he was also sweating, and the normally handsome man looked like he had just witnessed a ghost get up.

"Please, excuse me," she said standing up.

"Won't be but a moment..." said Lamont with his giant grin.

They walked quickly towards the door, Lamont holding her elbow as he whispered through clenched teeth. "We have a problem. A big problem. I need to call an ambulance, right now, or one of our employees is going to die."

She pulled her elbow away from him and stopped walking. Aware they were being watched, she kept her fake smile and spoke through clenched teeth. "Dr. White. Look around you. Don't be an idiot..."

"Dr. Hayes is the attending physician, and she insists..."

"Dr. Hayes works for GTWS! That means she works for me."

"She's going to call an ambulance..."

"Like *hell* she is. You go back to your table and entertain our guests while I have a little chat with Dr. Hayes."

One of the Secret Service agents, who never missed anything, casually walked over to the couple. "Everything okay?"

"Yes, just personnel issues. Make sure you get some steak."

"Maybe later, thank you, ma'am." He returned to his post near the door and melted back into the woodwork.

Kim stormed off towards the infirmary, where the mites were finishing off the last morsels of flesh, and shedding their exoskeletons once again for another growth spurt.

38

The Zoo

EMMET HAD SNUCK SOME food away from the kitchen.

He hadn't made the VIP list and had to work the night rounds. He finished his steak and walked down towards the zoo. A few doors were propped open as he walked, which was against every rule in the book, but he figured the VIPs had warranted breaking some rules. Emmet left them open as he walked. Once or twice, he thought he heard footsteps running around, but figured he'd better mind his own business, lest he walk in on some congressmen or senators grabbing a quickie in some back hallway.

With the Secret Service everywhere, he knew it wasn't the time to mess around.

When he arrived at Goliath's pen, which was on the way to the zoo, he froze. The interior passageway had been opened, likely releasing Goliath into the pasture. *That* was not some VIP exception.

"Holy shit," he muttered to himself.

Twenty thousand pounds of horny, pissed-off bull unleashed on a herd of heifers and steers was not cool. He reached for his phone to call Lamont.

The breeding plans were extremely specific. You didn't just "let Goliath loose" on the herd. Specific heifers would be brought to a breeding pen where he could sire calves in a controlled environment. This was *not* how it was supposed to happen.

"Don't you fucking move!" hissed a voice behind him. "Drop the phone."

Emmet started to turn towards the voice.

"I said *don't move!* I'll blow your fucking head off!"

Wally was already pointing his rifle, and Emmet had worked security for long enough to hear it in the man's voice.

Emmet dropped his phone and raised his hands. "Okay, be cool. Don't shoot."

"Who are you?"

"Emmet Waters. I'm just a worker bee, man."

"Who else is around? How many people?"

"You serious?"

"Do I sound like I'm playing with you?"

"No, I mean, you don't know who's here?"

Silence.

"Dude, listen up. I don't know who you are or why you're here, but you picked the wrong night. There's senators and congressmen here, and they're all here with security details. You'd better get your ass out of here now before you spend about a hundred years or more in jail."

"What the fuck?"

"Yeah. That's right. Secret Service. I'm telling you. Just go out however you came in, and I'll give you five minutes before I hit the alarm."

"Where are they?"

Emmet hesitated, which led to Wally shoving the barrel of his M4 into his ribs. "I'll fucking waste you. Right now."

Emmet closed his eyes and tried to be cool. "The cafeteria. Building one. Near the main entrance. It's a giant VIP dinner."

"How many people from Secret Service?"

"Tons, man, I didn't fucking count them. You should split..."

"How many?" He jammed the gun into his ribs harder, causing Emmet's knees to buckle slightly.

"Easy! Take it easy! I'm not sure. I saw at least four."

"And how many senators and congressmen?"

"Like fifty, I think."

"Oh shit. We hit the motherfucking jackpot..." Wally muttered to himself almost in a whisper

"Yo, man, I'm telling you..."

Wally dropped the rifle and thrust the hunting knife deep into Emmet's spine. The sentence never reached its end. Emmet dropped with a long groan and hit the ground face down. Just to be sure, Wally drove the knife into him a few more times, then ran back to the storage room next door where his people were setting up everything they could find that would burn.

He ran inside and addressed his army: "Yo! Listen up! Things just got way more interesting! Leave this stuff here for now. We don't start the fires until we're on our way out. We hit the jackpot, people! The motherfucking jackpot! We've got all those pig senators and congressmen here for free drinks and bags of cash, working their deals with these Franken-fuckers! We're gonna waste all of 'em!"

A few of the kids held up their weapons and cheered. Most of them looked scared. They were along to wreck an office and start a fire, then have something to talk about for the rest of their lives. They weren't ready to kill, and most of them were still far from being hardened murderers.

They exchanged nervous glances, then followed Wally out of the supply area through the hallway. A girl spotted a body lying in a giant pool of blood. She let out a scream, but Wally told her to shut up.

"I told you people! This is war! Now keep up!" He pulled out his phone and called Dean.

"Yeah?" whispered Dean.

"Listen up! There's a bunch of Washington VIPs here. Some dinner party or something. Secret Service is here, too, so pay attention. Where are you?"

"Just outside the lab, getting ready to take it out." He stifled a groan as the pain ripped through his torso. He pictured Hope and got pissed from the start. Whatever that whore had given him *hurt*.

"Okay, hit it hard, then haul ass to the front building. There's a cafeteria there. We're gonna hose that whole fucking place. Fifty senators and congressmen! Finally, we can make ourselves a *real* statement!"

Dean felt a nervous twinge. He turned away from his followers and whispered, "You sure you wanna do that? I mean, that's like a terrorist attack. They'll have every fed and cop in the country looking for us."

"This *is* a terrorist attack! I told you fuckers! This is *war*! Now hurry up!"

Dean hung up and took a deep breath, then turned around to face his worried army. "Okay, this is it. The lab where they make those freak animals. We go in, we wreck everything we see, then we go for a special bonus."

They stared at him with nervous smiles.

"Bunch of Washington DC VIPs are here. We're gonna' teach them a lesson. Now, get ready."

The lab was accessible only by swipe card, or in this case, shotgun. Dean took the shotgun from one of his guys, who reluctantly gave it up. He was dying to fire the giant gun, but had zero experience, so didn't protest.

Dean fired off one round after another at the heavy glass door until it broke open enough to kick out the remainder and step through the doorframe. The lab was a state-of-the-art facility, with rows of expensive computers, electron microscopes, and high-tech equipment. Luckily, it was devoid of people. Within seconds, the rampaging group had destroyed millions of dollars' worth of equipment.

Dean yelled at his group, impressed: "Okay, everybody out! We go to building one and link up with Wally." He ran over to a gas line and pulled out the hose, then turned the gas to full blast. He could smell the mercaptan additive in the natural gas and smiled. As he ran after the group, he stopped and took a knee, doubled over with agony. He felt like he might vomit.

"Yo, man! You okay?" asked one of the kids.

"I'm sick, man. Damn. I'll catch up. Just follow the signs for building one. You'll find Wally by the cafeteria, and he'll tell you what to do. If I can't make it there, I'll meet you at the van. Oh, man," he moaned, and got on all fours.

The kids looked at him, then just started running down the hall towards building one as instructed.

They weren't there when Dean started screaming and small armor-plated, prehistoric bugs began burrowing out of his skin. He bled out while screaming for help in the lab next to the hissing gas line.

39

The Zoo

CHLOE AND APRIL HID in the dark pasture until the rest of the group had run off down the hallway.

The two young girls were terrified. They'd seen Wally murder an unarmed man and wanted no part of any of this anymore. The giant bull didn't act like they thought he would when they set him free.

Instead of being happy to be free, he raced into the pasture and began crashing into the steers so hard the walls seemed to rattle. In a show of dominance, he raced after the smaller males and did his best to crush them with massive charges. They ran away from

Goliath as fast as they could, but not before they were already infected with a colony of Goliath's aggressive parasites.

When Goliath was satisfied that he owned the pasture, he turned his attention to the females. When he mounted the first heifer, he didn't get to finish what he started. He let out a long scream that didn't seem capable of coming from a bull. Chloe and April screamed at the horrific noise it produced, something they knew they would never get out of their memories.

Goliath rolled off the heifer and crashed into the grass, then began rolling and stomping and flipping around like a fish out of water—or more accurately, a whale out of water. He was so massive that the ground vibrated under April and Chloe's feet, and they clung to each other as they tried to stay invisible behind the hay bales.

The animal's screams made their hair stand up. When the two girls watched the bull explode, they froze with open mouths, not believing what they were seeing happen right in front of their eyes. Thousands of armored, horned, crab-like creatures raced out of Goliath's blown hide and streamed over the heifer. She tried to escape, but was instantly taken to the ground by thousands of slashing mouths and claws. In only moments, the heifer was reduced to raw, chopped beef.

When Chloe started screaming, April joined in. They hugged each other and screamed, closing their eyes and praying the nightmare would stop. As the heifer slowly disintegrated, the creatures re-emerged, now larger and just as hungry. They spread out across the pasture like a swath of locusts invading a cornfield, and it wasn't long before sheep and cattle alike began disappearing in clouds of blood, bone, and gristle. Now the size of softballs, the creatures' munching and crunching was loud enough for the girls to hear over the sounds of bleating, pained, and dying animals.

The girls were still screaming when the shiny black flood of mandibles and claws poured over them. They disappeared within seconds, whatever was left, seeping into the grass of the meadow.

Within moments, the bucolic meadow was silent, except for the crackling sounds of shells splitting, followed by the munching of empty exoskeletons.

40

Infirmary

KIM STORMED INTO THE infirmary ready for an argument. She threw the door open and stomped through the outside room calling out to Dr. Hayes. She wasn't using Laurel's doctorate title as a reminder of who was in charge.

"Laurel! Laurel Hayes!"

She threw the door open to the isolation room and froze. It took a second for her brain to understand what she was looking at.

The scattered remains of two human corpses were inside—one in the bed and one on the floor, but the skittering noise that enveloped her made no sense to her. She couldn't understand what was happening, even as she was taken to the ground with the lights spinning above her head.

She tried to scream—she wanted to call for help—but nothing would come out of her mouth. Instead, hideous creatures from some nightmare poured into her open mouth and tunneled into her flesh from everywhere, taking her apart in only moments. The last thing to go through Kim's mind was a baseball-sized arthropod.

41

Assault

Wally and his team arrived in building one only a few seconds before the second crew arrived.

"Where's Dean?" barked Wally, keeping his M4 at the ready.

"He got really sick." said one of his crew. "He said he'd catch up or meet us at the trucks."

"Are you shitting me?" he dialed Dean's cell, but he didn't pick up.

"Did you take his weapon at least?"

The kids looked at each other. None of them had thought of it.

"Oh great. Fucking great. The only other machine gun we have is going to be outside in a van? I'm gonna kick his ass." He started jogging with all of his remaining people in tow. "Let's go people. There's gonna be Secret Service inside, so be ready. When we hit the door, you just get inside and empty your weapons into the crowd. Kill everyone you see, you understand?"

A few of the kids exchanged nervous glances. One of them spoke up. "Who are we shooting at?"

"The fuckers who made those animals, and the ones who are gonna make it legal. Be ready when I open that door! Any of you fuckers chicken out and I'll kill you myself! Anyone with a shotgun or Molotov cocktail, get up front with me!"

The kids organized themselves by weapons as they ran down the hallway to the cafeteria. They slowed down as they reached the front entrance of the building on their way to their destination. Wally called out for everyone to slow down, and he took point as he approached the security desk. He ran behind it, ready to shoot, but no one was there. Banks of video monitors hung from the ceiling over the desk and showed rooms and hallways all over the facility. The monitors changed views routinely as they cycled through. Wally watched a few seconds, and then, satisfied it was quiet around the facility, ordered his people to barricade the front doors.

The group used their combined strength to push the entire security counter to the front doors and wedge it in tightly. They piled on the chairs, decorative tables and couches, and whatever else they could find around the front foyer. No one was getting in, and equally important, no one was getting out. Monitors and computers were ransacked, cables were pulled or cut, and furniture was overturned until the security desk was completely destroyed.

As soon as they were finished, Wally screamed, "Let's go!" and his army of reluctant killers ran after him to the cafeteria. A few of the nervous ones exchanged worried glances, but any hesitation was crushed by the more enthusiastic fanatics.

Agent Scott Keenan lifted his wrist to his mouth and whispered, "The steak looks killer."

The three other agents tried not to smile. They were a serious bunch and never made jokes on duty, but this was a lame assignment in a remote facility that was heavily secured.

The lead agent, Peggy Robins, stifled her smile and rebuked her agent. "Stay off channel unless it's security-related."

"If I steal a bite, is that security-related?"

Peggy looked across the room at him and gave her practiced "Mom-look." He wiped the smile off his face and moved back to a formal "at ease" position with his hands behind his back, looking like a plain clothes embassy guard. Peggy did a quick visual check-in with her other two agents, Sue Tyler and Thad Baker, who also forced serious faces. Once they nodded at their boss, they took casual strolls around the perimeter.

When the door burst open and Wally jumped into the room emptying his machine gun into the crowd on fully automatic, the guards were at four corners of the large room. Behind Wally, the group of Nature Power Movement soldiers ran in and fanned out, pointing and shooting their weapons. Unlike Wally, most of them had almost no experience firing a weapon, never mind murdering human beings. For the most part, they hesitated and missed the people who were screaming and diving for cover.

Wally's first target was the table closest to him. The table of three senators and six congressmen sitting with Jeannie Davis took immediate casualties. Jeannie was hit in the head and was dead before she hit the table, and two of the congressmen were also hit with mortal wounds. Scott Keenan was closest to the front door, and his pistol was up and firing instantly when the shooting started. He charged at the attacking crowd, and his first two shots hit Wally square in the face.

The instant Wally's head exploded in front of them, the kids dropped their weapons and ran. One of the girls was in the middle of lighting her Molotov cocktail when Wally was hit. She threw it on the floor and screamed. It exploded at her feet in a ball of flames before she had time to run. Agent Keenan killed her with two more well placed shots, and she fell into the spreading gasoline fire.

Paul leapt off his chair to the ground and immediately looked for Connie, but he couldn't see anything other than falling chairs and diving bodies. Everyone was screaming and trying to get away from the gunfire. Connie had also jumped out of her chair and hid under the table next to a congressman and senator who were equally panic-stricken. Paul crawled as fast as he could to where he knew Connie had been sitting and found her hiding. He grabbed her and rolled over on her, shielding her with his body.

With the machine gun out of commission and the attackers now retreating, the chaos began dying down, and the only sounds were the panicked screams of the guests and staff who were hiding under tables or scrambling away from the front door. The Secret

Service agents were now running to catch up with Agent Keenan. Flames stopped him at the entrance, and couldn't pursue his attackers, so he pulled a radio and called headquarters on their private emergency channel.

Keenan took a knee and called with one hand, while holding his weapon towards the door with the other. The other three agents assessed the situation, and seeing no threat and Keenan guarding the door, they sprinted to the casualties. Thad Baker, who looked big enough to play linebacker in the NFL, scooped up one of the victims and placed her on the table, shoving off all the remaining plates and glasses as he placed her down. He grabbed two cloth napkins and shoved them into her blouse, pressing down on her bullet wound. He began giving calm orders to the people around him and had everyone helping with first-aid within seconds.

By the time Peggy Robins got to him, Scott Keenan was on his feet and heading back to his group, weapon still at the ready. He turned to Peggy and screamed, "Birds inbound, but at least forty-five minutes out. State Police on the way now with EMS."

Peggy had to make a split-second decision. "Thad, you and Sue provide security and first aid here. I'll try and find some employees to help you. Scott, on me!" She began running towards the front entrance where the fire had burned out somewhat, although the carpet was still smoldering and acrid smoke was filling up part of the room. Peggy sprinted through the flames with Scott on her tail, never slowing down as they raced out the front door, their weapons held out in front.

Once they had cleared the doorway, they stopped and listened. They expected to hear their attackers head for the front doors, but they didn't. Instead, the sounds of running feet were headed towards the back of the facility. Peggy glanced up at the wall at the schematic and spoke into her wrist mic. "We're now team one, pursuing suspects towards the zoo. Team two, you are not to leave our people. Out."

Peggy and Scott raced after the sounds of the fleeing attackers. They were easy to follow as they dropped their weapons along the way.

42

Chaos

Lamont helped the two agents with the first aid, but they needed real supplies next. Laurel wasn't answering his calls. While he worked to stem the flow of bleeding on one of the congresswomen, he screamed over to one of the employees who was helping with the wounded:

"Frank! Take someone with you and get to the infirmary. Bring back everything you can find that even *looks* like medical supplies! We need pressure bandages, sutures, bandages, scissors, blankets—just grab everything you can goddamn carry!"

Frank and Jeff, who worked in the kitchen, raced off through the kitchen exit to avoid the smoky mess at the entrance. They sprinted as fast as they could, horrified at the amount of blood they had seen in the cafeteria. It wasn't like the movies. It was worse than that—it had been deafening, and the blood seemed to flow like rivers.

When they got to the infirmary, the two of them opened the door and walked inside, calling out to the staff.

"Dr. Hayes? Dr. Alonzo? Hello? It's an emergency! Who's here?" When no one answered, Frank yelled over to Jeff to go check the back office while he gathered supplies. Frank grabbed a pushcart and began opening drawers and pulling out everything he could find, throwing it on to the cart.

Jeff opened the door to the room in the back and stepped back in horror. Human remains? They had to be. There wasn't much there anymore, mostly teeth and bone fragments mixed in with bloody torn clothes and piles of the exoskeletons of some kind of large bugs. The room was littered with them. It stunk like something was rotting. Jeff made a face and turned back to the door. He opened it and screamed out to Frank.

"Frank! Come here, quick! Something's wrong!"

Frank threw what was in his hands on to the cart and took a step towards the rear door. He had a difficult time processing what he watched happen next. In one second, Jeff was standing in the door frame facing him, in the next, a swarm of insects the size of rats raced all over his body and literally took him apart in seconds right in front of Frank's eyes. The skittering noises and cracking and popping of skin, bones, and tissue under razor-sharp jaws and claws drowned out Jeff's screaming. As he fell back into the room, the door slammed closed again, locking whatever that was inside.

"Oh my God!" screamed Frank, his eyes wide with fear, shock, and horror.

He ran out of the infirmary, leaving all of the supplies behind.

———

With Wally dead and Dean nowhere to be found, the remaining army of the Nature Power Movement was nothing more than panicked amateurs running blindly through the halls of the giant facility. A few employees had confronted them as they ran, only to be knocked over or attacked briefly before the crowd ran off again. When one of them saw the directional sign for the zoo, they all took off in that direction.

"We just go out the way we came in! The hole in the fence is marked with the glow-stick, then we get to the vans and get out of here!" screamed one of them.

"We're missing people!" yelled one of the girls.

No one cared. It was every man for himself, and the panicked group raced along the halls all the way back to the zoo. The zoo doors had been purposely left propped open so they could get back in without access cards, and the group could see the final door to the field, and then freedom, up ahead. They were so close to escaping!

Behind them, Agents Keenan and Robins closed the gap, sprinting at full speed. They'd both reloaded and were ready to take on a superior force regardless of the odds. When they heard the screaming from up ahead, they stopped and waited.

"Hold up—what's that?" asked Keenan quietly.

The blood-curdling shrieks and cries of pain echoed through the hallways. It sounded like dozens of panicked voices screaming and begging, and it was getting louder. Peggy dropped to a firing stance on her knee, against the wall on one side, and Scott did the same thing across the hallway. They exchanged glances back and forth between each other and the long hallway. The noise was getting louder fast.

"They're coming back," said Peggy, half to herself.

"Whatever it is, it doesn't sound good," said Scott, his pistol aimed down the hallway.

43

Cafeteria

LAMONT WAS TYING OFF a leg wound with a tablecloth when Frank sprinted back into the room. He carried nothing with him.

"Frank? Where are the supplies?" screamed Lamont.

Frank ran until he almost crashed into Lamont and then grabbed him by his jacket. He was hysterical and started screaming into Lamont's face.

"We gotta get out of here! There's something in there! They ate Jeff right in front of me! Doc! We gotta get outta here!"

Lamont let go of the improvised bandage and stood up straight, grabbing Frank by the shoulders. "Slow down! *What's* in where?"

"In the infirmary! You can't go in there, man! Jeff opened the door to find a doc, and these fucking things came out of *nowhere*, man! They swarmed all over him and shredded him alive! It was horrible, doc! He just disappeared right in front of me. The door closed, and I think they're stuck in there, but there were millions of them!"

Thad walked over, catching part of the conversation. "What's he talking about?"

Lamont's mind raced for a second. "Call your people. Get them back here now!"

"What's going on?"

"We have a level five contamination. This whole facility needs to be locked down. No one in or out, and we need to secure this room. Now!"

"Doc, what are you talking about? We need to evacuate these people as fast as possible, and some of them need a hospital!" exclaimed Thad.

Lamont grabbed the agent by his lapel, who grabbed Lamont's wrist and twisted it off. Lamont was screaming at him. "Call your people back! *Now!*"

Frank was hysterical and started screaming at him, too. "There's millions of 'em, man! *They ate Jeff!* They'll eat your friends, too! Get them the fuck outta there, man!"

Thad spoke into his wrist mic. "Team two to team one, emergency. Return to the cafeteria on the double! I repeat, get out of there and *return to the cafeteria! Emergency!*"

Peggy and Scott both heard him in their ear pieces. Between that message and the sounds of a screaming, terrified hoard running at them from down the hall, they both hopped up and Peggy screamed, "Go!" They raced back the way they had come, a good hundred yards ahead of the group.

As they ran, the screaming grew louder and more panicked. They could also hear something else—a clicking, chattering, insect-like sound—like millions of locusts invading a field.

Peggy screamed into her wrist mic. "Thaddeus! What's going on?"

"I'm not sure, but maybe something got out of the lab that wasn't supposed to. One of the guys here saw something, and he's totally freaked out. I mean, like mentally *gone*!"

Lamont was holding the kid in a half-comforting hug, half-restraining hold. "Calm down, Frank. You're scaring everyone. Just calm down, okay? We're going to figure this out."

"We need to get out of here before those things get out," Frank screamed.

"They're locked in the medical exam room, right? That door closes automatically, Frank. They can't get out. You've got to relax." Lamont had no idea if the mites could get under the door or not, but he had to try to get Frank calmed down before he caused a bigger panic than they were already dealing with. The VIPs were screaming into their phones and at the two agents, demanding immediate evacuation and helicopters.

Lamont started thinking about all the people he hadn't been able to reach. Laurel. Mike at security. No one was answering. The last time he saw Laurel, she was with Andy in that exam room. He'd been in denial. There was no question now—the mites were infectious, predatory parasites that could now kill humans because of their size.

Connie and Paul had moved around the room trying to offer reassurances and help people get into chairs to calm down. They kept repeating that help was on the way, but the truth was, they had no idea what had happened, or if help was coming or not. Like everyone else in the room, they were in shock. The sudden rush of adrenaline had given them all a serious case of the shakes, and it was difficult to calm down. They finally worked their way over to Lamont, his clothes covered in blood that wasn't his. He had helped stabilize the wounded as best he could and now stood with a Secret Service agent.

"What have I done?" he mumbled out loud.

"What *have* you done?" snapped Thad.

"What's going on? What's happening?" stammered Paul.

Lamont looked at them with sad eyes. "I'm not sure what happened. I think an employee opened a live sample of skin mites and got infected. He somehow infected the whole facility, but these mites... They..." Lamont was shaking his head in disbelief.

"They *what*, doc? What's going on?" screamed Thaddeus.

"They have indeterminate size now, as long as there's a food source."

"I don't understand what you're telling me."

"Wait, I was asking about the attack. What are *you* talking about?" asked Paul confused.

"Look, we did some genetic engineering—some modifications of the gene code to unlock size limitations and increase growth rates. We started with small organisms first. Skin mites. Tiny things you can only see under the electron microscope. Only now…"

"Now they're the size of bugs and they're eating people? Are you shitting me, doc? I've got fifty senators and congressmen in here!"

"And I have almost fifty of my own staff here tonight, too. And I can't reach any of them!"

"Skin mites? What are you *talking* about? Who just attacked us?" asked Paul.

Thad's earpiece filled with Peggy's voice. "We're almost at the doors. Don't shoot us when we come through!"

"Roger! Be advised, the flames are out but it's smoky as hell over there. If you can come through the kitchen entrance, that's a better way."

"Two minutes!" she screamed, out of breath.

Peggy and Scott ran until they saw the kitchen entrance, then opened the door and ran through the messy kitchen. The workers had dropped everything and were up front trying to assist with first aid. Peggy and Scott came out of the kitchen into the main room and saw Thad and Sue standing with Dr. White.

Sue yelled at Thad, "They're back!"

They all converged in the middle of the room, ignoring Paul and Connie for the moment, who had followed them.

"What's going on in this place, Dr. White?" snapped Peggy. "No BS! What's happening?"

They were interrupted by Senator Carr. He stormed over and screamed at Peggy and Connie. "What are you people doing? We have casualties! We need immediate evacuation! Why aren't you people doing anything about those terrorists?"

Peggy took a quick breath and looked sternly at the senator. "The threat is gone for the moment. Right now, we have help on the way to assist with the wounded."

"Well, *Jesus*, you're taking too damn long! People are dying over here!"

"No one can go anywhere," said Lamont quietly with the most authority in his voice that he could muster.

44

Massacre

The Nature Power Movement soldiers had dropped everything and ran for their lives. They had almost reached the pasture, and their exit, when the mites appeared from what seemed like everywhere around them. After they had eaten their way through the animals in the pasture, the mites started attacking each other, cannibalizing the smaller of their kind first. When the colony detected human flesh arriving, they swarmed and attacked with greater speed then cockroaches scurrying across a kitchen floor.

The fastest of the group was closest to the zoo when the swarm attacked. He was a college-age kid, a runner, and was a good twenty yards out ahead of the group when the stream of shredding parasites engulfed his body in a tide of armor-plated ferocity.

The men and women behind him had only seconds to react. Those who hesitated were annihilated instantly. The people that reacted quickly slid to a stop across the slick hallway floors and turned tail to run back the way they came. One at a time, the slowest of the long line was taken down from behind. Their screams of terror and pain echoed through the hallways, but gradually grew quieter and quieter, until the last prayers for mercy disappeared in the crunching and munching of mandibles.

In less than thirty minutes, it was all over. Then came the crackling sounds of exoskeletons breaking as larger, nastier mites split out the back of their shells. The ones that were still hungry ate the exoskeletons. The ones that were *really* hungry ate the smaller mites, sending huge numbers of them off skittering in a dozen different directions. Once their new bodies hardened up like crabs, they began moving en mass—thousands of armor-plated eating machines, ready to mow through the next herd they found.

45

Cafeteria

LAMONT AND PEGGY MANAGED to get away from Senator Carr and the others to have a serious discussion about what to do next. Peggy and her detail had one priority—the safety and security of their people, several of whom were dead, dying, or injured to various degrees.

"Let me be real clear here, Dr. White—I'm calling the shots. I want my people evacuated as soon as possible. I have helicopters inbound and want the wounded triaged as soon as you can find me your medical staff..."

"That's just it. I can't find my medical staff. You want to know *why*, Agent Robins? Because they were eaten by giant predatory arthropods that have gotten out of the lab and risk getting out of this facility! You have no idea what you're dealing with!"

"All the more reason to evacuate this facility!"

"Let me ask you something. If there was a risk that these people had been infected with Ebola or Smallpox or some type of incurable, highly contagious disease, would you still want to evacuate them all immediately? Or maybe, just *maybe*, would you want them quarantined and then cleared medically before you sent them all out into the world?"

She stared at him, thinking of the proper protocol. "I think you'd be able to tell if someone had giant bugs attacking them and eating them alive," said Peggy.

"That's part of the problem. The mites started out *microscopic*. I think patient zero was Andrew Booth, and he was in our infirmary for a couple of days before we knew what happened. I also think he may have been infected even days *before* that. These mites, they get to a certain size, eat their host, and move on to another victim, except that victim is utterly torn to pieces in seconds. As they get bigger, their feeding patterns change. We don't understand their life cycle, we don't know how long they can live—you just can't unleash them on the world!"

She put her finger into his chest. "*You* doctor, *you* unleashed them onto the world! I'm just trying to keep my people safe."

"And what if you let this spread all over the globe?"

She stared at him. "You have any other suggestions?"

"Maybe. Just one idea."

She folded her arms across her chest and stared at him.

"They're bugs. We need an exterminator."

Senator Carr walked back over in a huff. "What the hell are you people doing? Where are the evac choppers?"

Peggy turned around to face him. "We're working on getting everyone out when it's safe. For now, I need you to take a seat or help with the wounded. What I don't need is you in my face right now."

Senator Carr was not used to subordinates standing up to him. He walked away, speechless.

"Tell me your exterminator idea," said Peggy.

"Down by the lab there's a supply area. We keep Nitazoxanide and other anti-parasitic drugs. We have hazmat suits and some chemical sprayers. If I can get down there and mix up a poison cocktail, maybe I can spray these things and kill them."

"It sounds like you'd need a lot of the stuff."

"We have plenty. We have bulk containers that we heavily dilute down to pharmaceutical doses. I won't dilute it. It'll be toxic to humans, too, in those doses, but if I gear up with the hazmat suit, I should be fine."

Peggy scowled. "Doc, at this moment, that's the only plan we have. Better to execute a mediocre plan than to do nothing waiting for the perfect one."

Dr. White looked at her eyeball to eyeball. "There's one more thing, Agent Robins. You need to call off the State Police and the helicopters. This entire facility needs to be quarantined until we know these things are dead. If only one little bug gets out, we could be looking at a mass casualty event. They lay eggs every day. In just a few weeks, you can have millions of these things."

"I have to get these people to safety..."

"Senator Carr isn't a doctor. Tell the cops to stand down. At least until I can see if this works."

"And if it doesn't?"

"Then I'll be dead and you can do whatever you want."

46

Cafeteria

PEGGY HAD ASSEMBLED HER agents and Dr. White and spoke quietly while eyeballing the wounded. "We can't get to the medical supplies—infirmary is off limits, so they'll have to just tough it out. In the meantime, we do a quick recon over to the security desk. There's a bank of monitors for the closed-circuit cameras. Maybe we can take a look and see if anyone else is around, or if we can see any of these critters. There's also a public address system. We need to tell anyone else who's still alive out there to shelter in place. Seal up all doors and windows and just sit tight until we can try and kill these things."

"How are we going to do that?" asked Scott.

Lamont reiterated his idea to the other three agents.

"How many employees are in the building right now?" asked Paul.

Lamont shrugged. "Saturday night, some went home. We had extra staff because of the party. Maybe fifty? But who knows how many have been killed by these things already. I can't reach Kim, Mike, Laurel—nobody. I even tried Emmet down in the zoo. Nothing. It's bad."

Paul shook his head. "I thought the people with the guns were the dangerous part. Who were they? Do they have anything to do with this?"

Lamont shook his head. "I don't know. Animal rights people? Anti-GMO activists? Terrorists? I have no idea."

Peggy cut off their conversation. "Look, it doesn't matter right now! Stay focused! One problem at a time. The terrorist threat seems to be eliminated for the time being. Now we need to deal with these bugs from the lab. Someone needs to stay here and babysit these VIPs. They think it was a terrorist attack and the bad guys split. They don't know about the mites."

"Should we tell them? They'd be less likely to try and run after we leave," asked Thaddeus.

Connie looked around at the group, feeling sick. She had cajoled all of them into being here. Now, some were dead, some were wounded, and they had no idea that some type of lab monsters were on the loose in the facility. She was living a nightmare.

"He's got a point," said Lamont. "If scaring them will keep them safe, I think we tell them. Even a modified version."

"What about finding another place to hold up?" asked Sue. This room is too big. We can't seal the doors in here. And there must be a dozen air vents. Can these things get through them?"

They all looked at Lamont. "They range in size from microscopic to who knows how big. I'm guessing they can get into a room a million different ways."

"That's comforting," said Scott.

"Maybe have everyone stay together in one back corner, and bring up the lights as high as they'll go. When microscopic and living on your skin, they're generally nocturnal. Maybe the light will help keep them away."

Peggy nodded and pointed to the back of the room nearest the kitchen. "Okay, then that's it. We move the wounded and everyone else to that corner and crank up the lights. We tell them we're concerned about a lab contamination and no one should leave the room. Just keep it vague. Let's move out. Sue, you stay with them and keep in contact with us at all times."

Paul spoke quietly. "I'll go with you. I'm ranking corporate officer. I go down with the ship."

"Me, too. I'll go," said Connie.

Peggy looked at the two of them quickly and said, "Paul, you come with us. Connie, you stay and try to help Sue keep these people calm. Let's get to the PA system and warn whoever's still alive out there to shelter in place, then go kill these monsters."

Paul gave Connie a quick hug. She kissed his cheek and whispered, "I'm starting to really like you. Be careful."

47

Cafeteria

Connie and Sue did their best to fend off the millions of questions that had been raised by Lamont's vague announcement of a parasitic threat being released from the lab. While the new information did serve to terrify an already-petrified group into staying put, these were intelligent, type-A personalities who demanded more and more information.

They also didn't know that Agent Keenan had called off the incoming helicopters and First Responders and continually asked where the ambulances and helicopters were. The State Police had been instructed to set up a perimeter and closed off the road leading to the facility from over a mile away.

"Look! Let's just stay focused on helping the injured!" said Connie.

Sue walked around using table clothes to cover the dead. She snapped a picture of Wally's dead face with her phone and sent it to headquarters, where it would be put through facial recognition software to identify the shooter. The body next to his was burnt beyond any type of recognition by the Molotov cocktail the young woman had thrown near her own feet. Sue threw another tablecloth over her corpse, happy not to have to look at it anymore. She could smell the burnt flesh, and it was revolting. It was thick and sweet, and clung to her nostrils like soot.

Once Sue had covered the bodies, she returned to the wounded and began assessing their wounds. Two senators and three congressmen were dead. Another congressman didn't look like he'd make it, with a chest wound that was being held together by another congressman using cloth napkins in a makeshift pressure bandage. Three others were injured with non-life-threatening wounds in their arms or legs, so long as the bleeding could be controlled. She shook her head.

Lamont, Peggy, Scott, Thad, and Paul moved cautiously out of the kitchen door and looked up and down the hall.

Lamont whispered to the group. "Look, our observations in the lab have us believing that these things use smell as their primary sense. They have eyes, but their vision isn't great. I'm not sure if they can hear or sense vibrations. Stay quiet, keep your eyes open for anything, and remember they may be tiny if they just hatched. Don't touch anything unless you have to. We have to pass the security desk on the way to the supply room near the zoo, so that's our first stop. I'll use the PA system and warn whoever's out there, then we get to the supply room as fast as we can."

They walked in silence, single-file. The agents had their weapons reloaded and were ready to face any terrorist threats, but had holstered their weapons. They were all fairly certain the group that had attacked them had fled. The possibility of them being infected and escaping out into the world had led Peggy to call the State Police and advise them that no one was to get past them, even if it meant lethal force. The state troopers had called in their SWAT teams, and their perimeter kept getting reinforced.

When they turned the corner, they spotted what should have been the security desk. Instead, everything had been piled up at the front doors. The PA system was somewhere jumbled up in the mess of desk, chairs, tables, and broken equipment.

"So much for warning our people," said Lamont. Wires hung from the broken monitors above where the counter had been. "We can't even see anything."

"I hope the second part of your plan works a little better," said Peggy.

They exchanged nervous glances, then started walking past the front doors in defeat. Lamont stopped and spoke to the group. "Okay, next stop, the supply room. There's no sense all of us going. I can go alone and bring back as much as I can carry..."

"We all go," said Peggy. She turned to Paul. "You can head back."

"We all go," he replied.

"The supply room is near the zoo. We may be walking into a horror movie," said Lamont.

"Go, we're following you." said Peggy. "We're going to need all of that bug spray and anything else that looks like it can kill your bugs."

They started up again, heading quietly towards the supply room and the unknown.

48

Dorm Area

DOCTORS BRIAN ARCHER AND Tim Silver were hanging out in Tim's room watching a movie and drinking a few beers. Neither lived locally, so going home for the weekend wasn't their typical routine. The movie ended and they finished their last beers.

"I'm out of beer. Want to head to the Pub and hang out there for a while? It's only eleven. You off tomorrow?"

"'Til two. Yeah, let's go."

The two of them left Tim's room and walked towards the pub in building one. The dorms, being in building four, were a decent hike, but there was a cart nearby. The two of them hopped in and cruised quickly through the long halls. They passed building three, the zoo, then building two, the farm, when Tim stopped the cart. The two of them just stared at a pile in the hallway and squinted, unsure of what they were looking at.

"What *is* that?" asked Brian.

Tim slowly drove closer. The pile was definitely moving. He got closer and closer until his brain could start processing what he was seeing.

"Holy shit!" He screamed, and slammed his foot on the accelerator, racing past the shimmering, slithering, pile of mites that were crawling all over each other and the remains of a human body.

Brian spun in his seat and looked back at the scene as they drove past. The piles of creatures moved like a swarm of bees, except they were running, not flying. The dark, bug-like mass raced off the remains of whoever that had been and took off after the golf cart, pouring across the floor like a raging river of snapping jaws.

"Go, man! Go! Fuckin' *drive*!" screamed Brian.

The cart rode over a few of the things, making a crunching sound. The crushed carcasses were instantly devoured by the colony as they poured over it like army ants.

"What *is* that?" screamed Brian, his foot on the accelerator to the floor.

"They look like giant mites! Like those arthropods in the lab! What the fuck man? I think they ate a *person*! Jesus Christ! They're chasing us, man! Drive faster!"

"This is as fast as it goes!"

Tim and Brian flew down the hallway, slowly increasing the distance between them and the pursuing swarm of killer mites.

"Don't stop for anything! Just keep going!" screamed Brian as he twisted in his seat to look behind them. They drove past the farm towards the micro lab. As they got closer, they could see it was destroyed inside.

"The labs wrecked. They must have gotten out," said Brian.

"What are you talking about? We never had thousands of giant mites in the lab!"

"We had a few—they must have laid eggs or something. Jesus, I gotta' call Lamont!" Brian pulled his cell phone off his belt and was just about to call when Tim swerved around a corner and almost crashed into Lamont, Peggy, Thad, Scott, and Paul. The group jumped to the side of the hallway to get out of the way, and Tim squealed to a stop.

Brian screamed at Lamont. "I was just going to call you! You gotta' get outta' here!"

"There's giant mites from the lab right behind us!" screamed Tim.

"You've gotta believe us!" screamed Brian.

Lamont ran forward. "We know! We know! How far behind you?"

"We outran them on this thing. They're fast as hell, though. You need to get out of here!"

"I can't. I need to kill these things. They're all over the building. You two—give me the cart. Run to the cafeteria and find the others. I've got to go back and get to the supply room."

"You can't go back that way, Lamont! It's suicide!" shouted Brian.

"I need the supply room. Go on, get out of here." He looked at the others. "I have the cart. You guys, too. Go."

"I'm going with you," said Peggy.

"Me too," said Paul. "I can get on the back."

Thad and Scott looked at each. "Okay, go!" said Scott.

Lamont hopped behind the wheel with Peggy next to him and Paul sitting on the back facing backwards. They raced off towards the zoo.

Brian and Tim shook their heads. "They're fucking crazy, man! You have no idea what's down there!" said Brian. "We need to move!"

Brian and Tim started running. Scott and Thad stood where they were.

Brian stopped and looked back. "Hurry!"

"You two go. We're going to try and help."

Brian mumbled under his breath and started sprinting after Tim, who was, in fact, running for his life.

When Tim and Brian were gone, Thad and Scott just stood and stared at each other. "So now what?" asked Thad.

"Let's try the lab. It's closest. Maybe they have stuff in there we can use."

"What do we do if we see those things running at us?" asked Thad. "I'm not sure we can outrun them."

"I don't have to outrun them. I just have to outrun *you*." Scott patted his friend's massive arm.

"Nice. Real nice. I'll just shoot you in the leg," said Thad. "Come on. Real quiet."

49

Cafeteria

When the cafeteria doors burst open the second time, everyone inside screamed and expected to be shot to pieces. Instead, it was Tim and Brian, out of breath and terrified. They slammed the door behind them and bent over, huffing and puffing, with hands on their knees.

Connie yelled from the back corner, "Over here!"

Tim and Brian walked to the group, looking at the bloody sheets on the floor all over the room. The room was trashed, and everyone was huddled into one corner with every light in the room plugged in and turned on in that area. Connie strode out to meet the two newcomers.

"What happened in here?" asked Brian.

"We were attacked."

"The mites did this?"

"You know about them..."

"We almost got *eaten* by them! They killed someone back near the zoo."

"Oh no! That's where Paul, Lamont and the agents were headed." she said.

"We just saw them. We gave them our cart. They had a plan to kill them." said Brian.

"Three of them took the cart. The other two, they just stayed back there. I told them it was crazy."

Brian looked at everyone in the corner. "Not a bad idea with the lights, although those things we saw didn't seem to care. They had eaten a person, I'm sure of it, right in the middle of the hallway. Right under the lights." He looked around. "Who attacked you?"

Sue walked up to the two men and Connie and broke the news. "We took out two of them. Maybe wounded a few others, I'm not sure. One of the dead perps is Walter Belville. He's got a criminal history. Violent repeat offender that was leader of the Nature Power Movement. They claimed to be earth-saving peaceniks, but they're just a fringe group of ultra-radicals. They firebombed a Prosanto office last year. Anyway, without Walter, they'll probably fold."

"So they planned the attack for when the congressmen and senators were here. Wow. Pretty brazen. You think they let the mites out of the lab on purpose?" asked Connie.

"I doubt it. If they had let them out, they'd all be dead. Those things were fast and vicious as hell. It was like watching a colony of army ants in super-fast motion," said Brian before Sue could answer. "If we hadn't been in the cart, I don't think we'd be standing here."

"They're huge," said Tim.

"Yeah," agreed Brian. "That's the other thing. I work in the micro lab. They were never that big. Not even close."

Sue squinted at Brian. "Why would you ever create such a thing?"

"It was early genome experiments. We were unlocking the genetic codes for size manipulation and growth rates. It was easiest in the beginning to work on simpler organisms. We made little things big. Then we worked on bigger, more complicated animals."

Sue shook her head. "Jesus. You're all fucking insane."

"Hey, we take every precaution. I have no idea what happened here, but don't blame science," said Brian.

"Science? This is a fucking man-made disaster. Why the hell would you make giant *anything*?" snapped Sue.

"You weren't inside for the video." said Connie. "We were trying to end world hunger."

"How's that working out for you?" asked Sue sarcastically.

"Hey," snapped Tim. "Science isn't perfect, but don't get on the wrong side of the arguments. All these anti-GMO groups—they have no idea about the real science. Almost everything you eat is engineered in one way or another. The ones who scream about our animals are the same people who've benefitted from polio and typhus vaccines, and every other kind of medicine on the planet."

"This isn't the time for an ethics in science debate." said Sue. "I've got three agents in the field with two of your people, and a room full of wounded and scared people. You're doctors. Go doctor. Maybe you can help with the wounded."

The two of them walked to the wounded and Connie asked Sue, "Can you call and check on them?"

50

The Lab

Scott and Thad walked to the lab as quietly as possible. They still hadn't seen the monster mites and didn't know what to expect other than what Brian and Tim had quickly described.

"Now would not be the time to tell me you're scared of spiders." whispered Scott.

"You're hilarious today."

Every step made their hair stand up.

"Serious pucker factor," whispered Scott.

"No shit."

They moved forward until they got to the door. The doorframe was wide open, with shattered glass all over the floor.

"Guess we know how they got in."

Thad stepped through the frame. It was dim inside with only about half of the overhead lights on. There was a huge bank of switches on the wall next to the door, and Thad started flicking them on. The overheads started to blink on, just as Scott smelled the natural gas and screamed.

The explosion was instant and immense. The entire lab exploded, blowing out every glass door and interior window into the hallway. Both Thad and Scott were tossed twenty yards out into the hallway in a cloud of fire, glass, and hot metal. For the next few seconds, it rained debris until going eerily quiet.

Scott and Thad were on the floor, unconscious for several moments, until the pain woke them up. They had too many cuts and abrasions to count, and Thad had suffered two broken legs. His feet pointed in impossible angles, and a bone protruded from his right shin. The second he awoke, he groaned in agony.

Scott blinked himself awake to the sound of Thad's suffering and tried to get up to help. He was bleeding from dozens of cuts and pulled glass out of his bleeding face. His earpiece and wrist mic were gone, his phone was shattered, and everything hurt. Scott managed to get to his feet and crunched across the broken glass, plastic, and metal. He was in agony, and his knee was blown, but his friend was badly injured. He forced himself to take each painful step until he got to Thad.

Scott mumbled, his ears ringing, "Oh shit, man. Broken gas line. Fuck—my head's pounding." He spotted the position of Thad's legs and feet. "Thad, your legs are bad, bro. Don't try and move. I've got to find us a cart or something."

Thad cried in agony. He was strong as an ox, but was now powerless to move.

Then they heard it.

The skittering sound of thousands of legs with hard, razor-edged claws clicking across the hallway floors. The noise alone was terrifying enough, just by its volume, but when they actually could *see* the colony racing towards them, they both knew they were dead.

"My service pistol's gone, man. Don't let them get me." said Thad.

Scott grabbed for his gun, which was mercifully still on his belt. He pulled it out and handed it towards Thad. Thad didn't reach for it. Instead, he just put his face to the floor and screamed, "Do it and get the fuck out of here!"

Scott hesitated. He fired a few rounds at the incoming swarm, but it was useless. He tried to pick up Thad, but moving him caused instant agony. Scott wasn't strong enough to sprint with a two-hundred-and-sixty-pound man, anyway.

Thad screamed at Scott. "Do it! Just fucking do it and get out of here before it's too late! I'd do it for you!" he closed his eyes and started praying.

"I'm sorry, man…" said Scott with tears in his eyes. He looked up at the swarm which was closing fast. Scott placed the gun behind Thad's head and fired two quick rounds, splattering his friend's face all over the floor. Then he got up as quickly as he could and stumbled out of the wreckage, running as fast as he could towards the cafeteria, crying as he ran.

51

Search and Destroy

"WHAT THE HELL WAS that?" screamed Paul, as he hung on to the back of the cart.

The explosion echoed through the hallways, and the lights flickered for a second.

"Oh God, please don't let us lose the lights," prayed Lamont.

Peggy called on her wrist mic. "Scott? Thad?" There was no answer. She tried again. "Scott? Thad? Come in, over!" Still nothing.

"What *was* that?" repeated Paul, hanging on tightly as the cart swerved around a corner.

"Had to be the lab," said Lamont. "Gas lines in there. Had to be it." He was half answering Paul, and half just thinking through it out loud.

"I can't reach my people!" said Peggy.

"Maybe you're just out of range," said Paul, trying to be optimistic.

"No way. Something's wrong."

"We can't stop now. We're almost at the supply room." said Lamont.

They made it to the supply area without seeing any of the mites and stopped outside the door. Lamont opened the door and looked inside. His heart sank. The invaders had trashed the room, throwing everything all over the floor. Some of the equipment and various supplies were broken, but he spotted the hazmat suits buried in the mess and grabbed them. They were folded up in plastic packages which were still intact, and Lamont threw them out to Paul, who threw them to Peggy back at the cart.

"Peggy! Get them open!" yelled Lamont.

She heard two feint gunshots that sounded far away and tried her guys on the radio again. Still nothing.

Paul went inside the wrecked supply area and asked Lamont what they were looking for. Lamont told him about the yellow drums, and they spent another five minutes rummaging through the mess until they found them. The last items were the backpack sprayers, which took even longer. They weren't broken, but they were disassembled and strewn about all over with the rest of the disaster.

Lamont spent a few minutes putting the plastic pieces and hoses together while Peggy opened the packages and pulled out the suits. "Hurry up, guys!" she screamed.

They emerged from the back with the drums and made three more trips to pull out chemicals and sprayers. They looked at the cart. Paul said what they were all thinking.

"We can't all fit in the cart with this stuff. Leave me a sprayer and a suit and just tell me what to do."

Lamont looked back and forth at them. "I'll stay—you go."

"No way, man. You're the only one that knows anything about these monsters. You have to make it back."

Peggy spoke up. "Look, we can try and stay together. We'll suit up and get the sprayers loaded up. Then you drive real slow and Paul and I will follow on foot. If you see any of those things, you can attack from the cart like a tank, with your infantry behind you."

"You watch a lot of war movies or something?" asked Paul.

"War movie my ass. Afghanistan twenty-ten."

"Let's get the suits on before those things smell dinner," said Lamont.

Lamont poured the chemicals into the sprayers and pumped them up to pressurize them. Then, the three of them pulled open the suits and stepped into them. They were a one-size-fits-all-deal on account they only had one size. The suit was large and baggy on Peggy, short and tight on Lamont, and sat just right on Paul. Once they put their hoods on, they sealed up the zippers and Velcro.

Lamont's head was tight at the top of his hood, while Peggy's flopped over on top like some weird clear beret. Paul's fit as intended, and he was the first to get his backpack on. They helped each other with the straps, and Lamont climbed into the cart that was full of chemical drums.

Each of them test fired a few squirts and adjusted the nozzles to maximize their range. When they were all set, Lamont started driving as slowly as the cart would move with the two astronaut-looking warriors walking behind him.

"How does the poison work?" asked Paul, his voice sounding muffled under his hood.

Lamont yelled through his own muffled hood. "It interrupts the metabolic pathways. The pyruvate-ferredoxin oxidoreductase enzyme-dependent electron transfer can't occur, so the anaerobic energy can't metabolize."

"You're fucking kidding me, right?" asked Paul.

Peggy laughed for the first time in what seemed like decades.

"No, that's it." said Lamont, not realizing Paul's sarcasm.

"Can you answer me in English?"

Lamont thought for a second and said, "The drug stops cell activity. Think of it as a nerve agent on a human. They'll drop and be paralyzed, and then they'll cease respiration and die. Assuming it works."

"Assuming it works? Are you fucking kidding me?" screamed Paul.

"The drug was designed to work on microscopic parasites, not rat-sized monsters. There's another issue, too..."

"Oh, great."

"Yeah. When administered orally on patients, it takes a few days to work."

Stunned silence.

"You *gotta* be shittin' me. Please tell me you're not serious."

"'Fraid so, but keep in mind, when used on infected people, we use very low doses to avoid injuring the patient. We're going to be spraying unheard-of amounts of the drug directly onto the mites. The reaction should be much faster."

"Oh that's great, doc. So like, maybe only a few hours instead of a few days?"

Peggy was horrified. "Lamont," she asked, "Could this really take hours? We'll all be dead!"

"No, no. Like I said, we're poisoning these things with mega-doses. Think of it this way, instead of you taking six-hundred milligrams of Advil for your headache—that's three tablets, this dose would be about *five thousand* tablets. *Instantly* into your system."

"That should take care of your headache," said Paul.

"God... I hope this works," said Peggy quietly.

"There is some good news. A theory, anyway," said Lamont.

"I can't wait to hear this gem," said Paul.

"I believe the mites use smell to detect food. We're sealed up airtight in these suits. If they can't smell us, they can't find us. Just a theory. Okay, we're getting closer to the zoo. Pay attention. These things were raised on beef in the lab. I have a feeling they'll seek out the cattle for food."

"God, I hope those cows stink to high heaven and we don't," said Paul inside his suit.

52

Hunting

THE COLONY OF MITES that had feasted on the retreating invaders had turned on each other when they ran out of food. After consuming almost thirty humans, they had molted repeatedly until some of them were larger than rats. Normally, the microscopic creatures couldn't survive independent of their human host for more than a few hours without dying, but these had evolved into something much stronger. No longer entirely reliant on the warmth from a human body, they were fast enough now to seek out food and warmth on their own. The change of behavior, coupled with the size of their colony, had manifested the creatures into something new on planet Earth.

Like most colony insects, the mites began forming a hierarchy, with the largest of them becoming dominant. When the largest picked his direction, the other simply followed. When he would occasionally stop and eat one of his siblings, the others scrambled for scraps

Dr. White had been correct in his theory. The mites lacked very good vision and saw the world only as tonal gray images. They were devoid of any type of hearing, but did feel vibrations and heat through antennae on their heads, and that, coupled with a keen sense of smell, allowed them to quickly identify food sources and attack. Their feeding style from the last billion years had evolved with their size.

No longer willing to accept the dead skin-cell scraps and sebum and bacteria found on human skin as their food, they now demanded meat. What had once lived inside the follicle of a human hair, coming out only at night to feed, was now capable of taking down twenty thousand pounds of genetically modified bulls. And, because they could keep growing as long as they could keep feeding, Mother Nature had built amazingly voracious appetites into their survival systems. The scientists had taken ancient creatures designed to feed on scraps and turned them into perfect little predators.

The largest of the colony froze and raised its dreadful head. Small antennae waved in the air, trying to pick up vibrations, and the olfactory cells in what served as a nose sniffed hungrily at the air. Food. Somewhere.

The creature raced down the hall towards the pasture where they had been born.

53

Irish Pub

Having not qualified for the VIP party, and not being on duty on a Saturday night, the majority of employees had descended on the "quasi-Irish Pub" for an evening of drinking, billiards, darts, and socializing with work friends. It was busy, and the crowd was livelier than usual for the simple reason that the crowd was larger than usual. Typically, some of them would have been at the cafeteria for dinner, then just gone back to their dorms, but with the cafeteria off limits because of the party, they'd all eaten dinner at the pub and just stayed to drink.

By eleven, the place was loud and fun, atypical for the "Nerd Lounge" as it was commonly referred to by the younger interns.

It was a little after eleven-thirty when an explosion rocked the building hard enough for the lights to flicker and the walls to shake for a fraction of a second. With some quick shouting and barking of orders by senior staff, the music was killed and the lights turned up all the way.

Janet Chung, one of the senior scientists, screamed at the bartender: "Joey! Get on the phone to security! Report an explosion! Then everyone get out of here!" Janet ran over and pulled a fire alarm, which set off flashing red lights in all the hallways.

The crowd in the pub filed out quickly and orderly, more than one of them carrying their drinks with them. No sense wasting a Guinness. Janet spoke calmly and professionally to the employees as they filed out of the bar, with a loud and steady voice.

"That's it, everyone keep moving. Follow this hallway to the right. The zoo is the closest exit. Just head down that hallway to the fire exit. Follow the signs, everyone." It dawned on her that some folks might be in the bathroom or kitchen, and she ordered everyone out through the fire exits, then ran back inside. Joey, the bartender, was on the phone.

"Okay, Joey—you made your call, now you get outside with the others. I'm clearing the bathrooms then I'll meet you outside."

Joey held up the phone. "I can't reach security. I even called Mike's cell phone. He's on duty tonight—I saw him earlier."

"He's probably dealing with evacuation and fire department calls. Just get outside until we see what happened." She ran back and checked the bathrooms, which were all empty, then ran outside to follow the rest of the crowd.

There was no fire or smoke around her, so maybe whatever had happened was minor. She walked down the hallway quickly, her heels clicking as she walked. She heard two loud pops, which made her cock her head and listen, but she couldn't place the noise. She picked up her pace and called Dr. White.

Lamont cursed himself for not thinking about it before he suited up, but his cell phone was inside his hazmat suit. He couldn't get to it without taking off gloves, hood, and unzipping the top. He let it go to voicemail as he drove the cart down the hallway heading to the zoo with his two-person mechanized infantry behind him.

"Damn it…" mumbled Janet when she got voicemail. She left a brief message, then hung up and tried security again. Still no answer.

The crowd from the Irish Pub walked and danced their way down the hallway towards the fire exit at the zoo. One of the happy drunks started singing "Satisfaction" by the Rolling Stones, which was joined by the rest of them, including many air-guitars, as the parade moved along. Not feeling particularly worried, without any actual smoke or fire, the inebriated crowd made the most of the Saturday night, regardless of the circumstances.

One of the women at the front of the procession, Michelle Jynkowski, a non-drinker who had taken it upon herself to make sure the partygoers behind her got out safely, froze. She stared at a shiny, shimmering mass that raced down the hallway towards them, not sure what she was looking at. The people behind her bumped into her, forcing her forward, and she began screaming at them to stop. It took a few seconds to be heard over the singing and guitar music impersonations, and as she was pushed forward, she began screaming louder.

When the skittering and clicking of thousands of legs and mandibles became loud enough for the group to hear, the singing stopped. Michelle's screaming had turned into terrifying wailing that had everyone looking to see what was wrong. When she began screaming to turn around and run, the people in the back were still trying to see why and weren't getting out of the way of the people up front trying to move. It was a traffic jam full of people, half of them panicking, and the other half too drunk to understand what was happening.

As the swarm closed in, Michelle fought her way through those too dumb to run and sprinted away from the onslaught with a few others who had seen the attacking mites. As the ones in the front smashed through the ones in the back, there was a bit of pushing and shoving, and a few tempers flared. The arguing didn't last long as the first of the rat-sized mites chewed into their victims. The sounds of arguing instantly turned to screams of terror and agony. Michelle never turned back, as the crowd began chasing after her to get away from whatever was shredding their friends behind them.

When Michelle turned the corner, she found herself staring at three people in hazmat suits. One was in a fully loaded golf cart with two people following on foot behind him. She began shrieking at them in terror, and the man in the golf cart accelerated towards her. He was screaming at her to keep running, to head to the cafeteria, and she didn't need to be told twice.

A handful of frantic people followed her past them, as the trio counter-attacked the colony of mites now in a feeding frenzy.

Lamont turned the corner to see a large crowd of people vanishing before his very eyes. Individuals would be standing one second, and then just slowly dissolve as thousands of creatures in various sizes bored into their flesh and began shredding them apart, chewing and biting and digesting human flesh faster than a food processor.

The few that had run past the cart would certainly be the only survivors. Lamont slammed on the accelerator and drove into the bloody screaming mess of humanity, pressing his sprayer as he blew through the colony. Peggy and Paul ran as fast as they could to catch up, horrified at the scene in front of them, but determined to kill the monsters that were annihilating their friends and co-workers.

Lamont drove through the colony at full speed, crunching over some of the creatures and flinging dead bodies everywhere. He continued spraying the toxin wildly until he cleared the carnage, then squealed his tires and whipped a crazy U-turn in the hallway, sliding and spinning the cart and almost tipping over. He drove back through it a second time, now assaulting from the rear as Paul and Peggy ran in from the front. With three sprayers hosing the colony down on full blast, the floors and walls were slick with yellow chemicals in seconds, and one by one, the mites began dropping off the destroyed human bodies.

The smallest mites died instantly, overwhelmed by the massive dose. The larger ones shook and twitched, all eight legs shaking as the creatures convulsed and spun around in circles before dying and excreting whatever liquids were inside their bodies all over the floor. Within a few minutes, almost all of the creatures were dead, strewn about with the remaining carcasses.

Lamont ended up back with Peggy and Paul at the front of the gruesome scene. All three of them had been screaming the entire time they were hosing the mites without even realizing it. It was pure terror and adrenaline. Now that it appeared to be over, they broke into nervous laughter and tears.

But it wasn't over. One of the human bodies, missing its arms and legs, burst open from the swollen abdomen. Out crawled something so big, all three of them began screaming until they were hoarse. The Alpha mite crawled out over the bodies of both humans and dead mites and appeared to scan the area. It got up on its back four legs and raised its antennae, now almost two feet off the ground. Its head shook as it sniffed at the air, but it was confused. It sensed human vibrations, but couldn't smell anything other than dead flesh.

Paul screamed—some sort of primitive war-cry from deep in his soul—and rushed forward aiming his wand and pressing the spray button. The blast of chemicals lasted a second and died, his tank now empty, it gave a hiss of air.

The thing turned its head and launched itself towards the threat, and Paul stumbled backwards. Behind him, Lamont and Peggy rushed forward and emptied their canisters at the hideous fiend. It flailed its front four arms at the steady stream of chemicals and then tumbled on to its back. With eight legs twitching wildly in the air, it spun round and round, using its antennae to try and right itself, but it was no use. Its mandibles snapped open and shut, giving glimpses of the razor-sharp teeth inside. When it puked up a long stream of bloody pulp that had at one time been human beings, Paul almost vomited himself, right inside his suit.

With one final twitch, the giant mite died.

The three of them rushed to each other and hugged, laughing and crying, ready to collapse. Their bodies were shaking from the adrenaline and fear. After a brief celebration for still being alive, Paul pulled away.

"I've got to reload. What if there's more of them?"

Lamont ran to the cart and pulled off another drum of Nitazoxanide. They all quickly refilled their canisters as they chatted nervously.

"It worked! Thank God, it worked." said Peggy.

"We'll need to douse every inch of this place, but at least we know we have a way to fight these things. My God, they massacred our people. So many…"

"There'll be time to grieve later. We have people that need our help right now," said Peggy, trying to stay focused. She avoided looking at the horrific mess piled up in the hallway.

"You're right. You should head back to the cafeteria," said Paul. "Look, you two can fit on the cart with the supplies. Go. You'll get there in half the time. I can defend myself if I come across any more of these things."

"You take the cart…" protested Lamont.

"No. You take Peggy and go. I'll meet you there. Get moving."

Lamont and Peggy gave him a quick smack on the shoulder and wished him luck, then hopped on the heavily loaded cart and took off towards the cafeteria. Paul walked back over to the dead mess and gave it a couple of quick little squirts to see if anything moved.

Satisfied that the creatures were all dead, he started walking quickly after Lamont and Peggy towards the cafeteria.

54

Survivors

MICHELLE JYNKOWSKI, JANET CHUNG, and Joey the bartender were among the eight survivors from the Irish Pub. They had run from the surreal massacre and kept running until they had to slow down and walk for a bit, now fully wound up.

"What *was* that?" asked Joey.

"They looked like the mites from the lab, but they were gigantic." said Janet, gasping for air.

"Mites from the lab? What are you *talking* about?" asked Joey, trying to hold it together.

"Hey! Shh!" said Michelle. They all froze, terrified that Michelle had heard those hideous creatures again.

"What?" whispered Joey.

"Listen. I hear someone calling for help."

They walked slowly and quietly until they saw blood droplets and bloody footprints leading from another hallway from the lab. When they got near a bathroom, they heard a voice inside. "Hey! Can anyone hear me?"

Joey opened the door and looked inside. A man was on the floor covered in blood. He had multiple cuts and burns all over his face and body and sat there with his back against the wall holding a SIG Sauer P229.

"In here!" yelled Joey to his friends.

The group entered the bathroom after Joey.

"Take it easy, buddy. I'm Joey. You going to shoot those fucking bugs?"

"Scott Keenan, Secret Service. And no. The gun was for me if they got in here. You've seen them?"

The rest of the survivors filled the tiny bathroom and collectively helped him to his feet.

"Yeah, we saw 'em," said Joey. "They massacred our friends. Must have killed forty or more people."

Scott nodded. "They got my partner. Well... *I...*"

They looked at him and waited for him to continue. He didn't.

"I can't walk too well. Can you help me get towards the cafeteria? If those things come at us, you just run and leave me. But until then, can you give me a hand?"

"No one's leaving anyone," said Joey. He pulled Scott's arm around his neck, and another survivor from the attack, Dan

Libonati, grabbed him by the other arm. Together, they helped Scott walk down the hallway towards the cafeteria.

Scott left a trail of blood behind him.

252

55

Cafeteria

Lamont and Peggy raced through the hallways as fast as their heavily loaded cart would move. They arrived back at the cafeteria and opened both double doors, then drove the cart right into the room.

The survivors of the shooting sat at tables they had moved to the rear corner, or walked around talking on their cell phones, or sat on the floor with the wounded. When the cart drove into the room, most of them stood up and walked over with surprised faces. Lamont and Peggy still had on full hazmat suits with tanks on their backs full of their improvised bug spray.

"You supposed to be the Ghostbusters or something?" asked Congresswoman Lisa Danfers.

It got a few smiles from the tired, scared, and stressed out group.

Lamont unzipped his hood and took it off. He was soaked with sweat. "Listen up, people!" he barked. The normally quiet gentleman doctor had seen things that no one could ever contemplate, and he wasn't playing games. "This facility is infested with giant mites. We told you we were concerned about a contamination problem. That wasn't exactly correct. This facility *is* contaminated, but not with anything viral. Swarms of giant mites are roving around out there. They're fast and extremely deadly. They've killed dozens of our people, but we do have a way to fight back. Peggy is going to stay here with you and protect this room with the sprayer. We have a chemical that kills these things. I need everyone to stay put until we clear the entire facility..."

The shouting started immediately.

"You can clear it without us in it! We're leaving!" screamed Senator Carr,

Senator Riccio started screaming at Connie. "You invited us to a death trap! This facility is as good as dead! My lawyers will eat you for lunch!"

"We need ambulances! We were told police were coming an hour ago!"

The crowd was on their feet and moving towards Lamont and Peggy, getting louder and angrier with each step.

The gunshot made everyone freeze and go silent.

Sue holstered her weapon and spoke with an even, professional tone. "No one is going anywhere until it's safe to do so. You are under the protection of the Unites States Secret Service, and you *will* follow instructions until we can safely move you all to a hospital or transportation home. Until then, you *sit down!*"

Peggy tried to stifle her grin.

"You go, girl!" she thought to herself.

There were mumbles and snide comments from the crowd, but they walked back to their seats. Lamont told Peggy to guard them and walked back out to the cart.

"Wait! You can't do this alone!" she said as she chased after him.

"You need to guard these people. Keep them safe. I'll start moving through the closest hallways and do some spraying like an exterminator would. Maybe I can create buffer zones around the room where those things can't cross over the liquid. It's worth a shot."

She nodded. "That's good. Real good. I'll do the same thing here. I'll spray real heavy around the doorways and make a little buffer around the group."

Connie interrupted them. "Where's Paul?" she asked, obviously worried.

Peggy forced a smile. "I'm sure he's fine. He's coming. He was on foot."

"You left him out there?" she snapped.

"We couldn't all fit on the cart. He volunteered, so we could get back faster to protect all of you. It was his decision," said Lamont.

"What are these things? These mites?" she asked. "Is it like that disgusting thing you showed us at the lab that day?"

"Yes. Exactly. Only larger. And now exhibiting predatory behavior. They're extremely aggressive, Connie. There were thousands of them. They attacked a group of our employees in a hallway and literally massacred twenty or thirty people. You couldn't even tell they were human bodies when the mites were through with them."

"Hey, what about the rest of them? Shouldn't they have been back here by now?"

"The rest of who?" asked Connie.

"There were survivors of that attack. We started spraying the bugs and some of the employees managed to escape. But you're right. We told them to come here. I need to go look for them," said Lamont.

"And Paul. Please. Find Paul." said Connie.

"He's in a suit with a sprayer. They can't smell him, and he can defend himself. He'll be okay. Just try and keep these people calm in here."

Lamont ran to the cart and hopped in, then took off down the hallway to the kitchen.

"Where are you going?" asked Peggy.

"Another experiment. I have an idea." said Lamont.

Peggy sprayed a heavy layer of chemicals around the doorway and outside hallway, coating the floor with the thick yellow liquid. Once she was satisfied, she closed the doors and returned to the room where Connie was being berated. She didn't see Lamont throw the piles of raw steak into the back of the cart before heading back out to find the mites.

Senator Carr began walking towards the door, followed by a few other congressmen and senators.

"Where do you think you're going?" asked Sue.

He ignored her and kept walking.

"Sir!"

He opened the door and turned back to face her. "You gonna shoot me?"

"I am ordering you to return to the others for your own safety!"

"And I am ignoring your order. Have a nice evening." He pulled out his cell phone and began speaking with one of his aids back in D.C.. "Listen! Al! I need you to get the Pennsylvania State Police. Get them over to the Global Tech facility to give me and a few others a ride outta here. These idiots don't know what they're doing."

"Senator? It's after midnight. Everything okay? What's going on?" asked his bleary-eyed assistant from his bed.

"No! Everything is *not* okay! These morons invite us out for a damn dinner, and it turns into a total shit-show! Isn't this on the news? We were attacked by *goddamn* terrorists and now they've got some kind of bugs running around the damn place. I'm leaving!"

He turned to the congressmen and senators that had followed him. "This isn't even on the news!"

The Senator followed the hallway signs to the front entrance and then stopped with his dozen followers when they saw the front doors barricaded by a huge pile of furniture.

"You've gotta be shittin' me," he sneered.

"It'll take us hours to clear that mess," said one of the congresswomen.

"We should go back," said another.

"Nonsense. We're getting out of here. There's got to be another way out. Fire exits. Something. This way," he ordered, like he knew where he was going.

"I'm going back," said one of them timidly.

"You do whatever the hell you want," said Senator Carr as he took off down the hall.

Everyone else followed him, so the lone dissenter hurried and caught up to the group rather than be left alone.

56

Rescue & Escape

Joey and Dan cradled Scott between them and helped him down the hall as quickly as they could. Scott stifled his grunt as best he could manage, but he was in agony. Joey and Dan had pulled out some of the glass shards, but there were dozens more pieces of glass, metal, and plastic in his skin, some fairly deep. Scott's right knee was already turning colors and swelling, and he could no longer even stand on it.

The small band of stragglers stopped at each intersection and peered around corners, expecting death at every turn. Taking care of Scott provided enough of a distraction to keep them from all out panic. As they turned another corner, they saw Paul in his suit, walking around with his sprayer.

"Hey!" yelled Joey.

Paul looked over and waved, then jogged over to them as best he could with his bulky suit.

"Scott! Good to see you!" Paul exclaimed. "Where's Thaddeus?"

Scott shook his head. "They got him. What's with the space suit?"

"It's working. Lamont found a chemical that kills them. They went back to the cafeteria. I was heading back that way but thought I heard them coming again and changed course. Got a little lost."

"We should get back to the cafeteria with the others," said Scott. "I can't walk. These guys saved my ass."

"Yeah. I'll escort you in case we see any more of them."

The group, now with their "fighter escort" continued their walk towards the cafeteria, but stopped when they heard arguing.

"Hold up. Who's that?" asked Michelle. She walked out ahead of the group and turned another corner. Senator Carr and a dozen other VIPs were walking and talking. Some of them were screaming into their phones, some of them at each other.

The two groups converged. "What are you doing out here? You should be sheltered in the cafeteria." said Paul.

"I don't think so," snapped Senator Carr. "We're getting the hell out of this house of horrors of yours. We've been attacked by terrorists, and now your friends back there are scaring the hell out of everyone with cockroach stories."

"They're not stories," said Scott. "You need to go back."

The Senator made a noise with his mouth and waved him off. He walked past them and said, "We're finding the nearest exit and leaving."

"You should come with us." said Paul.

Senator Carr and his crew ignored them and walked on, except for the one reluctant follower, who decided to leave the Senator and join them.

"It's your funeral…" grumbled the senator as the two groups parted company.

57

Scent

THE SECOND COLONY OF mites hadn't fed since Thaddeus and were skittering along the halls following the scent of Scott's blood. It was just a tease. They were ravenous. After feeding on Thad, they had molted and taken a moment to harden up their new exoskeletons before running on in search of more food. It was only those few moments that had allowed Scott to run and escape before his knee finally gave out on him.

The Alpha stopped and reared up on his back four legs, face to the air, antennae waving. Its mandibles slowly opened and closed, clicking and showing the rows of razor-sharp teeth inside. It dropped back down to its eight legs and hurried as it followed the blood trail, now sensing additional human smells, and then stopped.

It was sensing vibrations.

Footsteps.

Food was coming to them.

"...and we're gonna sue these idiots for so many millions of dollars they'll have to liquidate their grandchildren's college money just to pay us!" roared Senator Carr. The rest of the group was tired of his ranting, but just hurried along after him.

Carr looked up at the wall sign and pointed. "Finally!" He shouted. "This way. Looks like there's an exit down here..."

The group turned left at the corner and froze. They stared at the colony of approaching mites, their hard black and gray bodies shimmering under the LED-lighting.

"This is what all the fuss is about?" said Senator Carr. "In Texas, we call these cockroaches. Just step on the damn things!"

The colony picked up speed, now recognizing their targeted food source and moving into a feeding frenzy. Scout mites on the front outside corners of the mass pulled ahead of the colony, spreading wide to corral their prey. A few of the women in the group turned and ran, but they were slow in their high heels. They pulled off their shoes and sprinted. The men followed Carr as he stomped ahead, raising his knees like a marching band drum ranger.

"Stomp the damn things!" he yelled.

As the mites swarmed over his thousand-dollar cowboy boots and up his legs burrowing into his body, his dramatic stomping quickly turned to panicked shrieking. He and the men behind him dropped to the floor, flailing, as their insides were liquefied and chewed by the thousands of razor-sharp claws and mandibles.

The men's shrieking made the women join in with their own panicked screaming as they ran. A few hundred yards away, their echoing screams carried to where Paul and the others were heading to the cafeteria.

Paul spun around. "You go! Run! Get to the cafeteria!"

Danny and Joey had Scott between them, his arms around their necks, his knees held up by their elbows. As they ran, the pain made Scott groan. "Put me down. I'm slowing you down, just go!"

"Bullshit," said Joey. "We ain't leaving you. Just hang on! Danny! Come on, man! Faster!"

The two of them picked up speed, with Scott bouncing along, biting his teeth in pain. They were falling behind the rest of their group, but not by much.

Paul ran towards the direction of the screaming until he came upon the five women who were running as fast as they could in his direction. Two of them were younger and in good shape and had at least fifty yards on the three older women. In last place, Senator Riccio was having a hard time running at all. She was slightly obese and hadn't run since the early nineties. Her side was killing her, and she had to stop and catch her breath. The other women never stopped running when she went down in a shimmering black cloud of snapping jaws and slicing claws. One of her earrings rolled forward, spinning wildly around on the shiny floor.

Paul screamed at the women as he saw them. "Keep running! Faster!" He ran right at them as fast as he could, but it was tough in the plastic suit. The women saw him in his hazmat suit and sprayer and began screaming louder. "Help us! Help!"

Paul finally got to them and shouted for them to just keep running back to the cafeteria. They passed each other at an all-out run, and when Paul got closer to what had been Senator Riccio he slowed down and aimed his sprayer. He fired the chemical all over her shredded corpse, and the mites began dropping off and tunneling out of her corpse. They spun in circles and twitched, and then, thankfully, died.

Paul stood there, shaking, and realized he'd been screaming again. His voice was almost gone from his terrified shrieking, and he couldn't stop the shaking. He wanted to take his hood off and take a breath of fresh air, but the last remaining mites tunneled out of the body, and he fired another steady stream of yellow liquid on them. Like the others, they twitched and ran blindly until they spun in circles and died next to shredded meat that had been a human being. Bloody liquids seeped out across the floor.

When it was silent, Paul put his hands on his knees and cried.

58

Setting the Trap

LAMONT DROVE THE CART out towards the zoo, scanning each hallway he passed as he went by. It was scarier facing the things alone, but it was his lab. His disaster. His mess to clean up. As he drove the cart, he passed a few more victims. Now mere piles of shredded clothing, some heinous fluids, teeth and bones, these had been fellow employees and friends yesterday. It was overwhelming. He felt the hair on his body stand up. It was quiet and creepy, and he fought off the terror creeping into his chest as best he could.

When Lamont neared the zoo, he stopped the cart and got out. Walking around to the back of the cart, he pulled off the giant steaks he had taken from the kitchen. They were raw and bloody, and hit the hallway floor with a *splat*.

"Come and get it, you little bastards," he said to the empty hallway. "Dinner time."

Lamont sat back in the cart and backed away from the meat a few feet.

The trap was set. Now it was time to wait.

59

Cafeteria

Dan and Joey were exhausted by the time they got to the cafeteria. They carried Scott inside and brought him over to where the other wounded were on the floor. The wounded moaned quietly, trying to be brave, but suffered miserably.

Peggy ran over when she saw him. "Scott! Thank God—where's Thad?"

Scott's eyes filled with tears. He just shook his head.

"Get him over there, easy..." said Peggy, fighting back the urge to cry. Thad had been on her team for over a year, and was a reliable, likable gentle giant. She pushed the image of the mites out of her mind.

The other survivors converged on Connie and Peggy with dozens of questions. There were more questions than answers. The number one question was, "When are we getting out of here?" The response was "Soon..."

When everyone had settled down, Connie and Peggy spoke quietly off to the side. "Lamont's fear was that someone might be infected and not know it. Maybe that was possible in the beginning, but not now. These things aren't hitching a ride like a tick on a dog, they're massacring people. When Lamont gets back, I think we tell him we want to evacuate," said Peggy.

"I don't think anyone would argue with that. These people want out, and so do I."

"And what happens to this facility? How do we make sure it's completely sanitized? What if they laid eggs somewhere? It gives me the creeps just thinking about it. We should just drop a nuke on it." said Peggy.

Connie nodded and stared at the floor. "I saw myself as a rising star in G-Tech. I'm sure we'll all be fired now. Hell, we could be looking at lawsuits and jail for all I know. I *invited* these people."

"Don't blame yourself. You didn't make the monsters in the lab."

Connie shrugged. "Giant animals. We were going to feed the world and get rich doing it."

"It wasn't a horrible idea. Nothing wrong with making money and helping people at the same time."

Connie fought tears. "I'm a shitty person, Peggy. I used Paul. I used everybody. It wasn't about saving the world. I just saw myself making a few million dollars. I'll be lucky if I can get a job flipping burgers now." She thought about chopped burger meat and quietly said, "Ew."

"Look on the bright side..." said Peggy. Connie stared at her and waited. "We might get eaten by giant monster bugs and you won't have to worry about your job."

Connie wiped a tear and said, "Thanks a lot."

Peggy patted her arm. "I need to go check on Scott."

Connie stood by herself, looking out at the wrecked scene in front of her. She took a long deep breath, straightened out her posture, and followed Peggy to go check on Scott.

60

Lamont's Trap

LAMONT SAT ON THE cart, waiting silently. He was pretty sure they couldn't smell him, and with his suit on, probably couldn't even recognize him as human. The wand of the sprayer lay across his lap, and he sat like a deer hunter in a tree stand.

Something echoed through the hallway. It wasn't the chattering sound of the hard bodied mite's claws on the floor, it was more like a *shush-shush-shush*. Lamont picked up the sprayer and strained to listen as it got closer. The hair on his arms stood up again.

Paul came around the corner in his hazmat suit, the plastic legs rubbing together as he jogged, making a funny noise that seemed

271

hilarious even in the seriousness of the situation. Lamont smiled broadly.

"Paul!"

"Lamont! What are you doing out here...?" he spotted the meat on the floor. "Was that...?"

"No, no. It's beef from the kitchen. Setting a little trap."

"Only you would try and attract monsters that everyone else on the planet, including me, wants to avoid."

"You're out here hunting, who are you kidding?"

He shrugged. "I did manage to save a few women. I think. I mean, I hope they made it back to the cafeteria. Four of them. Senator Riccio didn't make it."

Lamont nodded. "Well, you saved four. That's something."

"Shh," whispered Paul. "Oh, God. Listen." He got goosebumps, too.

"Get on the cart and don't move," said Lamont, moving quickly to the driver's seat.

The two of them sat and listened as the chattering grew louder. A few seconds later, the mites came around the corner. Thousands of tiny claws clicked over the floor sounding almost like gentle rain. These weren't as big as some of the others they'd seen, but there were a lot of them. Paul swallowed hard and said a quick prayer.

The mites raced straight for the steaks and tore into the bloody meat. Lamont pressed the accelerator lightly and slowly rolled towards the pile of carnivores.

"Now!" shouted Lamont and he and Paul unleashed a torrent of the yellow spray all over the feeding monsters. The creatures ran and spun and flipped and died within a few seconds.

"If we live though this, I don't think I'll ever sleep again," said Paul.

"Yeah. And I'm pretty sure I'm now a vegan," said Lamont quietly, as he watched the last few mites crawl out of the beef flesh and drop off to die.

61

Politics

PAUL AND LAMONT SAT in the cart waiting to see if more mites would show up to attack the bloody meat.

"You know, those VIPs aren't just going to sit in that room and wait to see if some hideous parasites start crawling out of their skin." said Paul.

Lamont nodded. "I was wrong about the quarantine, anyway. I based that on my observations of Andrew Booth, our first victim. He walked around with those things inside and didn't even know he was infected. But I think each generation gives birth to larger sizes now. There's no doubt in my mind that you'd damn-well know if one of those things burrowed into your skin now."

"Yeah, no kidding," said Paul. "I've never seen anything like it. I mean, I've seen army ants on TV and stuff, but damn. It was like fast motion of a shark feeding frenzy."

Lamont nodded. "It's horrific, what's happened, so don't take this the wrong way, but I'm a scientist. I find it fascinating, in a way."

Paul turned and stared at him with disdain, his plastic suit crinkling.

"I know, I know, but look. We took a billion-year-old creature and made changes that created a whole new species on this planet. They instantly evolved into something else, and damn successfully, too."

"Lamont—they murdered maybe a hundred people!"

"No. They didn't *murder*. They hunted and ate. But that's my point. They *hunted*. You saw them. These were creatures that never hunted. They simply fed on detritus. But when made larger and faster, they no longer had to eat dead cells and waste. They demanded *respect*. Right to the top of the food chain."

"You are one fucked up individual, Doc."

"You're not getting it. We took them for granted. Invisible things that ate dead skin cells that no one even new existed. Well now they're supreme predators. In less than a few years of research, they moved up the food chain a few billion years of evolution."

"That's not evolution, Doc. That's you acting like Frankenstein in your lab. Trying to play God to animals and plants..."

"Oh please, Paul. Don't give me that 'playing God' speech. I'm tired of those arguments. God gave us brains to experiment and try new things. If not for this disaster, we'd be producing enough food to feed the planet. Now this facility will be closed, we'll be fired, and the world can keep starving."

"Listen."

They both froze, straining to hear it. The clicking of thousands of mandibles and claws on hard hallway floors.

"Let them get close. Right to the meat, and we zap them," said Lamont.

"I swear, I hate spiders and bugs. I'm gonna freak out." said Paul.

"Shh. Wait."

The shimmering colony of mites scurried across the floor in a mass of shiny shells and skittering legs. The armored mandibles opened and shut with snapping noises, amplified by the sheer numbers, echoing off the floors and walls. The ones out front ran through the yellow liquid on the floor near the bloody meat and began twitching and spinning before dying. The mass of mites behind them hesitated, their antennae twitching as they sensed their kin dying, and they ran off in a hundred directions as Lamont and Paul tried to spray them down.

"Oh my God," said Lamont. "They're *learning*!"

"Drive! Get after them!" screamed Paul, leaning out to spray whatever he could reach.

Lamont floored it, and they took off after the mites as best they could, but the hoard was splitting off into smaller groups down separate hallways. They sprayed and killed a few hundred of them down one hallway, but knew that others had disappeared in another direction.

"Amazing. You saw that! They turned and ran and split up!"

"I swear I'm going to punch you in the face if you talk about them anymore. Drive! They went that way!" snapped Paul, pointing down another hallway.

62

Cafeteria

MICHELLE AND JANET SAT on the floor, calling everyone who worked in the facility on their cell or room phones in their dorm. They were zero for twenty-two when they finally reached someone.

A terrified voice answered. "Hello?"

"Deena? Thank, God. Where are you?" asked Michelle.

"I'm in Natalie's room."

"We heard an explosion earlier and went to go see if everyone was okay when the fire alarms went off, and then... And then..." She started crying.

"You saw them, didn't you?"

She started screaming. "What was that, Michelle? There were millions of them! They attacked Tony at the end of the hallway—they just swarmed all over him, and he was screaming and bleeding! We just started running! Oh my god! What's happening?"

"Listen! You've got to stay where you are. Tell Natalie! We're trying to find out where everyone is. We'll come get you. Make sure your phones are charged and keep them with you. Do not go outside! And shove some towels under your door. These things can smell you. They're deadly, Deena! Stay inside!'"

Michelle hung up and looked at Janet. "Natalie and Deena are alive. They're the only ones I've been able to reach so far. My god, Janet. Is everyone else dead?"

Janet wiped a tear and tried the next number on her phone. "Just keep dialing."

Peggy and Connie walked over to them. "How's it going? Any luck?" asked Connie.

"Two. That's it so far," said Michelle.

Connie nodded. She looked at Peggy. "Paul and Lamont have been gone a long time."

"They have suits and sprayers. We just need to wait. This is a huge facility. Lots of ground to cover," she walked over to Scott, who sat with his knee propped over some rolled up tablecloths. "How ya doing?"

He forced a smile. "Might have to cancel yoga tomorrow, but I'm okay."

Peggy smiled. "You didn't strike me as the yoga type."

"I look great in a leotard."

"I bet. Hang in there," she said, and checked on the other wounded. One of the senators marched over to her, red in the face with anger.

"Hey! You!" snapped Senator Collins from New York. "I've made a dozen phone calls. Where the hell are the ambulances? I was told they'd be here an hour ago, then I find out the State Police won't let them past some perimeter you decided to set up! We've got people dying over here!"

Peggy looked over at the wounded. Most would be okay, but Congressman Burress was on his back with chest wounds, tied up with makeshift bandages. He was pale and unconscious.

"As soon as Dr. White and Mr. Dodds return, we'll come up with a plan. Right now, just be thankful you're in here and safe."

"Safe? You call this safe?"

"I understand your frustration..."

"If he dies, this is on you!" he snapped, walking away. His peers began peppering him with questions.

"What did she say?"

"Are we getting out of here?"

Janet ran over to Peggy. "Hey, we called the entire staff. We have four survivors out there in the dorms. That's all we could reach."

Peggy nodded and stiffened her posture. She eyed the hazmat suit that she'd taken off earlier. "Okay. Tell them to sit tight. I'm going to go get them."

Peggy walked to Sue and pulled her aside. "I'm going to gear up and head to the dorms. If Paul or Lamont return, tell them that's where I went. I need to show you how to use a sprayer. Until I get back, you're going to be in charge of security. Stay by the door. Any of those things come through the door, you soak them good."

"You're going back out there?" asked Sue.

Peggy shrugged. "I have a suit and sprayer, and we confirmed a few survivors. I need to get them together in one place and protect them until we can get back here. When Paul and Lamont get here, start coming up with an evacuation plan. I have my cell phone, but can't answer it with the suit on. Leave me a voicemail and tell me the plan. I'll listen to it when I'm in a secure area and meet up later on."

Sue nodded and followed her over to where some supplies were piled up. They assembled another sprayer and filled it with the yellow liquid, said a quick goodbye, and Peggy suited up and left out the main doorway. Sue looked at the yellow liquid all over the floor outside and prayed it would keep the things outside, then shut the door and took up her post inside.

Peggy started walking towards the dorms, listening to her pants make that plastic *shush-shush* noise as the baggy legs rubbed together, feeling very much alone.

63

The Zoo

LAMONT AND PAUL PATROLLED the hallways looking for more of the insidious creatures. They found themselves back near the zoo.

"Let's go take a look." said Lamont, now feeling more confident.

"You think there's any left alive?"

"Who knows?"

Lamont made a right turn and headed down the hallway to the pasture entrance. The door remained propped open from their attackers.

"Creepy as fuck in here, Doc. Let's just get out of here." said Paul.

"My life's work is inside here. I have to see if any of them made it."

Paul reluctantly followed Lamont inside and through another door into the open pasture. It was eerily quiet. They stood for a long moment and then walked across the grass. Other than a few empty mite shells from molting, and several piles of teeth with bone fragments, there was no sign of life.

"Doc. Seriously, man. Let's get the fuck out." said Paul. The hair on his body was standing up again, and he was trying not to freak out.

"This way..." said Lamont, ignoring him.

They walked into a smaller hallway, and Lamont saw the empty pen that had housed Goliath. He shook his head, wanting to sit and cry, but pressed on. There was another set of doors, which were locked. Lamont punched in a number combination and they popped open. Inside, twenty-five giant hogs milled about in the pen.

"Pigs made it," said Paul.

"We kept them inside. They can get a little more rambunctious, and we didn't want to scare the VIPs."

"How's that working out for you?" asked Paul.

Lamont gave him a dirty look and resealed the door. "I guess that's it. That's all we have to show for a decade of research and a few hundred million dollars."

"Expensive bacon," said Paul. Lamont gave him another nasty look. "I mean, if you're figuring it by the pound."

"You're not funny." said Lamont.

"Actually, I'm hilarious. All things considered, I'm doing quite well handling my desire to scream hysterically and start running and never stop. If I live through this, I may need a padded cell."

Lamont made a sad face and nodded.

"Asians consume a lot of pork. Giant hogs would have fed a lot of mouths in China and Southeast Asia."

"Doc, no one's ever going to let us sell anything out of this lab. Ever. Face it. This place is as good as condemned, and so is everything in it—including our careers."

Lamont nodded. "You're right." He redialed the combination and opened the door again, then pressed a button that released a side door which opened into the pasture. The hogs began trotting out into the grass.

"What did you do that for?" asked Paul.

"Might be their last night on Earth. I'd prefer to think they were enjoying the grass and open pasture."

"Going to draw the mites back in with them?

"Might. They've never eaten pork before, but they might recognize them as food."

"Holy shit, doc. *Everyone* loves bacon."

"You're still not funny."

"I'm scared, okay? When I'm scared, I make jokes."

Lamont followed the pigs out into the pasture. "Well, if the mites like bacon, we'll be here waiting for them."

64

Dorms

PEGGY WALKED DOWN THE hallway for a long time. Occasionally, she passed what she knew had been a human being. Clothes and teeth and some fluids in a pool on the floor, along with exoskeletons that had been shed after they ate and molted. When she came across a random golf cart, she said a thank you to the Almighty and hopped in.

Now driving, her pace was more than doubled. She hadn't been to the dorm area before, so it took some navigating to find the right hallways. Once there, the number of human remains on the floor increased. The alarm after the explosion had roused anyone that wasn't in the Irish Pub. Those who had heeded the alarm were devoured in the hallways.

Peggy slowed down and started calling out as she drove. "Hello? Is anyone back here? Hello?" She kept it up for ten minutes before someone banged on a door and shouted, "In here! Is it safe to open the door?"

Peggy pulled up next to the door. "Open up! I have a cart. Come out!"

The door opened, and Dr. Marty Kessler peered out from his room. "Did you see them?"

"The mites?"

"Yes! Giant arthropods from the lab! They were killing people out here!"

"Yes, I know. Hop in. Anyone else in there with you?"

"Just me." Marty ran around the cart and got in. "We need to get out of here fast!"

"We have to pick up a few more people."

"How many?"

"There's four of you, as far as I know."

Marty looked at the golf cart. "We won't all fit." He was six-five and filled his side of the cart.

"Yes, you will. Someone will sit on your lap, and on the back and on the fucking roof if they have to! We're getting everyone out of here." She drove a little further, calling out to anyone who might hear her. Two doors opened up ahead, and Deena Cohen and Natalie Olesinski ran out of one side while Doris Chen ran from the other.

"Thank God you're here!" they screamed as they piled on.

Doris sat on Marty's lap, and Deena and Natalie hopped up on the back. The two-person cart now had five people crammed together, and even at maximum speed only puttered along. Peggy drove with her left hand and held the wand with the other. She had removed the hood of her hazmat suit to see better in the crammed cart.

"Head over to the lounge area, over on the right," said Marty. "There's always a few carts over there."

Peggy made a right turn and drove, barely moving at quarter speed, to where she hoped to find carts. They were close enough to see the extra carts when they heard the skittering and clicking.

"Oh god! They're coming back!" shrieked Deena.

"Faster! I can see them!" screamed Natalie. She and Deena were facing rear and watched the shiny river of black approaching them.

"We're too slow!" said Marty. He shoved Doris off his lap towards Peggy and hopped out of the cart. "Go! I'll get another cart!" He started running as fast as he could towards the carts, and Peggy wheeled around to head into the mites and spray them.

"*What are you doing?*" screamed Doris, panicking and grabbing the wheel. "Go the other way!"

They fought over control of the cart, which came to a stop in the middle of the hallway as Marty ran for the extra carts. The black horde swarmed around the cart and went under it for the easy target, while Peggy and Doris fought over the wheel. Natalie and Deena were screaming at the top of their lungs as they watched the mites swarm towards Marty.

"*Runnnnnn!*" shrieked Deena and Natalie. "*Runnnnnnnnnn!*"

Marty made the mistake of looking over his shoulder. It slowed him down just a little. Just enough for those first mites to get onto his feet and run up his legs, biting and tunneling deep inside his flesh. He screamed and began swatting at them, but was no longer able to sprint away. By the time Peggy punched Doris in the face and freed the wheel, Marty was on the ground screaming in agony. Peggy drove to him and began hosing him down, killing the mites still outside of his body, but the ones inside were busy slicing through muscles and organs. Marty let out one last blood curdling scream before falling back with wide eyes and mouth. A mite crawled out of his mouth and died from the spray while a few dozen others took off away from the chemical.

All four women were screaming hysterically as they watched Marty bleed out in front of them. Doris was still screaming to get away when, finally, Peggy stopped spraying.

"Shut up! All of you! Shut up!" she snapped.

She drove past Marty without looking at him over to the carts. She looked at Doris. "Get out! Get your own cart and take someone with you."

Doris ran and hopped behind the wheel on one of the carts, Natalie and Deena ran to another one, not wanting to share the cart with Doris after she'd panicked and gotten Marty killed. The caravan of three carts took off towards the cafeteria with Peggy out in front, sprayer in hand. Peggy was outraged, but reminded herself these were civilians, and they were traumatized.

If they could just make it back to the cafeteria...

65

The Zoo

LAMONT AND PAUL WALKED the pasture for a while, watching the Clydesdale-sized pigs trot around and root through the grass. Occasionally, they'd hear munching when one of the giant animals chewed up what they hoped was an exoskeleton and not human remains.

"Maybe they're all dead," said Paul in a hushed tone.

"Maybe."

"So maybe we should head back. To the cafeteria."

"You go," said Lamont.

"Come with me."

"Not yet."

The lights in the perimeter hallways started popping off until half of them were out, making it much darker.

"What's going on?" mumbled Paul.

"It's midnight. The whole facility cuts to half-power to save energy. We can override it in each section as we go, but this will be happening all over the facility now."

"They come out at night, you said..." stammered Paul. "The mites, they're nocturnal..."

"Well, when they were microscopic, yes. The light didn't seem to bother them today."

"But you don't know that for sure. They might get more active at night, right?"

Lamont shrugged and squinted as he looked out into the pasture. When the colony of mites had demolished the entire herds of cattle and sheep, they'd laid thousands of eggs in the grass before moving on. With the lights lower, the hatchlings began crawling up out of the dirt looking for a meal. One of the giant hogs began squealing wildly and sprinted across the pasture before crashing into the grass, howling in excruciating torment.

Its eerie scream sounded human.

"Jesus. They're back," said Paul.

"It would appear you were right. They like the night."

The sound of thousands of the things rushing through the grass sounded like rain in the cavernous space. One by one, the hogs began to go down, squealing and screeching.

"Everybody likes bacon," said Lamont flatly.

"You're right—that's *not* funny. There's too many of them. We need to get the fuck out of here, Lamont."

"You go."

"Come on, man. Come *on!*"

"You go. This is my mess to clean up."

"I'm not leaving without you."

"Then stay and fight." Lamont looked at Paul and gritted his teeth, then screamed a war-cry that echoed through the pasture, before charging forward out into the grass.

Paul, in total terror, overcame his fear and joined in the crazed howling, charging behind Lamont, screaming like a Confederate soldier across the fields of Antietam. The two of them ran side-by-side, hoses spraying all over, as they charged into the midst of the scurrying black horde.

66

Hallway

PEGGY DROVE AS FAST as her cart would go with the three other women following in their two carts. They were halfway back to the cafeteria when the lights started going out.

"Oh no," she muttered under her breath, slowing down so she didn't crash in the dark.

The two carts behind her slowed down, but Doris was panicking again. "What's going on? What's happening?"

Natalie was scared, but also annoyed. "Calm down, Doris! Jeez, the lights go off at midnight every night! Shut up, will you?"

"*Everyone* shut up!" said Peggy. It was distant, and it was barely audible, but it was there and getting louder. That sound like rain, when thousands of tiny claws run across hard hallway floors.

"Oh my God! They're coming back!" screamed Doris. "We have to get out of the hallway!"

"Quiet! Get moving!" said Peggy, starting up again, at quarter speed in the very dim hallway.

Doris raced around her, swerving and almost crashing into her as she passed by Peggy in the dark hallway. She was screaming and talking to herself hysterically as she drove, the other women shouting at her to calm down. As the noise of the colony grew louder, Doris began breaking down.

"We have to get out of the hallway!" she screamed.

The mites were almost invisible in the darkness, but there was no mistaking the snapping of their sharp mandibles and clicking of their claws.

Doris spotted a bathroom and swerved, crashing into the wall. "Get out of the hallway!" she screamed, pushing the door open and running inside.

"No!" screamed Peggy. "Don't stop!"

Doris slammed the door shut behind her and leaned against it. She wouldn't have opened it for the others even if they begged.

Peggy drove faster, even though it was hard to see.

"Don't stop!" she screamed at Natalie and Deena.

The chattering and clicking had gotten so loud, the sound was like driving in a torrential downpour. Their carts put distance between themselves and the invading mass behind them, which took a sudden left turn and raced under the door of the bathroom.

Doris's screaming was heavily muffled by the door as the mites drilled through her skin and ate their way into her organs. They feasted there long enough for Peggy, Natalie, and Deena to make their escape.

Ten minutes later, the three women arrived back at the cafeteria. The employees there had turned up the lights outside that hallway and inside the cafeteria. Peggy ran in with Natalie and Deena, who were greeted with cheers and hugs from their friends inside, as they shared the news on Marty and Doris.

Connie ran over to Peggy. "Have you seen Paul or Lamont?"

"No. I thought they would have been back here by now."

Connie wiped at her eyes and shook her head.

"I know Dr. White was against an evacuation, but we need to get these people out of here. If we don't organize it, they'll just start leaving on their own like Senator Carr and his group."

"You won't get any argument from me, but what about Paul and Lamont?"

"I'll go back out."

"I'll go with you."

"I don't have another suit."

"I don't look good in yellow plastic," she said, forcing a smile.

Peggy nodded. "Okay. You and me. But after we get these people out of here."

Peggy found Sue, and they walked back to Scott, who looked fairly miserable sitting on the floor. "How you doing there, Agent Keenan?"

"Just peachy."

"Excellent. We're getting you and the rest of these folks out of here. Sue, call the State Police. Tell the major to assemble trucks outside the emergency exit of the kitchen. The front doors were heavily barricaded by those whackos. We can't get out that way. We need enough room for fifty people. One trip. They stack up their vehicles, motors running. We open the doors and these folks haul ass to the trucks, and they take off. We'll take the wounded out second, since that will take a little longer. We need four ambulances."

Scott motioned to the covered bodies. "Can't leave them, can we?"

Peggy nodded. "Seven ambulances. For *our* people. Those two murderers can stay here and be food for all I care.

"I'm on it!" said Sue, and she dialed the State Police major.

Peggy walked out to the center of the room, her hazmat hood under her arm, barking out instructions to the weary guests and employees. "Listen up, people. In a little while, the State Police will line up trucks outside the fire exit in the kitchen. You'll form a single-file line and three at a time you'll exit the building to fill an SUV. We'll get you all out in one trip."

There was some applause and cheering.

"Quiet! As soon as you're out of here, the police will assist us getting the wounded out. You'll all be taken to the hospital for observation and treatment for those that need it. Sue will be organizing your departure, so listen to her!" She walked quickly to the cart and refilled her canister with more chemical. A *step-clomp-step-clomp* sound behind her made her turn around. It was Scott Keenan, using a chair as a cane to limp over to her.

"What are *you* doing?" he asked.

"I'm going to try and find Lamont and Paul. Maybe there are more survivors out there, who knows?" replied Peggy.

"Load me up one of those tanks. I'm going with you."

"Like hell. You're going to the hospital. Get out of here."

"You ain't the only bad ass in the room. I did a tour in Afghanistan. These little cockroaches don't scare me. They'd choke on me."

"Scott! You can't even walk."

Connie walked in on the end of it. "It's okay, Scott. I'm going with her."

"Good, the more the merrier. I'll sit on the back, you two up front. Everyone gets a hose and we drive around like an M2 Bradley Fighting Vehicle, wasting everything we see."

Peggy smiled at Scott. "Crazy bastard. Fine. If you can get on, you can go. But I ain't helping you up."

Scott hopped over on one foot and sat on the back of the cart facing backwards. "Tail gunner, like the old bombers. Just give me a tank and I'm good to go."

"You fall off and you're bug food," said Peggy.

"Yeah, well I've seen you drive, so that's a real possibility."

Peggy assembled and filled the extra tanks and gave them to Connie and Scott, then threw her hood on the floor and got into the cart.

"Let's go play exterminator." said Peggy, driving them out the front doors.

67

The Zoo

Both Paul and Lamont attacked the colony with as much violence as the mites exhibited on the pigs. As the pigs squealed and screamed under the massive assault, Lamont and Paul also screamed. Some of it was obscenities, some of it was just animalistic screams from fear and adrenaline. They hosed down everything they could see in the dim light. Black, shiny shells twinkled as the mites ran and swarmed, many of them twitching and spinning as they died.

When Lamont's nozzle went from spraying chemical to air with a loud *"Phhhht!"* he knew he was in trouble. He cursed and screamed at Paul. "I'm out!"

Paul screamed back at him. "Get behind me and follow me out!"

The two of them ran in a single line with Paul spraying bullets until his ran out too. They were still a long way from their cart.

"There!" screamed Lamont pointing up. "Climb!"

At the nearest wall, part of the steel superstructure was exposed. They jumped up and started climbing, and the pursuing mites below quickly lost their scent and ran in circles looking for their prey. Lamont and Paul didn't stop climbing until they were fifteen feet above the field. They both started laughing nervously.

"Tell me something, Doc. These fuckers know how to climb?" asked Paul, somewhere between laughing and crying.

"I don't know. Probably," said Lamont.

"You shitting me?"

"They climb eyelashes and hair, why not steel?"

"Come on, Doc! Can't you just say no?"

Lamont shrugged. "Maybe they can't grip the metal. So far so good. We have plastic on and we're fifteen feet up. Maybe they can't find us."

"Thank you! Was that so hard? Cut me a break, man. Just once I want to believe we're going to get out of here alive."

Lamont nodded, suddenly feeling overwhelmed with sadness, guilt, and shame. "What a *goddamn* disaster," he muttered.

"But everybody likes bacon. Am I right?"

Lamont laughed. And cried. "So many dead," he whispered.

"Yeah, well, we're still kicking. We just got to figure a way out of here."

"Can we just rest a minute? I don't think I can move," said Lamont.

The adrenaline rush had left them now, and the shaking and exhaustion replaced it.

"Yeah. Sure, Doc. We'll just sit here and watch those things finish dinner before they come up here for dessert."

The sight of a golf cart blasting into the zoo was a surprise. Peggy was driving with Connie next to her, and a very banged up Scott Keenan hung on facing backwards. All three had the nozzles out as they raced out into the pasture at the skittering creatures that were eviscerating the dead pigs.

"Hey! Up here!" screamed Paul.

"Paul!" Connie responded, flooring the cart. "Stay there!"

The three of them hosed the feeding frenzy as they drove around the grass through the melting carcasses. Paul and Lamont cheered like spectators at a football game from up in the stands, as they watched the cart cut in and out of the dead pigs, spraying the chemical all over. The cart made a wide turn, spraying as it went, and stopped below Lamont and Paul, spraying the remaining mites.

Paul and Lamont climbed down onto the roof of the cart, and as soon as they were on, lying on their stomachs, banged on the roof.

"Go!" they screamed together, and Peggy took off, albeit much slower with such a full load.

When the cart had cleared the pasture and arrived back at Lamont and Paul's cart, Paul and Lamont slid off the roof.

"Thanks for coming back for us," said Paul, smiling at Connie. "You saved our ass."

"I wasn't done with you," she said quietly.

"Even if I'm out of work and unemployable?"

"We'll both have very flexible schedules. Unless we're in jail."

"All right, let's get the hell out of here," said Peggy.

Lamont and Paul jumped into their cart and raced back to the cafeteria.

68

Cafeteria

By the time the two carts rode back into the cafeteria, most of the guests were racing out into awaiting police vehicles. The five of them got out of the carts, with Paul and Lamont helping Scott, and walked quickly over to the cops who were helping the EMTs load up the wounded and dead.

The Troopers looked at the group and saw the three hazmat suits. "You have a biohazard in here?" asked their sergeant.

"Something like that. Parasitic invasion of immense magnitude. We need this place cleared as fast as possible in case there's more of them," said Lamont.

"Parasitic invasion? Like fleas and ticks? I hate ticks," said the Trooper.

"Then I seriously suggest you get these people out of here as fast as possible. You do *not* want to see what's out there," said Paul.

He made a face and helped to move the wounded. Lamont walked over to Peggy.

"I was wrong about keeping these people here. I was just being cautious. Those things can't ever get out of here."

"And how do we ensure that?"

"I'll take care of it."

"Doctor, whatever you're thinking, you need to tell me."

"It's my mess, I'll clean it up..."

"Doc, I'm not playing with you. What are you thinking?"

"This facility will never be allowed to reopen."

"Agreed. So?"

"The explosion in the lab was from a natural gas line. There are several high-pressure lines in this facility. We heat the zoo and the farm—they're big areas. I can open the lines and blow this whole place to hell."

"And get blown up in the process?"

"I haven't worked out all the details yet."

"Yeah, well, I'm ordering you out of this building."

"You have no authority to order me anywhere. I'm the director of the lab..."

"And that doesn't mean you're personally responsible for everything that happened here today. We were attacked by some fringe group of lunatics, who unleashed monsters from the lab. That's not your fault. We've had enough casualties for one day."

"We need to be sure they're all dead."

Peggy stared at him. "And you think fire's the best way?"

"Yes."

Paul had been listening and finally spoke up. "Doc, not to act like I know more about this than you do, but a million years ago I was a volunteer fireman. We had a fire in a Chinese restaurant one time. I was up on the roof trying to hose it down. There must have been a million roaches running out of the flames. What if you light this place up and they all just scatter?"

Peggy looked at Lamont and raised her eyebrow. "Well? He's got a point."

"I was picturing more of a massive explosion making a giant black crater. I let the place fill with gas before I set it off. I told you—these are high-pressure lines. Way bigger than the one in the lab."

"And how were you going to get out?"

He shrugged.

"Oh great. I see. Psycho. Enough macho crap for one day. You're out of here."

Paul spoke up. "Hey, wait. I've got an idea. I think Lamont's right. We crank open the high-pressure lines and turn up all the fans in the HVAC control room to really push it through the building, then we have one of those troopers fire a few rounds from half a mile out—might do the trick."

Lamont nodded, "I like it."

"Okay, so where are the gas lines and the controls?"

Lamont made a funny face. "Back towards the butcher shop. Building five, all the way on the other side."

"Hey, it's okay. We don't have to go through the building. The State Police have a million vehicles outside. We drive around on the outside, key in from over there, and then get out," said Peggy.

"That's it. Let's get it done," said Lamont.

Connie ran over to them from the kitchen. "Everyone's out! Come on!"

Paul shook his head at the others so she couldn't see. "Okay, we're coming"

They all went outside and started piling into the SUVs. Paul held the door for Connie, and as she got in, gave her a quick kiss. "One more job to do. See you in a bit." He yelled at the driver, "Go!"

Connie protested as the driver took off with her locked inside. Paul ran to another truck where Peggy and Lamont were explaining the plan to the State Trooper behind the wheel. Scott understood he'd slow them down and reluctantly allowed himself to be loaded into an ambulance. The Trooper driving wouldn't let them have the truck without him behind the wheel.

"You realize we can all get blown up, right?" asked Peggy,

"I am way less scared of getting blown up than I am of explaining to the major how I let you borrow my vehicle, and then watched *it* blow up."

Peggy shook her head. "Drive."

They roared through the soft earth and grass, tearing up the ground as they four-wheeled around the building, leaving the long line of vehicles. Overhead, a police helicopter circled with lights.

"Hey, do you have a sniper on that thing?" asked Peggy.

"Pretty much all the time," said the Trooper. "I'd assume they'd have one tonight."

"Problem solved!" said Peggy, smacking the man on his thigh.

They stopped on the far side of the building near a loading dock. The large air conditioners and heaters were all located in one central area, and the high-pressure gas lines were clearly marked with yellow pipes and dozens of warnings.

"Hey. One thing," said Lamont. "We don't have the sprayers."

"Oh shit. We have to go back." said Peggy.

"We were just about out of the stuff anyway," said Lamont. "We went through a five-year supply in three hours. Maybe they didn't make it over this far."

"That's a great plan, Doc. *Maybe they didn't make it over here. Maybe they won't eat us.'* That's just great. Let's go back and grab the sprayers," said Peggy.

"We don't have time, and I'm telling you, they were almost empty! I'll go. Just stay here in the truck."

"And let you be the big hero? Not on your life," said Paul, getting out of the truck.

"Yeah. What he said," said Peggy, opening her door.

69

The Colony

THE REMAINING MITES USED their highly sensitive olfactory receptors to begin finding each other. In simple terms, they could smell each other.

Like a colony of bees, termites, or ants, the hierarchy fell into place through the same mysterious process that had developed over the millennia in the insect world. They were evolving—and specializing. The mites swarmed all over, and with a split-second examination of each other, knew who were the workers, the soldiers, the alpha, and the queen.

They came from every corner of the building, splitting and shedding and growing as they assembled. They'd eaten every morsel they could find throughout the facility and now grew even more agitated and hungry. Like a single organism, the mass began to move down the hallway outside the farm. The largest of the mites, as big as a toy poodle, remained with the queen, who was just slightly larger and full of eggs. Their attendants and guards whipped around them constantly, taking chemical orders from their antennae, like bees in a hive.

The majority of their kind had been killed, but like any colony of insects, a threat to the queen or hive was met with a lethal counterattack. They were now hunting not only for food—they also wanted to eliminate any threats to the future eggs carried inside the queen's swollen abdomen.

The alpha male stood on his back four legs and waved his antennae around. The slamming of doors and pounding of human feet hundreds of yards away carried across the vast empty spaces of the facility. The alpha began moving faster towards the back of the facility, with thousands of clicking claws and snapping jaws...

70

Building Five

LAMONT, PEGGY AND PAUL ran into the hallway, the heavy doors clanging shut behind them. They'd taken whatever tools were in the Trooper's truck, which amounted to a tire-iron and hammer, and raced through the building towards the HVAC control room. Lamont had been part of the original design team of the facility, and knew every inch of the place, even though he wasn't familiar with the running of the actual system.

They arrived at the control room a minute later, out of breath. They were unarmed and defenseless. All they could do was pray they'd killed most of them. Once inside the room, they had to pause and look around. There were dozens of pipes, color coded with arrows, connectors, and valves. It was a confusing mess for those not familiar with it.

"Holy crud," mumbled Paul. "Now what?"

"Yellow! Yellow pipes are natural gas. Trace the pipes back to the biggest yellow pipe you can find," said Lamont.

The three of them worked their way through the room's maze of piping until they found the main pipe from outside which came up from the ground.

"Here! Now what?" shouted Peggy.

"Now crank the main cut off shut, then we get the pipe open and turn it back on," said Lamont.

The pipe was a twelve-inch high-pressure main and heavy metal.

Paul looked at the pipe and then at Lamont. "There's no way we can just break this open."

Lamont looked around quickly. "You're right. Damn it. We'll need to find where it branches off and... *There!* Use those pipes and redirect them right into those ducts!"

After a second of looking, both Paul and Peggy understood. They'd open the smaller lines and push them into the ductwork, then turn on the fans pushing the gas out into the facility. While Peggy cranked the large wheel to turn off the gas, Paul slammed the smaller pipe at a connection, clanging and banging as hard as he could without any luck.

"It's no good, man. These metal pipes won't break," said Paul after breaking a sweat with zero progress.

"They have to!" screamed Lamont. He grabbed the tire iron and began smashing at the pipe with the same results. Lots of noise and nothing else. "Damn it!"

They stood staring at the pipes in silence.

"Okay. Okay. I have another idea," mumbled Lamont. He walked over to a far wall and began smashing the sheetrock under a pipe. He tore at it like an animal until it began splitting open, then he ripped it open with his hands. Peggy and Paul had no idea what he was doing, but helped him tear open the wall anyway. Inside was a yellow flexible hose.

"Flex piping! Inside the walls they used flex piping. They're much smaller lines, but they can be unscrewed at the connections!"

The three of them pulled at the line until they found a connection and then unscrewed it after a few minutes of groaning. They ripped the end out of the wall and kept pulling out more of the hose until they had enough to reach the intake ducts that brought fresh air in from outside. Lamont shoved the hose into the duct and then ran over to the outside vents. There was a lever to close the vents and recirculate the air, which he pushed closed.

"That's it! Now get the valve open again!"

Peggy ran over and cranked the wheel of the valve until they could all hear the hissing of the open line into the ductwork.

"That line is so much smaller than the one I wanted to open. This may take a long time," said Lamont. "I have to make sure it's working. Stay here!"

He ran down the short hallway, and out the door of the control room, then down a longer hallway that led out of the HVAC area into the butcher shop. He climbed up on a table and put his nose by the ceiling vent. Sure enough, he could smell the mercaptan that made natural gas smell like rotten eggs.

Lamont screamed up into the vent. "Hey! Can you hear me?"

"Yes!" screamed Paul from the other end back in the HVAC room.

"I need to make sure this is getting out to the other buildings. Go wait outside, I'll be back in five minutes!"

"No! Wait! Don't go by yourself! Those things could be anywhere!" screamed Paul.

"No sense all of us going! Wait outside!" He hopped down from the table and ran down the hallway until he got to building four, which housed the dorms. As he ran down the hall, he cringed at the sight of the shredded clothing and piles of teeth and bone fragments sitting in small puddles of coagulating bile. Lamont ran into the first open lounge area he saw and climbed up on a table to sniff near the vents.

"Thank God," he whispered.

The smell was getting strong here, too.

Back in the control room, Peggy and Paul argued about what to do next. After a minute of back and forth, they decided to wait for Lamont where they were, by the exit door outside the HVAC room.

71

Building Four

LAMONT WAS UP ON the table sniffing around when he first heard it. The sound of rain. For a split second, he thought something was leaking from the pipes. And then, as the goosebumps flashed across his arms, he recognized the sound.

The skittering and clicking of thousands of hard claws across the hallway grew louder by the second. He started to climb down off the table to sprint back to the exit, but it was too late. The first scouts of the colony ran under the table, antennae waving as they tried to locate the smell of food. They ran in circles below the table, and Lamont wondered if the smell would confuse them enough to mask his presence. He froze and waited, wishing he still had the hood to his hazmat suit to completely cover himself.

When the Alpha entered the room in a shimmering pile of smaller soldiers, Lamont's heart skipped a beat. It was gigantic. A second later, another giant, this one even bigger followed him in. Lamont was terrified, but as a scientist, he was also amazed. He stared at the creature and held his breath.

The giant male stood up on his back legs, as big as a dog, antennae moving and flicking back and forth. The antennae stopped, and pointed at Lamont, and the hideous creature cocked its head and seemed to sniff the air. It began clicking its mandibles, razor-sharp teeth showing every time its jaws opened. The four front legs in the air began snapping their lobster-like claws, until they fell into a rhythm.

Within a few seconds, the rest of the mites followed suit, clicking in unison, like a crowd cheering death in an ancient Roman Colosseum.

Lamont's face fell. They had cornered him, and they weren't going to leave.

"What's taking him so long?" snapped Paul.

"How far was he going?" asked Peggy.

They stared at each other worried. Paul climbed up on the duct and screamed again. "Lamont! Lamont!" He coughed. The gas was so thick it made him nauseous. "We can't stay in here!" he coughed.

Peggy ran to the short hallway and called his name, *"Lamont!"*

Lamont heard his name, ever so faintly over what sounded like clapping by his tormentors.

Lamont put his face by the duct. "You need to get out! They're in here! Get out now!"

"What's he saying?" asked Peggy. His voice was feint and far away, and the loud hissing of the gas made it difficult.

Paul listened and closed his eyes, held his breath, *focused*—it was Lamont, telling them to get out.

"Where are you?" screamed Paul.

"I'm trapped! They're in here. You've got to get out!"

"I'll find a cart and get to you! Stay where you are!"

"No! You don't understand! You can't come in here. Get out now before it's too late!"

Paul looked down to Peggy, coughing. "He says to leave. He's trapped. He must be cornered somewhere." Paul climbed down and took a few breaths.

"We can try and get back around to the cafeteria. There's a little left in the sprayer."

Paul stared at her. They both knew they'd never get there and back in time.

"This place is full of gas, Peggy. It's getting worse. We need to get out of here."

"He's down by the dorms. There were carts down there."

Paul nodded. He wouldn't want to be abandoned to die in there, either. "Okay."

The two of them ran towards the dorm until they found a cart and hopped in. They were unsure where Lamont had gone and started driving and calling out his name every few seconds, listening for a reply.

A minute later the awful screaming began. Peggy and Paul drove towards the sound of the horrid shrieking, Paul pounding on the wheel as he drove. The horrifying screams seemed to end in a quick gurgle seconds just before they turned into the open lounge.

Inside the large room, on top of a table, Lamont's body lay on his back, his face frozen in agony, his abdomen splayed open. Hundreds of mites were climbing and crawling all over the legs and top of the table like ants at a picnic, but they weren't shredding his body and consuming him. The giant male sat on his legs, front claws up and out, like a lobster defending itself. The female was on Lamont's neck with the back of her abdomen shoved into his open body cavity, where thousands of glistening eggs slid out into his guts.

Peggy threw up all over her lap with a loud gag. The noise and smell caused the things to freeze, antennas waving for a target. Paul didn't have to be told—he screeched the tires in a wild U-turn and sped off as fast as it would go. Peggy was spitting and crying, and Paul fought back his own horror and panic. They raced for the exit as the soldiers scurried down the legs of the table after them. The alpha male was clicking away, sending his soldiers on the attack as his mate continually pushed out eggs, building their next generation of soldiers.

Peggy craned her neck and looked back at the shimmering bodies that filled the hallway floors like a rising black tide. "Oh, God! Paul! Faster!"

Paul was pounding on the wheel, willing it to drive faster. As they got closer to the HVAC area, the smell of gas was overwhelming. Paul drove straight for the exit door. He slammed on the brakes, the cart sliding towards the door, with the two of them coughing from the gas fumes. Paul crashed into the door, throwing it open, and Peggy ran out behind him. Paul slammed it closed, then sprinted after Peggy to the SUV. The instant they were inside, they were screaming: "Drive! Drive!"

The State Trooper peeled out throwing mud and asked, "Where's your other guy?"

"He's dead! Drive!" screamed Paul, completely hysterical. The image of Lamont being turned into a nest for the eggs was too revolting to contemplate. "Get on the horn! Get that sniper firing at the ventilation shafts!"

The Trooper pulled his radio and called the pilot. "Big Blue Six, this is Trooper McGowan. I am instructing you to fire rounds at the ventilation shaft to ignite a fire in that building. We are trying to ignite the gas and contain an infestation. Burn that facility to the ground! Do you copy?"

"I copy, Trooper McGowan, but I'll need authorization before I can order my shooter to start a fire. Please standby, over."

Peggy grabbed the radio from the cop. "Big Blue Six, this is Special Agent Peggy Robins of the Secret Service, I am authorizing you, hell, I am *ordering* you! *Shoot that damn ventilation shaft and keep shooting it until it explodes! Now!*"

The argument inside the helicopter was short. The sniper trained for this moment and rarely got to do it for real. He wasn't about to miss his chance to fire his sniper rifle. The helicopter side door slid open, and the Trooped spun his legs out until they rested on the skids of the helicopter. He was strapped in around his waist and leaned out of the stationary bird.

Three shots.

That's what it took.

The third shot sent orange sparks down into the duct work where it ignited thousands of pounds of liquefied natural gas. As the building exploded in a rolling cloud of flames, the State Police SUV was lifted for a second and pushed forward, the rear window popping into millions of little squares.

Trooper McGowan never slowed down. They sped across the grassy field until they reached the fence and slid to a stop. The three of them piled out of the SUV and looked back at the facility as it continued to explode, over and over, with orange and red and purple flames reaching up to the heavens. With the high-pressure gas lines wide open, there was no stopping the fire, which roared through the house of horrors. Inside, the popping sound of roasted exoskeletons bursting was drowned out by the sounds of whining metal, as steel I-beams melted and collapsed into the raging inferno.

"Burn. Burn, you fuckers..." whispered Paul.

They stood for a long time watching in silence until another SUV sped across the grass and stopped next to them. Connie got out and ran over to Paul, who hugged her. A genuine caring hug from both of them.

"Maybe we can start a little farm stand or something," said Connie as the tears rolled down her face.

"Organic," whispered Paul as he closed his eyes. "Only organic."

Epilogue

THE NEWS CYCLE STARTED the next morning.

The typical Sunday morning stories, gentle in nature, with coverage of travel and food, were replaced with the horrific story of a tragedy inside the Global Tech World Solutions lab facility.

The anchor read his teleprompter with the same horror as the viewers listening to the incoming news.

"Over fifty people were killed in the domestic terrorism attack that claimed the lives of the majority of the Global Tech staff, as well as almost a dozen United States senators and congressmen. The members of the group responsible were killed by Secret Service and the ensuing fire. That fire continues to rage out in the Pennsylvania facility, but due to its remote location, no homes or businesses

are being impacted. The destruction of the Global Tech plant is expected to send stock prices tumbling when trading opens Monday, as the facility was the flagship of Global Tech's research arm, and shareholders were expecting a big announcement on Monday morning. Global Tech Director Paul Dodds, who was at the facility during the attack and fire could not be reached for comment. The investigation is ongoing..."

ABOUT THE AUTHOR

DAVID M. SALKIN IS the author of sixteen published thrillers in various genres, including military espionage, crime, horror, science fiction, action-adventure, and mystery. With a writing style reminiscent of the late, great Michael Crichton, he keeps his readers turning pages into the late hours. His books have received gold and bronze medals in the Stars & Flags book awards, and he has appeared as a guest speaker all over the country, including three times as a panelist at Thrillerfest in New York City. David has also written two screenplays, and continues to work on getting those produced.

David served as an elected official in Freehold Township, New Jersey, for twenty-five years in various roles including mayor, deputy mayor, township committeeman, and police commissioner. He was inducted into the New Jersey Elected Officials Hall of Fame in 2019, and has a street named after him. He is a graduate of Rutgers College with a Bachelor of Arts in English Literature. When not working or writing, David prefers to be fishing, Scuba diving, or traveling. He is a Master Diver, gourmet chef, and wine aficionado.

DavidMSalkin.com
facebook.com/DaveSalkin
X: @DavidMSalkin

THE END?

Not if you want to dive into more of Crystal Lake Publishing's Tales from the Darkest Depths!

Check out our amazing website and online store or download our latest catalog here.

We always have great new projects and content on the website to dive into, as well as a newsletter, behind the scenes options, social media platforms, our own dark fiction shared-world series and our very own webstore. Our webstore even has categories specifically for KU books, non-fiction, anthologies, and of course more novels and novellas.

Readers...

Thank you for reading *Little Things Big*. We hope you enjoyed this novel. If you have a moment, please review *Little Things Big* at the store where you bought it.

Help other readers by telling them why you enjoyed this book. No need to write an in-depth discussion. Even a single sentence will be greatly appreciated. Reviews go a long way to helping a book sell, and is great for an author's career. It'll also help us to continue publishing quality books.

Thank you again for taking the time to journey with Crystal Lake Publishing.

You will find links to all our social media platforms on our Linktree page.
https://linktr.ee/CrystalLakePublishing

Follow us on Amazon:

MISSION STATEMENT

Since its founding in August 2012, Crystal Lake has quickly become one of the world's leading publishers of Dark Fiction and Horror books. In 2023, Crystal Lake officially transitioned into an entertainment company, joining several other divisions, genres, and imprints, including Torrid Waters, Sinister Smile Press, Crystal Lake Comics, Crystal Lake Games, Crystal Cove Press, Crystal Lake Kids, Memento Mori Ink, and The House of Shadows & Ink on YouTube.

While we strive to present only the highest quality fiction and entertainment, we also endeavor to support authors along their writing journey. We offer our time and experience in non-fiction projects, as well as author mentoring and services, at competitive prices.

With several Bram Stoker Award wins and many other wins and nominations (including the HWA's Specialty Press Award), Crystal Lake puts integrity, honor, and respect at the forefront of our publishing operations.

We strive for each book and outreach program we spearhead to not only entertain and touch or comment on issues that affect our readers, but also to strengthen and support the Dark Fiction field and its authors. Not only do we find and publish authors we believe are destined for greatness, but we strive to work with men and women who endeavor to be decent human beings who care more for others than themselves, while still being hard-working, driven, and passionate artists and storytellers.

Crystal Lake is and will always be a beacon of what passion and dedication, combined with overwhelming teamwork and respect, can accomplish. We endeavor to know each and every one of our readers, while building personal relationships with our authors, reviewers, bloggers, podcasters, bookstores, and libraries.

We will be as trustworthy, forthright, and transparent as any business can be, while also keeping most of the headaches away from our authors, since it's our job to solve the problems so they can stay in a creative mind. Which of course also means paying our authors.

We do not just publish books, we present to you worlds within your world, doors within your mind, from talented authors who sacrifice so much for a moment of your time.

There are some amazing small presses out there, and through collaboration and open forums we will continue to support other presses in the goal of helping authors and showing the world what quality small presses are capable of accomplishing. No one wins when a small press goes down, so we will always be there to support hardworking, legitimate presses and their authors. We don't see Crystal Lake as the best press out there, but we will always strive to be the best, strive to be the most interactive and grateful, and even blessed press around. No matter what happens over time, we will also take our mission very seriously while appreciating where we are and enjoying the journey.

What do we offer our authors that they can't do for themselves through self-publishing?

We are big supporters of self-publishing (especially hybrid publishing), if done with care, patience, and planning. However, not every author has the time or inclination to do market research, advertise, and set up book launch strategies. Although a lot of authors are successful in doing it all, strong small presses will always be there for the authors who just want to do what they do best: write.

What we offer is experience, industry knowledge, contacts and trust built up over years. And due to our strong brand and trusting fanbase, every Crystal Lake book comes with weight of respect. In time our fans begin to trust our judgment and will try a new author purely based on our support of said author.

To date we've published around 300 books, and with each launch we strive to fine-tune our approach, learn from our mistakes, and increase our reach. We continue to assure our authors that we're here for them and that we'll carry the weight of the launch and deal with third parties while they focus on their strengths—be it writing, interviews, blogs, signings, etc.

We also offer several mentoring packages to authors that include knowledge and skills they can use in both traditional and self-publishing endeavors. This includes Shadows & Ink Creators on our The House of Shadows & Ink YouTube channel and our Crystal Lake Academy.

We look forward to launching many new careers. This is what we believe in. What we stand for.

This will be our legacy.

Welcome to Crystal Lake Publishing—
Where Stories Come Alive!

www.ingramcontent.com/pod-product-compliance
Lightning Source LLC
Chambersburg PA
CBHW020908060726
47591CB00004B/1141